SEVERED

Kelly Masters

NEWMAN SPRINGS PUBLISHING
320 Broad Street
Red Bank, NJ 07701

First originally published by Newman Springs Publishing 2019

ISBN 978-1-64096-944-5 (Paperback)
ISBN 978-1-64096-945-2 (Digital)

Printed in the United States of America

I dedicate this book to my lovely wife Cristi. You make me want to be the man that my parents tried to make me.

CHAPTER 1

Another lonely evening watching *Sports Center* on ESPN. It was the third time he had watched the same highlights that night. This seemed to be the norm lately since his wife had left him ten months ago. Sitting on a piece of crap floral couch that his brother had given to him since his ex had taken all of the furniture. The couch had a dip in the middle of it, and he couldn't keep the cushions from sliding off onto the floor. When the cushions would fall off, they would reveal some green funk that came with the couch, no extra charge. Who knew what had made that stain; maybe it was best he didn't know. Jackson missed his ex-wife from time to time, but what he really missed was his old couch. It was one of those with recliners on both ends and pillow top cushions that just begged you to fall asleep every time you sat down. He had become rather fond of that couch the last four months of his marriage as he slept on it ninety percent of the time.

Jackson flipped through the channels to see if he could find something else to watch. A rerun of *Grey's Anatomy* was on, the one where George has an affair with the hot nurse, what was her name again... Izzy, yes, how could he forget her name. While married, Jackson and Camille had started watching this show to have some bonding time together. He never told her that he actually liked the show; he wanted her to think that he was just sitting through it because he wanted to spend time with her. Near the end of the relationship, he was glad he liked the show because they weren't doing much bonding. Now Jackson used his DVR to tape the new episodes because he didn't want to miss one. *How pathetic is he?* he silently wondered.

The weekend was coming, and that meant one of two things, trekking up to his icehouse on Lake Mille Lacs with his brother, or having his ex-stepdaughter spend a night or two with him. Haley was truly the only bright spot he had left in his life. She had just turned eleven this past winter, but it sure seemed like she was closer to twenty than ten. Haley was very mature for an eleven-year-old, but then she had been through a lot lately, so Jackson was hoping it wasn't a front to hide her true feelings. He really loved that girl, even though she wasn't really his by blood. The past eight years had brought them together real close, as if they were truly father and daughter. He really missed coming home to her every night, helping her with her homework, and then playing with her. Haley was a sports nut and was the best athlete in her class. Her soft-flowing, straight blonde hair made her look like one of her American Girl dolls that she loved to play with a while back but was slowly growing out of her doll phase. She was Jackson's best friend.

Jackson stepped outside onto his front porch to have a smoke. Normally, he would go out on to the back deck so nobody would see him smoking, but when he did that, his faithful black lab, Raider, would expect to be petted. It was midsummer, and Jackson didn't want to deal with all of the fur that shed all over his clothes when he messed with the dog. Plus, he just wanted to think.

Jackson lit up and hoped nobody he knew would drive by and see him. Haley would have a shit attack if she found out that he smoked. Just as he flicked his Marlboro Light toward the street, he could see two shadowy figures striding up the street. He didn't recognize the woman on the left, but he definitely knew the other woman. They were both wearing oversized T-shirts and spandex as they were pretending to exercise. Everyone knew the real reason they walked was because neither one could stand their husbands; this got them both out of the house, and they got to gossip at the same time.

"Well, hello stranger," he hears Tami yell from across the street, "how are you doing?"

"Not bad," he replied, "out working up a sweat, are you?"

"Yes, we are actually walking over to the workout center to work off some of our flab."

"Now, Tami, I don't see any flab that you need to work off, but if you want a real workout, I'll give you the best three minutes of your life," he flirted.

"Sorry, hun, even my husband can go longer than that."

"Oh, I wasn't talking about sex. I was going to have you help me move my freezer, ha-ha," was his witty comeback. *Oh my god, how stupid did that sound?* he wondered.

"I was hoping you would be better than that in the sack," Tami quickly spouted. "I've heard things about you, you know."

"Really? Like what, and from whom?"

"I can't give up my sources, but I'll message you what I've heard tomorrow on Facebook."

What is this world coming to? The most action I get anymore is flirting with married women on Facebook. At least that is free, unlike match.com or eHarmony. Jackson had tried both of them plus a few more, and he had two women eventually ask him for money, probably weren't even women, just some crooks looking to make a buck off some lonely idiot. The only real person he really connected with was a hot little number from Wisconsin, who turned out to be not so hot when he got recent, updated photos of her. She must have gotten hit with the ugly stick between the ages of twenty-six to thirty because it was *not* the same as her previous pics.

As the two women walked away, he couldn't help but be drawn to Tami's perfectly toned legs that led up to her... Oh, how he wished that shirt wasn't so long, couldn't the wind blow it up so he could catch a glimpse of her ass? Her friend wasn't near the looker that Tami was, but hey, she might do in a pinch. *I'm a pig*, he mumbled, barely audible as he went inside for the evening.

CHAPTER 2

Thursday at work seemed to drag on and on. Trying to figure out why invoices aren't paying is not the most exciting thing in the world. His official title was accounts payable research specialist, a fancy name for fixer of other people's problems. But as Jackson and his work buddy, John, always said, if other people didn't make mistakes, we wouldn't have a job. They didn't have any reason to worry either because there were plenty of people who liked to make mistakes at Mayo.

Jackson logged onto his Facebook account, and there was a message waiting for him from Tami. Opening it, he was surprised to see that not only had she written some things that she had heard about him that were flattering but a few other things that Tami said that she would like to try with him. Tami said in her message that she was leaving her husband, and if he was interested, she would like to stop over and show him how serious she was and that she wasn't all talk.

Now for a man who hadn't enjoyed the company of a woman in a sexual manner in over a year, this got his heart pumping. Even though it went against his better judgement, Jackson replied back to Tami that she could stop over anytime. At the end of his message, he wrote, "I don't know if your husband ever goes down on you, but I guarantee to satisfy you before I ever penetrate you, and you won't need to work out the rest of the week by the time we are done."

Almost as if Tami was waiting for Jackson's reply, she had shot back a message to him. "OMG, you actually like doing that because I *love* it when a man does that. I'm actually getting wet thinking about you down there on me. I may have to go home on my lunch break and have a little me time!"

Jackson went back to work, but all he could think about was Tami going home and thinking of him while she touched herself. Isn't that what every man dreams of? Well, that and maybe twins, but this was pretty cool!

Five o'clock came eventually, and since Haley was going to Wisconsin Dells that weekend with her mother and some friends, he was headed up north to the lake. He changed quickly in the bathroom before leaving. Being careful to not touch the floor because who knows what is on the floor in a work bathroom stall. This can be difficult when changing socks and pants, but carefully stepping on top of his black work shoes, he managed to not touch the floor. The stall was actually fairly clean looking, but that didn't really matter; it still grossed him out.

After packing up his work clothes, Jackson made his way to the parking ramp where his 2005 Yamaha 1100 V-Star was waiting to make the four-hour trip. He loved his bike but dreamed of the day he could afford a custom chopper. That would make him cool. Then he thought to himself, *You can't polish a turd, nothing will make you cool.* He grinned at this thought as he bungee strapped his clothes bag to the backrest of the bike, pulled the key out of his pocket, turned the key forward, flipped the stop/run button to run, pulled the choke halfway out, and pushed the start button. As the engine roared to life, that sound meant the official start of the weekend.

There aren't many things that bring a smile to Jackson's face lately but a sunny day, running down the highway at 75 mph with the wind in his face is one of them. He had only been riding for five years now, why hadn't he bought a bike before that? Oh yeah, his parents had forbidden it, but his ex talked him into purchasing one. Surprisingly, his parents thought it was cool to have a biker in the family. They could have said that years earlier, but I guess they were just trying to keep him safe during his partying years.

Stopping for gas a couple times, Jackson pulled into the makeshift campground of ice houses on the North end of Mille Lacs. He didn't know how many ice houses were there, but it was around sixty or so. Their "cabin," as they referred to it, was light blue, almost gray, and it was pretty much in the center of the campground, close to the shower house and toilets but far enough away that you couldn't smell the pungent aroma of sulfur that it omitted when it got really hot out. It wasn't the nicest house there, but it was in the top ten, he thought. The sign on the front still bore the name and address of its previous owner, with his brother's name and address written over the top of it with a black magic marker. The sign looked like shit, but their sister, Emily, was making them a top notch sign with a picture of a cabin on a lake with a couple deer standing next to it and a fish jumping out of the water. Emily had started making things with her artistic skills of wood burning a couple years ago, and she was quite good. She had volunteered to make it for free, but both Jackson and Chad knew she just wanted to use it as advertising. That just meant she would do a good job on it though, so neither one argued.

The deck on the front of the cabin had the look of five pallets stuck together on cinder blocks, but that is what most of the decks here looked like; they had to legally be mobile, and it also made it easier to adjust them when their shack was pulled back off the lake each spring and put back in the park. The antenna was a mangled mess of aluminum since the resort owners pulled it through the trees as they moved it onto the lake the previous winter, and it no longer worked. Jackson saw that nobody had mown the grass since his last visit three weeks earlier. They would have to mow in the morning. He thought it was ironic that he had to mow the grass here, when he paid his neighbor at home to mow his grass there. This was more like a short-weed bed than grass, but when it was mowed, it didn't look half bad.

It was a long ride, so he grabbed the shared restroom key off the hook in the cabin after taking the padlock off the cabin door. As he walked toward the newly constructed restroom with its white siding and bright-red door, the smell of sulfur got stronger the closer he got. After inserting the key into the lock and walking in, the smell disappeared and was replaced by the smell of cleaning solution.

After relieving himself and washing his hands, Jackson walked back toward the cabin just in time to see the familiar white GMC four-door pull up, pulling a boat. The boat wasn't very exotic, but it worked well for the two of them. Only a fourteen-foot Northwestern that many considered too small for the big lake, they had never had any problems with it.

Jackson guided his older brother while he backed the boat and trailer into its parking spot. The driver's side door opened and with it came the wry-crooked smile of a clearly frustrated man with a good sense of humor. No hi, how ya doin, just "Man, traffic sucked. How the hell did you beat me here?"

"Well, it wasn't by driving the speed limit like you," the younger brother quickly spouted off. "Did you ever get that governor removed from that thing?"

"Funny man, funny man, wants his ass kicked already, I see."

Chad opened the rear door on his side of the truck and out pounced his black lab Gunner. Gunner ran up to the nearest clump of tall weeds and quickly watered them. He didn't need any bathroom key, he seemed to say. He sprinted over to Jackson to say hi and to get some attention before he proceeded to snoop around and mark his territory. Jackson liked this dog but didn't care for the fact that he was allowed in the cabin. He was a firm believer that animals shouldn't be let inside. Raider was not allowed in his house at home, but he never said anything to Chad on the subject.

"What are you waiting for, an invitation? Help me unload this shit!" Chad said with a hint of irritation in his voice, "Mister, I have to ride my bike up and can't bring any supplies. The least you could do is carry some of it the twelve feet to the cabin."

They unloaded the truck, and Chad walked the dog, while Jackson smoked a couple cigarettes while he watched other people arrive in the campground. Most vehicles held couples which made Jackson a hint jealous, but then his ex would have never let him buy this cabin, so that feeling went away quickly.

Chad, Jackson, and Gunner decided to hit the hay early since they would be up in a few hours to get out on the lake early in hopes of catching their limit in walleye, with a couple of northern mixed in. Jackson climbed the small-step ladder, all of two steps, into the top bunk that was unofficially his, being the younger of the two. As Chad made a dog bed and climbed into the lower of the two double beds with matching candy cane striped sheets and burgundy comforters, he socked Jackson in the shoulder and said, "No farting tonight!"

Jackson rubbed his shoulder and said, "Don't tell me, tell the dog! Ha-ha," then he rolled over and pulled the covers up to his neck and was sleeping within a minute.

CHAPTER 3

Friday night for Samantha meant a break from watching the children in the cancer ward suffer. Eight years of this was starting to wear on her, but she knew that she could never give it up. Every child that beat the dreaded *C* word was enough to get her to come back the next week. Even though she was a secretary, she saw the pains and the triumphs of each child and their families. This had been a good week, and her doctors all seemed to be in good moods, which made her job a lot easier.

But now it was the weekend and time to have some fun. She had plans to go out tonight and tear up the town, and who knows, maybe Mr. Right would finally show up. She was going to be the dreaded 30 in a couple of months, and she hadn't had a serious relationship in nearly six years. It was girls' night out again, which meant some serious drinking and flirting with men. Her girlfriend Joan was picking her up at eight, and they were meeting up with some other friends at Coyote's in Chatfield, where they would do some shots and dance on the bar if they got wild. Samantha considered herself to be fairly good-looking, but she just had to lose five more pounds. As she stood in front of her full-length mirror in her bedroom, she squished the skin on her stomach together. Five more pounds, why was she worried about five stinking pounds, most of her girlfriends outweighed her by a good twenty.

Samantha finished getting dressed and was waiting for Joan. In typical Joan fashion, she was late. "Heck, I could have walked the six blocks to the bar by now," Sam told her fish as she fed them.

Eventually, Joan showed up, and since Samantha had been watching out the window, she had already gone outside, locked the door, and was standing patiently in her Harley Davidson tank top and short little jeans shorts that revealed what she thought were her best assets, her legs. As Joan's Chevy Lumina came to a halt in front of the condo, Samantha hopped in.

"Hey, only forty-five minutes late, a new record for you! Congrats, I wasn't expecting you for another half hour," Samantha joked with her best friend of nearly twenty-five years.

"Bite me," quickly replied Joan. "It takes me a little longer to make me beautiful. You can just fall out of bed and look like a supermodel."

"Well, you did a good job. Look how cute you look—OMG, you are wearing a mini skirt? You do realize you will be dancing on top of a bar later tonight, right? Unless you have tamed down since last Saturday?"

Shyly smiling and trying to look innocent, Joan shrugs her shoulders and says, "I'm just doing a little advertising. I really need to get laid."

"You slut! Ladies don't talk like that!"

They both turn to each other and exclaim at the same time, "*Yes, they do!*" and they hi-fived.

CHAPTER 4

He waited in the darkness on the backside of the bar parking lot. It was almost bar time, and he almost couldn't contain his enthusiasm. This would be the first time he had done anything like this, but it was necessary. Wearing all black from head to toe, he should be completely camouflaged by the darkness. There were no security cameras or anything like that to worry about. She just needed to walk out by herself. He could see her dark-green minivan right in front of him and her husband's piece of crap truck up next to the door, indicating that he had been one of the first patrons of the evening.

The door to the small town bar flew open and the sounds of the Dixie Chicks could be heard, along with about sixty drunken Iowans doing their best to sing along. Two men in their early thirties stepped out of the bar, clearly intoxicated. As they stumbled over to a new Ford pickup, the owner dug for his keys while the other guy was struggling to light his cigarette. His hands just couldn't hold steady enough to have the lighter meet the end of his smoke.

The driver unlocks the truck with the remote and dangles the keys above his head and says, "You honto dive?" with his slurred fat tongue. "I, I'm a little...drunk."

"Surrrre, I just need to take a pee," the other one says as he unzips and begins urinating on the fire hydrant.

Again the door opens and a woman exits the bar, snapping the hidden man back into focus quickly. It was her, the reason he was here.

The woman had shoulder-length dirty-blonde hair. It was somewhat curly, but it looked greasy. She was around 5'9", 145 lbs., and her body wasn't bad at all. She had what he considered a butter face; her body wasn't bad, but her face. She had lots of acne scars and a rather large roundish nose. She wore a low-cut lacey blouse with a god awful floral pattern on it. It was cut low enough to expose the top of her bra and a good portion of cleavage. She clearly wanted to pull the focus from her face to her chest.

"I told you that all men were dogs, now put that thing away, Spot, before you hurt yourself," the woman yelled to the guy by the hydrant.

"Ooouuwwe!" was all he could reply, and the two guys hopped in the truck and peeled out of the parking lot, loose gravel flying and spraying the remaining vehicles.

"*Dumb asses!*" she yelled, though nobody could hear her. Or so she thought.

Now she was alone. As she unlocked her minivan and opened the door to get inside, she heard footsteps. Before she could turn to see who it was, it was too late.

CHAPTER 5

The morning came too quickly; the good thing about being at the cabin was you didn't have to shower and shave. The fish don't care what you look like or how bad you smell.

Chad had to walk the dog quick before they went out in the boat, so Jackson sat at the picnic table and cracked a Diet Dr. Pepper and lit up. The table was a green color, but half of the paint had flaked off already and was in bad need of a paint job. It didn't sit level on this make-shift deck, but it was good enough. He was on his third smoke by the time Chad returned with Gunner. The dog looked lighter.

"When you going to quit that nasty habit?"

"Everyone needs a bad habit. I'd prefer mine be sex, but cigarettes are cheaper."

"Maybe you should just start drinking again? Ha. Just kidding, we don't want that. But seriously, smoking is just gross and not good for you."

"I know, but it is the only thing that relaxes me. I'll quit next week."

The two brothers drive to the landing and launch the boat in silence. They have done this so many times, it is old hat. They know their jobs. Chad has to make sure he has a lifejacket on because he is deathly afraid of falling in and drowning. Jackson, on the other hand, isn't even sure where his life jacket is; it should be in the boat somewhere.

"Buck for the biggest fish?"

"You're on, little brother, you might want to get you dollar ready."

"Paleez, you couldn't catch a fish if I tied one onto your line."

So began a weekend of bad jokes, picking on each other, lots of laughter, and not much fish catching.

CHAPTER 6

I t was dark and damp, and her head was all fuzzy as she came to. She was trying to figure out where exactly she was and how exactly she got to be wherever it is that she was.

As Roxy was still gathering her bearings, she noticed that she was tied to the chair that she was sitting in. She tried to move her arms, but they were tied down with some sort of white rope. Her legs and chest also were bound by this smooth white rope.

Roxy attempted to free her hands, but the more she struggled to free herself, the tighter the ropes got. If she could only get to her cell phone, she could text her husband, Ronald, and he could come find her. Assuming he hadn't passed out. Oh, and assuming he could find her anyway.

While working her left hand toward her pocket to where her phone should be, suddenly, a light appeared in the corner of the room. It was her phone, but how was it suspended in the air? she wondered.

"Are you looking for this?"

Holy shit! She hadn't even noticed the man sitting in the dark corner, and that is how the phone was seemingly floating; he was holding it!

Roxy couldn't see his face, and she didn't recognize the voice, so she asked, "Who are you, and what are we doing here? *Untie me*!"

"I'm the last person who will ever see you alive."

Not realizing the trouble she was in and thinking she could call his bluff, she said, "Well, if you just want sex, you didn't have to tie me up, but it is kind of a turn on. I've cheated before, and I can keep a secret. Why don't you bring yourself over here, and we can get started?"

"You are as dumb as everyone says, aren't you?"

"You don't have to be insulting! I'm not dum—" Her head is severed off with one swift blow before she could even finish her sentence.

Fresh blood dripped off the machete as he stood over his first kill. His heart felt like it was ready to explode with the excitement of it. Every hair on his body was standing on end, and his senses seemed to be heightened with this adrenaline rush.

"Not dumb, huh? Wasn't even smart enough to be scared."

He was very surprised to see her head come completely off with just one blow; he was expecting to just sever her windpipe and watch her suffocate to death, so that was pretty cool. He must have hit her just perfect; he can't expect that every time.

As the murderer prepared to clean up and move the body to the predetermined dump site, he thought to himself, *If I didn't have a purpose, I think I would still enjoy this.*

CHAPTER 7

*M*onday mornings are the worst, thought Jackson as he walked the three blocks from his house to where the Rochester City Lines bus picked him up to bring him to work. It was starting to get a little chilly in the mornings as it got closer to the fall. *Might have to start wearing a jacket*, he thought. As he got on the bus, the only thing he could think about was getting his nap in before he got to work. The town of Preston was about forty-five minutes south of Rochester, so he got a good nap in every day he rode the bus. He had contemplated moving closer to work after the divorce, but Jackson was not a city man. Preston was too big, as far as he was concerned.

The day was dragging as usual when about two-thirty, an e-mail popped up on Jackson's preview that shows who sent it to him and usually the title of the e-mail. It said, "Might want a bike ride." It was a coworker who he had ridden with her and her husband; they all rode together a few weeks back. Jackson opened up his e-mail, and it said that the girl that worked in travel was just talking about wanting a bike ride but had nobody to take her. Maybe Jackson should ask her to go on a ride?

Jackson had never even said more than hi to Klaire, and frankly, he knew she was way out of his league, but he decided to man up and ask her. Jackson instant messaged Klaire, saying he heard she wanted to go on a ride and that he would be glad to take her if she wanted.

Bla-ling, came the little electronic notification sound identifying an instant message had arrived, accompanied by a flashing small box with Klaire's name on it. Bla-ling, bla-ling, bla-ling. Wow, she could type fast!

"I'd love to go on a ride with you!"

"How did you know I wanted to?"

"Never mind, I know who told you."

"When can you go? I am free this Saturday."

Jackson's mind was a complete blur, and he was nervous as hell. Here he was not only chatting with, but did he just set up a date with the most beautiful woman he had laid his eyes on?"

"Yes, I am free this Saturday. Is one good for you?"

"Yes, that is perfect, let's meet somewhere halfway between our places, you live in Preston, right?"

"Yes, that is fine."

"Oh great, I have to drop my daughter off at my parents, so that will work if we just meet in Chatfield."

"Okay, sounds good."

"See you at one on Saturday. I'm so excited!"

"Okay."

Jackson didn't even know what to think. Was this a date or does she just want a motorcycle ride? She has a daughter? Wonder how old and if she would get along with… Haley… *Oh crap*, Haley!

Getting caught up in the moment, he completely just spaced the fact that this was his weekend with Haley! What was he going to do, he couldn't and wouldn't miss his time with her, no matter how sexy the woman was. But damn, she was sexy.

Not even a minute into his thoughts about what on earth he was going to do came the answer. The answer came from an unlikely source, his ex. Camille just sent a long e-mail explaining how Haley wanted to spend the next week with him before school started. If that was okay, she could do that, but she couldn't spend this weekend also. That was just too much, and she didn't even know why she let Jackson take her at all, seeing that he wasn't her *real* dad.

That always made Jackson's heart sad whenever he heard or read that he wasn't her real dad. He knew that, heck, everyone knew that. Everyone also knew how much he loved that little girl. Loved her not only like his own daughter, but that he would do anything for her. She was his life; and Camille knew this as well. She just liked to get a dig in whenever she could.

Jackson decided to overlook the comment as he hated conflict. He replied to Camille's e-mail. He wasn't near as wordy as his ex-wife, pretty much like when they were still married. She would talk and talk…and talk. It was the only thing her mouth was good for, remembered Jackson, as his mind seemingly always found something dirty in almost all situations.

"Well, I did have plans for the two of us, but I suppose I can change them," was all he replied, not wanting her to know how perfectly that actually was going to work for him.

So it was set. He not only still got his Haley time, he was about to take a super-hot chick on a bike ride.

Jackson's mind immediately started trying to figure out a nice route to take her on. He didn't actually know anything about this girl, but he knew she was gorgeous, and he didn't want to fuck it up!

What do I wear? he found himself thinking. *Oh my fucking god, did I really just think that? Tell me I didn't think that.*

"How gay am I?" he actually mumble out loud, "How…what am I going to wear? Ya, I'm so gay."

Just as he was mumbling, his good buddy, John, walked by his cube. "You're pretty gay there, but who talks out loud asking what he is going to wear. If this is you coming out, can I make you a rainbow sign to hang outside your cube?"

"Shut it!"

"Now that you are officially out, would you take my wife to Phantom of the Opera on Ice? She got us tickets to it and says if I don't go, she will cut me off."

"I'm not gay, butthole!"

"Oh, why you talking about buttholes then?"

"*Augh!*"

"I can do this all day if you want. So what are you all flustered about anyway?"

"I'm taking Klaire on a bike ride this Saturday."

"No, shit! Klaire, who sits over there… Hot Klaire?"

"Yes, that's her."

"Wow, I'm actually impressed, congrats…what are you gonna wear?"

CHAPTER 8

Emily called a little after seven that night. He couldn't tell if she was excited or hysterical. She rarely called, so he wondered what the heck was going on. Jackson was pretty close to his sister, but they normally just e-mailed, or he stopped by her house when he was on a bike ride.

"She's dead! She's dead, OMG, have you heard?!"

"No, I haven't heard, who are you talking about?"

"Roxy!"

"No shit! Car accident? You didn't kill her, did you? Did you throw water on her, and she melted?"

"I didn't do it, but she was murdered! I wonder if Ronald did it? Finally had enough?"

"Wow!"

"Ding-dong, the witch is dead, which old witch, the wicked witch."

"Are you giddy that someone just got murdered?"

"No, it is so sad, I must just be in shock…she'd gone where the goblins go below-below-below yo ho!"

"Okay, *Wizard of Oz* soundtrack. I get it, you aren't very sad."

"She was the most evil woman ever, and she treated my boys like crap. I hated her."

"Well, you don't have to put up with her anymore now."

"Nope, okay, I gotta go, have to make more calls. I'll probably e-mail you tomorrow."

"Okay, catch ya later."

Jackson didn't give the subject another thought, and he went about his routine of flipping through channels, he stopped on the

MN Twins game for a few pitches. Although he grew up and lived in MN most of his life, he wasn't a Twins fan, but he loved baseball. His Dodgers weren't on very often in this part of the country, so he settled for the Twins or Brewers games that he could normally get.

Bert Blyleven and Dick Bremer were calling the game. Bert was fun to listen to because he tells it like it is. Jackson was just getting ready to make a bowl of popcorn and grab another Diet Dr. Pepper, when there was a light rap on his door. Who the hell would be knocking on the door this time of the day. He got up and made his way to the door, all five steps from the couch. He opened the door to find a cute, little blonde lady standing there, in a gray oversized T-shirt and black spandex shorts with new-looking Nike running shoes. He pushed open the screen door, and they just stood there looking at each other.

"Tami…I wasn't expecting you, what's up?"

"Well, I just came by to make sure you know that I am not all talk, and that I have been thinking about you all day. I had to see you tonight."

"Well, you know I'm very attracted to you, but you are still married, so I think it would be wrong for us to do anything."

She stepped in closer and looked up at him with her large cool blue eyes and sort of a puppy dog look and said, "Makes it a little more exciting though, knowing that we would be doing something forbidden, doesn't it?"

Her breathe smelled minty, like she had been chewing gum recently, and for having her work out clothes on, she smelled pretty damn good. She was now standing close enough that he could feel the tips of her breast barely touching his chest. The testosterone in him was telling him to grab her, pull her in, and pin her against the wall and have his way with her, but not all of his blood had flowed south, and he had a little left in his brain.

"As soon as you are divorced, you need to come over, but I'm afraid, we can't do anything until that as much as I may want to." His breathing was getting a little heavier, her being so close to him and knowing that she wanted him was starting to get to him.

She stretched her body to make herself taller, reached up, touched his face gently, and kissed him. It was a nice kiss, soft and gentle, with a just enough of her tongue moving into his mouth. He didn't resist, and he kissed her back. It was their first kiss, a forbidden kiss, and it was amazing.

They separated and just stood there looking into each other's eyes, not saying anything, just enjoying the moment.

"We can't be standing in my doorway for all the world to see us making out, you are still married, and I don't need a reputation like that."

"I'll be back when I get moved out because I don't want you to go anywhere. I had to give you a small taste. I'll be back soon."

As she turned to walk away, she ran her hand down his chest. She started to walk away and was looking back at him over her shoulder with those eyes, those dangerously seductive eyes.

Jackson slowly closed the doors and locked the deadbolt and put his forehead on the door and thought to himself, *How am I going to wait until she is divorced, this is going to suck.* He just then realized that he was fully erect, and he was suddenly self-conscious and wondered if she had noticed. Oh well, with any luck, she'll be seeing it fairly soon anyway.

This had been a strange day for sure, first getting a date with a hot coworker for the coming weekend, the ex helping to make that happen, his sister's ex-husband's wife being found murdered, and now this, a horny married woman stopping at his house and kissing him.

"I wonder what tomorrow will bring?" he asked out loud to one of his mounted deer heads that adorned his walls in the living room. "Maybe, I'll get a raise?" He chuckled to himself and flopped back onto the couch to watch the remainder of the Twins game.

CHAPTER 9

Wednesday morning, the alarm went off as usual in the upstairs bedroom Jackson slept in. It was the same bedroom that he used to share with Camille, and it hadn't been used for anything but sleeping for a very long time.

I'm going to have to wash the sheets, my luck seems to be turning. Who knows, maybe I'll have a visitor sometime soon. I am going to have to do some cleaning around here, so whoever it is doesn't think I'm a slob. I might even want to put my twelve gauge and shells away that have been lying on the floor for over a month since he'd went target shooting. He was just making sure the sights were still on for the upcoming shotgun deer season. He always hoped that he wouldn't need to even buy a shotgun license since he bow hunted also, but he hadn't had much luck with his bow that last few seasons, so he kept his gun ready to go. That might scare women though, so he better put it in the closet where it belonged.

Jackson stepped out of his shower, dried off, and wrapped his towel around his waist. Shaved, threw on some deodorant, and began brushing his teeth, when he heard a firm knocking on his door. What the...who could this be, it is five in the morning!!

He walked to the door, unlocked it, and stood there in his towel around his waist and toothbrush hanging out of his mouth. He didn't recognize either man standing there on his front steps, but he recognized the uniform of the one. Both men were built pretty good and right around six-foot tall each. They filled the door frame.

"Mr. Ackerman, I'm Sherriff Osborn, Fillmore County sherriff's office, this is Detective Holmes from Winneshiek County. He would like to have a few words with you."

"Detective Holmes, like as in Sherlock? Ha-ha-ha."

"Ya, that never gets old, never heard that before," said the detective, dressed in a sport coat, cloth tie, and brown dress pants. None of it seemed to match. "Do you mind if we come in?"

"Ya sure, come on it, will this take long? I'm getting ready for work, and I have to catch my bus."

"You may want to call in and let them know you will be late today," replied the Sherriff.

He let the two men in, and they stood around the island in the kitchen. "Sorry, I don't have much for furniture since my divorce, so we'll have to stand."

"Been there, done that, went through that a couple years ago myself, at least you got to keep the house. My ex lives in mine with her new husband, and I still am paying the mortgage," Sherriff Osborn related, with a hint of angst in his voice.

The detective informed Jackson, "Mr. Ackerman, we are here investigating the murder of Roxy Monroe. She was found dead this last weekend, propped up against a mailbox down by Decorah, holding her head in her lap. It was *my* mailbox, to be precise."

"Holy crap, I'd say that is either some bad luck on the part of the killer, or someone don't like you." Jackson almost sounded amused at this news, and it didn't really go over that well.

"Do you find this funny, Mr. Ackerman?"

"A little bit, but I'm sure you don't, my apologies."

"So a woman whom you know is murdered, and you think it is humorous. Maybe we did come to the right place."

"What do you mean, came to the right place? Just because I happen to not like someone who is married to my ex-brother-in-law isn't a crime, last time I checked. I know that Iowa is a little fucked up, but it isn't that bad."

"Well, cutting off the head of someone you happen to not like, who was married to your ex-brother-in-law, is a crime even in my 'fucked up state of Iowa.'" The detective was clearly agitated and used his fingers as quotation marks when he spoke.

"If you think I did that, you aren't a very good detective. I haven't even seen that witch in probably ten months or so, and that was at my nephew's football game, and she was about as far away from my family as you can get in the stands."

"Then can you tell me why the last text message she sent to her husband said that you were following her, and she was scared?" the Iowan detective enjoyed asking that question, and he couldn't help but smirk a little bit, thinking that this was going to be a pretty simple case to crack. He'd been a police officer for twelve years, and this was his second year as a detective, his first murder case, so he wanted it to go well. A lot of people would be watching this case.

"Well, I don't have any idea what the texting habits of her and her husband might be, but I can assure you that it wasn't me following her, and if you think I killed her, you might want to look in a different direction. If she was killed this weekend, I was up on Lake Mille Lacs with my brother, and I'm sure I can prove that. Wanna see my twenty-six-inch walleye that won me a buck?"

Jackson could see the once smug look of Detective Holmes change to something else; he wasn't sure, but it looked like failure. The detective would actually need to do some real police work to find the killer.

Still standing in just a towel, he asked if the officers had anything else they wanted to know, or if he could get dressed and get going to work. He was already going to be late because he had his morning ritual down to an exact science and left little to no room for delays.

"We don't have anything else right now, but we may be back. If you hear anything about who may have done this, I'll leave my card." Detective Holmes placed his card on the counter and made his way to the door. "You wouldn't know anyone else who may have wanted to harm Ms. Monroe, would you?"

"Sir, you may get fewer writers cramps if you looked for people who *did* like her. She was not a nice person, treated everyone as if they were beneath her, treated my nephews and her husband like slaves. Maybe look at her husband, isn't that normally the first suspect anyway? I watch a lot of TV. I know stuff. Ha-ha-ha."

"Good day, Mr. Ackerman."

They let themselves out, and as Jackson stood in his kitchen, holding his toothbrush in nothing but a towel, he had an idea. It wasn't every day that he could call in to work and tell them that the police had come to pay him a visit; he was going to call in for the whole day and go riding. He would put his jeans and a beat-up Sturgis shirt on, grab his sunglasses, and just ride, no destination, who knows where he would end up.

A new sense of anticipation filled his heart, and he was dressed quicker than he normally does when getting into dress clothes for work. He placed a call to his supervisor letting her know that he wouldn't be in because he was being questioned by the police; he'd explain tomorrow. The good thing about living so far from work, when he called in, there wasn't anyone in the office to answer the phones, being as it was so early in the day, so he could just leave a message.

Raider needed water and food and of course a little treat. The black lab was his baby; he spent a little extra time with him this morning since he had it. Started his bike in the garage and let it warm up and went out back on the deck to smoke and pet the dog for a bit. He was getting pretty shaggy; his pitch-black fur had started to get really thick in spots and needed a good combing. As he was getting his body stroked, clumps of fur would come off on his owner's hand, so it felt double good to the canine, not only getting petted, but removing some of his excess fur that made him hot.

It was early morning, but it was already warm enough to not wear a jacket; it was going to be a great day. Jackson hopped on his bike and moved it out of the garage. Not knowing how long he would be gone, he stopped, put the kickstand down so that he could go back and close the garage door behind him.

Hopping back on without hesitation, grabbing the clutch, and kicking down the shifter into first gear, revving the throttle up, he was off for the day. The smile on Jackson's face was almost immediate. The kick back of the throttle gave him that adrenaline rush he loved so much. You can't substitute that rush with anything. Wind therapy he called it. All your problems were forgotten once in the wind.

CHAPTER 10

The detective left the house of his lead suspect with more questions and doubt than he had when he arrived. His alibi seemed pretty solid, but he would still be checking it out. He couldn't figure out the motive, unless, he just really didn't like this lady so much that he did her in. He had gotten word from the coroner's office that there was indeed no sexual assault. The ligature marks on the body showed that Ms. Monroe had definitely been bound and restrained for a while.

The detective had to chuckle to himself every time he said or thought of her name. Ms. Monroe. She surely was not Marilyn Monroe, or any relation to her, because even before her head was cut off, she was not an attractive woman. The decapitation almost enhanced her appearance, as sad as it was.

The most disturbing part of this case was the fact that whoever the killer was dropped her off at his house. Was the killer trying to slap him in the face and say, you can't catch me, or did he want the body found for some reason.

The puzzling part was why would the last text try to implicate Jackson Ackerman? Did the killer send that text message, or was it really sent by the victim? Too many questions. Hopefully some of them would get answered soon because his ass was on the line.

CHAPTER 11

It was Saturday morning, and time to get ready to go on his date-ride with Klaire. Today is the day! Jackson loved the feeling of taking a shower and hopping on the bike. The summer air while going down the road and a clean body was probably one of the most refreshing feelings he had found in life. Today though, he put a splash of cologne on, something he hadn't done in years. He actually wondered if cologne went bad, sitting in the bottle for so long, so he didn't put much on.

The dog was already fed, and he went to the garage to warm up the bike, started it up, and opened the garage door. *Crap, looks like it is going to friggin' rain! Seriously? Of all days, this could be a disaster.* He thought that he better call Klaire to make sure she still wanted to go. *Boom, another roadblock. I don't have her phone number. How do I get ahold of her?*

Just then his pocket vibrated. He always keeps his phone on vibrate so he knows if someone is trying to get ahold of him while going down the road. It was an instant message on Facebook from Klaire. This Facebook thing is starting to become pretty darn handy!

The message said, "Hey, didn't have your phone number. Was just looking at the radar, and it looks like rain. It isn't raining now, so want to still meet, and go from there?"

"Sure, I was just leaving. I'll be there in twenty minutes. I need to stop and fuel up the bike first."

"Okay, see you in a bit. I'm so excited!"

Jackson felt a little excited himself, but he still wondered, was she excited for the ride on the bike, or did she want something else? He was hoping, maybe a combination of both.

He headed out of the driveway thinking to himself, "This may be the greatest date ever!"

*****

As Jackson pulled into the parking lot of the bar that they agreed to meet at, he didn't know if she was there or not; there were only a couple vehicles, and he had no idea what Klaire drove. He soon found out; she walked out of the bar and opened her Lincoln Navigator's door and grabbed her sweatshirt and sunglasses. As she bent over into the SUV to get her sunglasses, Jackson caught a glimpse of her perfectly shaped ass. It looked even better in her jeans than it did in the dress pants she normally wore to work. Her white tank top that she wore was super tight, and he could tell that she must work out because her stomach was about as flat and tone as he had seen.

Klaire pulled out her phone and showed Jackson the weather. "This says it won't be here for a couple hours, so we should be good to go."

"Perfect, let's ride!"

"Do you have room in your saddle bags for my sweatshirt and purse?"

"Sure, stick them in here," and Jackson opened one of the bags, and she stuffed her things in there, and she latched it closed.

The slender young lady went to put her leg over the back seat of the bike and said, "Where do I put my feet?"

"Oh duh, I forgot to put the pegs down," Jackson said, feeling embarrassed. *Not like I haven't been thinking about this all week. I could have at least put the pegs down for her*, he said inside his own head.

She hopped on, placing her feet on the foot rests for the passenger, and grabbed onto the sissy bar, which was behind her. She slid all the way back to the rear of the seat, so they were barely touching. Jackson felt the disappointment stream through his body; he had hoped she would snuggle right in behind him and wrap her arms around him, pressing her small but very ample breasts against his back. She just wants a ride.

They sped off down a two-lane highway and did some zigzag-ging on different country highways, slowly working their way to the Mighty Mississippi. The river had some of the best riding roads in the country, and Jackson wanted to give Klaire the full experience. They hadn't gone much more than twenty miles, and it started rain-ing. Since Jackson's bike didn't have a windshield on it, all that rain hits the driver and passenger right in the face, and all those romantics out there who think that riding in the rain is peaceful and serene have never taken little drops of rain in the face at sixty-five mph. It was like someone was throwing small stones at your face. Klaire ducked down behind Jackson's body so she wouldn't be pelted with the small mid-evil style torture device, otherwise known as raindrops.

It wasn't long until they were to the river, and they headed up and over the big bridge, which took them to the Wisconsin side of the river. About a mile after that, Jackson steered the two-wheeled vehicle into what looked like an overgrown, shabby wayside rest. Nothing there but a crappy parking lot, with a view of the railroad tracks, and the dam that blocked up the Mississippi's water and turned it into power. Klaire wasn't quite sure what she had gotten herself into; there were no other vehicles around, and she couldn't see the highway from where they parked. She nervously asked, "What are we doing here? Why did we stop?"

Jackson could sense her fear and decided to play with her a bit, "Why, I brought you here to take advantage of you."

"Listen, bud, I don't know what sort of ideas you have in your dirty little biker head, but I'm not that kind of..." and she started smacking the back of Jackson's head.

"Hold on, hold on, I'm kidding! I'm kidding! Ha-ha-ha. I thought we would get out of the rain for a bit and grab something to drink," he said, trying his best to defend himself while keeping them from tipping the bike over.

"What on earth are you talking about?"

"Follow me."

They both got off the bike and started toward the railroad tracks along a gravel path. She trailed a way behind him, as she was still very leery of where he was leading her to. Was he leading her into the woods to rape her? She knew she shouldn't have gone for a ride with someone she barely knew!

As they crossed the railroad tracks, he stopped and said, "There it is."

"What the hell is *it*?"

"Ha, it is a bar. The Dam Saloon, to be exact. It is a floating bar, only open during the summer."

"It looks like an abandoned barge."

"Come on, be careful on this ramp, it isn't very stable." Jackson held out his hand, and she reluctantly took it, and he led her up the steel grate. The grate was at an odd angle; the baby-blue paint that once adorned it was mostly gone, replaced with rust. It swayed with the waves of the river as they ascended. Klaire was glad she had his hand to steady her as she climbed onto the old barge. He wasn't a large man by any means, but she could feel the strength in his hand, and that comforted her. His hands were soft from doing office work, and not manual labor, yet strong and masculine at the same time. They were hands that she would like to feel running over her body, caressing her firmly, but not all gross and callused up so they scratch.

She looked around and wasn't impressed at all. Two outhouses looked to be the only rest rooms available, and the floating bar was dirty but somehow kind of cool at the same time. As they ducked into the cabin, where the horseshoe-shaped wooden bar was located, she noticed all the beer posters with scantily-clad women all over the walls and the ceiling, while a video of half-naked women danced for hundreds of drunken men.

She asked why they would play that, and the bartender over-heard and said, "Oh, that's last year's wet T-shirt contest, got a little wild, and most of the girls forgot to keep their T-shirts on."

"Wow, all those people were on this little floating barge?"

"Yup, had 2,500 people here that day, most of them on the barge, until the Sherriff floated up and told us we better get down to capacity. So we had to kick a few people off until they left."

Jackson was still trying to read Klaire, trying to figure out if she was disgusted with the place, or if it was a good idea. She seemed to be okay with the nudity, so that was good.

"So, are you a little more at ease that I didn't stop to rape you, and I just wanted to stop and get out of the rain?"

"Well, it is dry in here, but I might be on edge until you get me back home," she said with a smirk. "You know, I've lived within a half hour of this place most of my life, and I've never even heard of this place."

"I stop here a couple times a year. I like going places where there aren't a ton of people and where nobody judges you. Look around, nobody here is going to judge you." Jackson waved his hands to show that the only people there were the bartender, who was probably closer to seventy than sixty, and two old guys, sitting at the corner of the bar, who must have come up the river in the little boat that was tied up outside. They looked like they had been there a while, and it wasn't even noon.

"They may ask me to take off my top, though, from what I've seen so far!"

"Hey, I wouldn't be opposed to you doing that either. Go for it!"

She punched him in the shoulder, "Nice try, it takes a little bit more than taking me to a nice swanky bar for my shirt to come off. You will have to try a little harder than that."

"Hey, speaking of wet T-shirts, how come your shirt is dry, and I look like a drowned rat?"

"Like I said, you have to work harder to see my stuff, did you plan on seeing my boobs today or something, riding in the rain and bringing me here? Ha! I tucked in behind you and barely got wet at all. But…that was a nice try, you get points for that one, calling on Mother Nature, you must have some connections."

"Well, to be honest, I would *love* to see your boobs today, but if I do ever get to see them, I'm hoping it is in a place that is a little more private so I'm the only one who gets to see them. I don't really share very well."

"For the record, you will not be seeing my boobs today."

"You said today, so there is a chance some day!"

"Ha, wow, you men are all alike."

"No, I'm actually quite different. Hopefully, you will stick around long enough to see that."

They ordered drinks, her's a Mich Golden, and he ordered a Coke, knowing that a small bar like this wouldn't have his Diet Dr. Pepper. They sat for a good hour talking about work, picking on people that they worked with, telling each other about their week and about their kids. She was actually quite impressed that this guy still was so active in his ex-stepdaughter's life. Most men just moved on; maybe he is different. She was starting to see this guy, who she always saw as a goof at work, and quite a few of the other ladies there always wanted to date, but he wouldn't, as someone she could actually be interested in. He was slightly older than her, but age didn't matter to her. Maybe she wasn't just out for a ride today?

The rain let up, and they decided to take the long way home, but they needed to head back. Jackson was hoping to ride all day, but Klaire needed to pick up her daughter. The ride back was completely beautiful, sun shining and a beautiful woman on the back of his bike. Jackson was in complete heaven. The smile on his face couldn't be bigger, and his passenger could see it in the rearview mirror. She knew that he really liked her, but she hadn't made up her mind yet.

When they pulled back into the parking lot where they started their journey earlier that day, she climbed off the back of the bike.

"I really enjoyed our ride today, maybe next time we can go for a little longer, when I don't have my daughter. We should try to get another ride in before it gets too cold."

"I really enjoyed our ride also, and we will definitely have to go again. In a couple weeks, the leaves will be turning, and the river roads are so beautiful to ride that time of year. I'll even try to pull some connections and see if we can stay dry next time."

"Deal. I'll see you at work on Monday, ride home safe."

"Don't forget your purses," as he reached down to unfasten his saddlebag.

"Oh duh."

Jackson was really hoping for a kiss or something. Something to let him know that she was interested in him. That is when it happened. That thing all guys dread. She stuck her arms out straight and motioned for a hug. It was the friend hug. He accepted it like you are supposed to but hugged her back with a little more passion than she hugged him, just so she knew that he was interested but not too much so it wasn't awkward.

"Okay, see you Monday." And Jackson took off. He got to the stop sign and thought about lighting it up, burning some tread off the tires, but noticed the town cop, staring at him. *Son of a...* He pulled out nice and easy.

She watched him go. She threw out the friend hug, but he went right through it and showed her he had feelings. Maybe he is different...maybe.

CHAPTER 12

Saturday night, and it was becoming almost routine that Joan and Samantha headed to the local bar for some drinks and scoping out the single men.

"Why do I always let you drive to the bar, I end up walking home, and you leave your car here and go home with some random dude?" Samantha asked.

"Why don't you just drive my car home? That way other guys don't see my car parked here every Sunday morning, and they won't think I'm such a slut."

"I have two things to say about that. Number one, everyone already knows you are a slut. And number two, I'm not going to drive your POS car."

"My car isn't a POS!"

"I noticed you didn't defend not being a slut, but you defended your car, ha-ha."

"Well, honestly...I shouldn't have defended either one. This car is a pile."

Joan and Samantha pulled up to the curb of the bar, and Samantha noticed a biker pulling away from the stop sign. "Hey, I think that is my friend Camille's ex-husband, Jackson, on that bike."

"Too bad he isn't coming here, instead of pulling away. I'd straddle his bike in my skirt if he'd let me," Joan said and bit her bottom lip lustfully.

"You are so bad...but ya, might be better than anything I've brought home in years," Samantha replied. "I wonder if the statute of limitations has run out for time you have to give a friend's ex before you jump his bones?"

"From what I heard, she don't deserve any time. Her and Frank were bumping uglies way before she finally told Jackson about it. But I'm not one to judge. Either way, I thought of it first, so I got dibs on him."

"Ohhh no, he's fair game until one of us gets his digits, or he wakes up in our bed," she said with a shy devilish smile.

Joan knew she had no shot with him if Samantha was interested in him. Not only was her best friend super hot, but she was never interested in anyone. So if she was showing any interest in someone, she knew the game was over, assuming she would actually ever talk to him. Maybe she would have to set it up for her. Although Joan needed to get laid, she knew her friend had been on a lot longer dry streak, but it wasn't for the lack of interested guys. That was one of the best things about having her as a friend; she brought the men to the table. Joan just took them home after Samantha shot them down. Now that Sam had Jackson Ackerman in her head, Joan was pretty sure she was getting some action tonight because Samantha was going to shoot everyone down again tonight.

"It's gonna be a good night," Joan mumbled, barely audible. But her smile was big enough for her friend to see.

"What was that?"

"Nothing, let's go have some fun!"

CHAPTER 13

The same hick bar in Iowa that he was at last weekend. Sitting in the dark, dressed in black, truck parked blocks away. This one would be a little harder than the first one. A lot more people paying attention to this lady.

Jackson's high school sweetheart was back from Los Angeles, where she just finished her latest modeling job. It was a modeling job that you get when you are in the twilight of your career. A job where you only can see your face, and there is a ton of makeup involved, and the photographer couldn't afford someone younger. Since turning thirty a couple years ago, jobs were hard to come by, and living in Los Angeles was not cheap. Brandy was seriously thinking about moving back home to Iowa and working the books for her dad's trucking company. She had managed to get an accounting degree while modeling, something most girls don't do. She had a good head on her shoulders and knew her looks would eventually fade.

Most of the people from her small-town high school class showed up to see Brandy, who "made it in Hollywood," even though it had been years since she had done anything substantial. Everyone knew who she was, and she never bought a drink for herself, which was good, because even though she dressed in the latest fashions, she didn't have a lot of money.

*****

He sat there in the dark for hours, couldn't see inside, but it sounded like they were having a blast. This bar was absolutely hopping tonight, busiest he had ever seen it. To see the amount of people there tonight, you would think it was an all-school reunion. It was just the homecoming of a has-been model. That is when he saw someone pull up that he wasn't expecting to see. *It was Emily, shit, what the fuck was she doing here?!* She could totally blow this whole thing! She knew his vehicle, hopefully, she didn't notice it as she drove by it down the street.

Emily got out of her car and walked up to the door but paused and decided to light up a cigarette before going in. As she was taking her first full drag of her Marlboro Light, out came Brandy.

"*Oh my god! Oh my god!* What are you doing back!" Emily snorted out through her smoke-filled mouth.

"I just came to visit my family and some friends," replied Brandy. "Never thought in a million years I'd run into you here. How the hell are you?"

"I'm doing exceptional actually, thanks for asking. How are you, still looking like a million dollars, dang girl, wish my brother wouldn't have messed up your relationship."

"Oh, we were young, don't be so hard on him, we wouldn't have lasted. It was a good run, but we were done."

"Well, I still love ya anyway."

The two ladies hugged, and Emily could feel Brandy's augmented breasts that she had gotten since the last time they had seen each other. She was instantly jealous; she thought hers looked like a rock in a tube sock since her second child.

"So, Emily, what made you decide to show up here, tonight of all nights? Did someone tell you I was back, or do you always venture down here?"

"Truthfully, it is actually morbid curiosity. My ex's wife was here last week, and it was the last time anyone saw her alive. I thought I'd come down and see if I could run into the guy that did it and buy him a drink."

"Wow, that was here?! I heard something about it from my parent's, but I didn't know she was here. Dang, that is eerie. You got an extra smoke I can bum?"

The door swings open and drunken men pour out of the bar. "*Brandy*! There you are, come back in. I want to dance with you!!"

"No way, I'm buying you a drink first," explained a second drunk.

"You better go, your public awaits. I'll be in when I'm done. See you inside," Emily said while simultaneously inhaling her nicotine-filled smoke.

Nobody saw the danger, lying in wait, across the street in the trees. He was starting to get bored with waiting, so he decided to have a smokie treat of his own. He got up and walked behind a building and lit up his own cigarette, which calmed him down enough for the rest of his wait.

Getting close to bar time and the place was still hopping; it seemed like every single person that came out tonight stayed the entire night. This was going to make it harder than originally planned. If everyone came out of the bar at the same time, it would be impossible to grab Brandy and get her out of here without being seen. His truck was parked in the right direction if she headed to her parents' house, but with it seemed like every guy in the bar was there for her, so there is a good chance that she wouldn't be going straight home, or by herself.

The music finally stopped, and the bartenders started yelling, "Time to go home, we need to close up! You don't have to go home, but you can't stay here!"

Wow, that was original, they need to come up with something new to say that is more up with the times. Made them sound like they were stuck in the eighties.

People started pouring out of the bar, one after another; there must have been over a hundred people in that little shitty bar that would hold sixty-five to seventy tops. She wasn't hard to spot, being the center of everyone's attention. Sitting patiently in the dark, trying to figure out his next move, he was trying to hear what was being said. Everyone seemed to be in too-good-of-a-mood to go home, and they were trying to figure out where to have an after-bar party.

One of the drunkest guys there shouted out, "Everyone, list-ten up!! Afterbar at Big Rock!! We're gonna party all night lonnnggg!!"

"Yaee!! Whahoo!!! Fuckin-a right!!" cheers came up from the drunken mob.

The man dressed in black knew exactly where Big Rock was because he happened to have spent many after-bar parties there himself throughout the years. He also knew where the girls went to pee when they were there because he had silently watched them drop their pants to pee many times. He chuckled to himself. Who would have ever guessed that his sick need to see naked girls would turn out to actually help him? As he slipped off to his vehicle, the only thing that troubled him was figuring out how to take out the other girl that would be with Brandy. Everyone knows that girls don't go pee by themselves.

*****

Big Rock, oh, the memories. Able to pull up as close to the bathroom area was the key to this. The bathroom area was an area surrounded by tall weeds; it was actually mowed in the middle by the land owner, who obviously knew the ladies liked their privacy but didn't want the hassle of getting a porta-potty put in, not to mention the added expense. It was pretty dark there, with trees overhanging, but with a bright moonlit night, you could see who was coming and going. You could definitely see who was…going.

This was a fairly good-sized after-bar party, almost everyone from the bar showed up. Coolers were pulled out of some trucks, firewood, old pallets, and lighter fluid pulled out of others. It didn't take long for the women to start finding their way to the pee area. Some pretty darn good-looking women too. Hiding in the weeds, he had a clear shot of most of them as they took turns pulling down their drawers and emptying their bladders of the beer and mixed drinks from the bar. He was very excited sitting there. His manhood was almost as solid as the granite rock that he was sitting on. His right hand had a small club in it, and his left hand had somehow maneuvered its way down to his pelvic area, and he was stroking himself over the top of his jeans and wasn't even aware of it.

About forty-five minutes after arriving there, Emily and Brandy were having a great time catching up with each other. When Brandy and Jackson were dating, they spent more time with each other than

Brandy did with Jackson, sitting together at his football, basketball, and even his baseball games. Baseball was the worst, and neither of them even watched other than when Jackson came up to bat, and maybe if the other team had some hot boys. They weren't very good and always got killed, so there wasn't much to cheer for. The other two sports they were actually pretty good, so they were interesting, but still they chatted more than watched the games. Emily would point someone out and ask Brandy if she remembered them, and if she didn't, would remind her. They would laugh at who hadn't aged well, and they were both getting pretty loaded.

Brandy said, "I need to hit the little girl's room."

Emily laughed, "You remember where you are, right? We do the weeds thing here, no running water at Big Rock."

"Oh ya, I remember. I was just trying to bring some class to this hill-billie rodeo." She snorted when she laughed at her own joke, which made them both laugh even harder.

"I don't have to go, but I'll go with and stand guard," Emily said.

"Oh-oh, I need to go too, I'm coming with," spouted some girl they had both just met. She was dating a guy from Brandy's old high school class, and she literally didn't know anyone else there.

"Sure, the more the merrier!" both girls exclaimed simultaneously.

There were a couple of girls just leaving the "bathroom area" when the three showed up. Hiding in the dark, weeds covering him so that he couldn't be seen, his penis hard as he could ever remember it being. He was having a hard time not taking it out and taking care of business, like he had in his past encounters in this hiding spot. He saw Brandy coming but was very disappointed to see that Emily was with her. She could ruin this, and he'd have to wait. He wasn't going to hurt her; that wouldn't be smart. What he didn't know is that she was just coming to stand guard, and he was very happy to see her stop outside the entrance and start playing with her cell phone, texting someone and not paying attention to inside the area where the real threat was. She yelled something like hurry up, there's beer to be drank, or something to that effect. But there would be no more beer drunk for those who entered.

44

There was another girl with Brandy, he didn't know her, but he would have to take her out in order to complete his mission. As they pulled their pants down and started to do their business, he made his move, first, hitting the girl he didn't know with his club and knocking her out with one smack. Brandy thought she heard something and glanced at the other girl just in time to see the cloth with the chloroform shoved into her face. Quickly, she was dragged into the weeds. He then went back to grab the other girl.

Great, she fell directly into her piss, and she was still urinating onto and down her leg, even though she was not conscious. She was completely covered in her own piss. Strangely, he found this turned him on, but he had to hurry and get the two girls out of there.

Getting both girls into the weeds was easy, but now he had to carry both back to his truck. Luckily, both only weighed a little over a hundred pounds each, and even though it was a struggle, he somehow managed to get them both onto a shoulder and haul ass out of there. Both girls' underwear and shorts that they were wearing still around their ankles; he didn't have time to pull them up. His hand on their naked asses, piss soaked, he moved as fast as he could. Still fully erect and excited as he had ever been. He made it to his truck, where he put them in the bed of the truck instead of the cab. It was dark; nobody would see them in there. One was alive, the other, he wasn't sure.

*****

Emily was fully engorged in her texting with her new boyfriend. She didn't even realize how long it was, and the girls had not come out yet. A couple other girls were coming that way and went in and came out.

Emily yelled in, "Are you two coming, or are you taking a dump? If you are taking a dump, do it in the weeds so nobody else steps in it!"

No answer. So she decides to go in and see just what the hell is taking them so long. She knew Brandy wasn't into chicks in the old days, but she had lived in California for a while, maybe her and the other girl were making out or something? Naw…that shit isn't happening; she must be hanging out with her sick brothers too much, got her thinking like that.

When she got there, nobody was in there. The other ladies coming to use the bathroom came in, and Emily asked if anyone had seen Brandy, and they both said nope. They hoped she went home because all of the drunk guys were starting to forget she was there and were starting to pay attention to them finally.

Emily thought, *Maybe I was too stuck on my phone, and they walked right past me and went home. Strange she wouldn't say bye to me though.* Oh well, she better get herself home; it was getting late, actually, it was getting early.

CHAPTER 14

Sunday morning, Jackson was not a fan of mornings, but he needed to get his butt going. He had a volleyball tournament to go to. Haley was in JO Volleyball, and that season was starting. Not only was there school volleyball, but JO also, so he was going to be getting some serious bleacher time in this fall. He hated going by himself, so he decided to call his little sister and see if she wanted to go with. So he dialed her cell phone.

"Hello," came the voice on the other end of the line, clearly struggling with the fact that she had to form words and wasn't sure she knew how.

"Wow, long night, sis?"

"Yahhh, Big Rock...afterbaaar."

"So I guess you aren't interested in going to watch Haley's v-ball games with me today then?"

"*Faa-k* no, sleeping until I have to work tomorrow."

"Okay, I better get ready to go then. C-ya lat."

She interrupted him, "Hey, guess who I was partying with last night?"

"God, who knows, you didn't go try to get back with Ronald, did you? Since his wife is now dead."

"Holy crap, you are gross, that fat sloth will never touch me ever again! You F-n dildo head, how can you even think that?!"

"I don't know, just tell me, I suck at guessing."

"Brandy!! She is back from Cali and sounds like she may be staying."

"No, shit. Does she still look good?"

"No, she looks like crap, got all fat-n-shit. She's only a model, you moron. She looks amazing. Got some nice fake titties now too. You totally f'd that one up, bro."

"Ya, I know, you only remind me all the time. Well, good for her, she deserves only the best. I better get going, talk to you later."

As he hung up, he remembered how poorly he had treated her, and how he had promised himself that he would never treat anyone like that ever again. He saw how much he had hurt her, and he never wanted to make anyone feel like that again.

On the other side of the phone call, Emily was feeling bad, and not only because she was super hung over. She vowed to let her brother off the hook finally for messing one relationship, which was in high school for fuck sake up. She could tell he still felt bad about it. She knew he didn't want her back but just knew he was wrong, and she needed to give the guy a break. After all, he was a pretty good guy. Oh god, she threw up in a pail that she had next to her bed, wiped her face with a shirt that was on the floor, and laid back in bed and just wanted to die.

CHAPTER 15

Jackson pulled into the Chatfield Elementary School parking lot on the bike, just as Camille and her dumb-ass looking, extremely younger boyfriend, Frank, and Haley pulled in.

"Wow, can't you just stay home for one of these tournaments?" Camille blurted out as Haley ran to hug her stepdad.

"Nope, don't worry, I don't come for your sake. It's this one here that I love," Jackson replied, still hugging his little girl. "How's my jeep running?"

"It isn't your jeep, it's mine."

"That's right. I just paid for it. Let's go watch some volleyball!"

Haley was actually quite a good athlete, clearly got her skill from her real dad's genes and the fact that Jackson had worked with her on basically every sport since Haley could throw, catch, and hit a ball. Her team won the first two games against a team that wasn't very good at all. The first few games were just for seeding; the real game came in the afternoon.

After the second match, another win; Camille slowly came up to Jackson, who just happened to be filling his face with a walking taco. He had a little bit of sour cream on his lip, and she motioned for him to wipe it off.

"You know you are actually pretty easy to get along with when your boy toy isn't around. Why don't you get rid of him and get someone better, maybe closer to your age?"

"Because the sex is amazing!"

"Oh, for fuck sake, Camille!"

"Sorry, but you asked."

"Noted, I won't be asking anything along those lines again."

"Speaking of him, I was wondering if you happen to run into us in a bar, would you beat the shit out of him? Or have one of your friends do it? I think he is kinda scared of you and jealous of your relationship with Haley, and he thinks you want me back because you come to all of her games."

"Ha-ha-ha, sorry, but that is funny. No, he is safe, he isn't worth it, and I'd probably go to jail for assault or something. And he don't need to worry. I don't want your cheating ass back either. No offense."

"None taken. I may even deserve that comment…once."

Just then Haley walked up with a couple of her friends. "Jackson, Jackson, did you see my spike?! Almost hit that girl in the face!"

"Ya, that was awesome, hun, try to hit her next time. Ha."

Back to the gym, where Jackson sat as far away from his ex as he could and pretty much by himself. He didn't care what people thought about him being there. All of them knew he wasn't Haley's real dad; she called him Jackson, and her real dad still showed up every now and then. He actually would sit with Jackson most of the time since they shared a lot in common. They both loved the same little girl, hated her mother, and they both loved to hunt, so they actually had stuff to talk about. He wasn't there today, though, so alone it was.

CHAPTER 16

Two girls, both tied to chairs, sitting in a dark cabin, facing each other. It was now light outside, but the cabin was still dark. Their shorts and underwear had been pulled up and fastened. The smell of urine coming from the girl with a bad-looking head wound, dried blood, half-red, the rest a kind of black color. Brandy had been awake for what seemed like hours. This other girl sat facing her, with her head sagged down in front of her, limp. She started to stir and slowly lifted her head and looked at Brandy.

She attempted to wipe the dried blood that had pooled on her neck and almost completely filled her left ear, only to discover that her hands were not able to move. She suddenly freaked out and began to try and loosen her hands and legs from their restraints.

"It's no use," said Brandy, calmly. "I've been trying for hours, and I can't get free. I was starting to think that you were dead. Glad to see you are alive."

"What…what happened? Where are we?"

"I'm not sure. I was peeing. Next thing I know, I wake up here, tied to a stupid chair, looking at a girl, who I don't even know her name, who is also tied up in front of me. I didn't know if you were dead or alive. All I know is that I went to piss, and now I'm here. Wherever the fuck here is." Brandy seemed almost too calm; even to herself, she was amazed at how calm she was, given the situation. Perhaps she was in shock, she didn't know.

"My head hurts."

"I bet, looks like half your brain leaked out!"

"I think it is still in there. How are we going to get out of here?"

"Well, I'm all ears if you have any ideas, that's all I've been thinking about all morning, and I got nothing. Unless you have a knife or something in those cute little shorts you have on," Brandy said sarcastically.

"I do have a nail clipper! At least I did…it feels like it is still in my pocket," said the petite girl. "I can't reach it though, with my hands tied like this."

They both sat silent for a few seconds. Brandy had an idea. "What if we use our feet and try to maneuver ourselves so that I can grab it with my hand? Then I can work on your ropes, and we get you free!"

"Worth a shot!"

They were both tied to old wooden chairs with rounded backs. Like ones from an old farmhouse. They had rungs on them, where their hands were tied together behind their backs. Each foot had been tied separately to a chair leg in the front, so their legs were separated.

"Try to get your weight a little bit forward so you can get onto your toes and move. Don't get too far forward, or you might fall, then we are screwed." Brandy was actually surprising herself with how clearheaded she was thinking, but she thought she had to be since the other girl had a head injury, and she couldn't expect that from her.

The two girls slowly started to figure out how to get their chairs to move. It wasn't an easy process, basically only being able to pull with their toes to get to where they wanted. Worried that whoever had brought them there would return soon, they started to get more and more panicked with each passing moment. They had to maneuver around so that Brandy could get her hand into the left front pocket of her fellow captive. To get the angle right, they had to be at almost a ninety-degree angle, with Brandy's back to the other girl's side. To make things more difficult, they were having a hard time getting a firm grip with their toes, and the chair legs kept getting caught on the tarp that was covering the cabin's floor. Finally getting close to the right place they needed to be in, Brandy was able to touch the other girl's leg, and she stopped.

"Okay, before I go feeling you up and digging in your shorts, can I get your name? I know it may seem a strange time to ask, but I just gotta know."

"My name is Anne, and thank you for asking. Strangely enough, it is the first time since I've been up here with my boyfriend that anyone has even bothered to ask me my name. My name is Anne."

"Nice to meet you, Anne, now, I'm going to run my hand up your leg," and they both smiled and laughed a little, somewhat out of nervousness, but also because they had both been so scared that they needed to laugh.

Brandy slowly ran her hand up Anne's leg, moving her fingers trying to find the opening to the pocket. She finally found it, and she tried to get her hand in it, but the angle wouldn't allow it. She wiggled her chair to get a better angle. It was hard not being able to see what she was doing and going only off feel. After a bit of finagling, she was finally able to get her fingertips into the tight pocket and feel the cold metal of the fingernail clipper. She pinched it between her index and middle fingers, like chop sticks, and pulled at it. It took her a couple of times pulling on it to get it all the way out, but she did get it out, and she grabbed it with her whole hand. She held onto it, like it was the last thing on earth that could save her life. And she truly believed that it actually was the only thing that could save her from whatever this nutjob had in store for her.

"Okay, now we just need to get to work on these ropes!"

Brandy and Anne had to change positions again, and the small nail clipper wasn't exactly the best tool for the job, but it was all they had to work with. Anne could feel the rope slowly getting looser, and after what seemed like an hour, finally cut enough of the rope to where Anne broke the rope and got one hand free.

"I can't reach my other hand's knots, or even down far enough to get my left ankle free, what do I do?!"

"Reach over and untie one of my hands, and then I'll be able to get your other hand, and you get us both out of these ropes," Brandy said hurriedly.

Anne reached over and slowly untied Brandy's right hand. It was a lot harder than she thought it would be since the ropes were so tight, and she couldn't pull at them with both hands. She did finally get it and quickly turned her chair so that Brandy could undo her other hand.

Brandy also found it difficult to get the knots out with only one hand, but she did it. Finally, with both hands free, Anne reached down and untied a leg and then the other. She was completely free, and she stood up and grabbed Brandy's knot that bound her left hand and then let go of it and just stood there.

"Tie her back up." They both heard a voice say, simultaneously as they saw light from the open door. "You shouldn't have untied each other, now you are going to make it more difficult, so tie her other hand back up.

"*Tie her back up, I said!*" This time with a more forceful, clearly anger-filled voice that was as scary as any human voice the girls had ever heard.

Anne started to whimper and said softly to Brandy, "I'm soo sorry, I'm sorry."

Brandy was tied back up, but Brandy still had that clipper in her hand, and she palmed it in hopes that she could have an opportunity to use it again later.

"You see, you were not my target, you were just in the way. Brandy here. She was the target. Little Ms. California, Ms. Hollywood, finally came home. I've been waiting and didn't think you would actually come back to this little rinky-dink place. I guess I'm just lucky, and you…well, you're not so lucky Brandy."

"What do you want with me?" Brandy was finally starting to lose that calmness that she had carried through her ordeal.

"I need you dead. You may want to take a step back, Anne. Don't want you to get in the way again. Oh, that's right, you are tied up, you can't step back. Here, let me help you." He grabbed her chair and pulled her a couple of feet farther away from Brandy.

"How do you know who I am?" Anne asked. Nobody in this area knew her name, how did this guy know who she was?

He held up her driver's license. "I'm not clairvoyant. I just know to check your pockets. Got your license and cell phone. Must have missed whatever it was that you got to cut that rope. Now, if twenty questions are over, we have business to attend to."

He swung his machete like a baseball player, hitting Brandy right square in the middle of her chin. This shattered her jaw, and teeth went flying, blood squirted everywhere.

As Anne watched in horror, she saw this beautiful model's face go from gorgeous to hideous in a second. She listened to her gagging on her own blood. It was the worst thing she had ever seen, or heard.

"*Holy fuck!* I guess I missed. I was trying to cut her head off!" exclaimed the evil man standing there, with his big cutting weapon.

He just sat there, watched, and listened to her die a painful and horrifying death, choking to death on her own blood as it drained into her lungs. It took a couple minutes and was the most horrifying thing Anne had ever witnessed. It seemed like it took forever, and finally, Anne had to just close her eyes as she couldn't stand to watch anymore.

As the last bit of breath gurgled from Brandy's body, he heard something drop behind her chair. He looked around and saw the nail clipper.

"Guess she won't be using that any more. Ha-ha."

Anne started screaming, and she was so terrified that she didn't even notice the pee running down her legs. But the killer saw it and smelled it. It reminded him of the previous night and how he watched half a dozen different women drop their panties and go right in front of him.

"I've changed my mind with what I'm going to do with you." He dropped the machete and grabbed Anne and forcefully tore her shirt off and took out a small pocket knife and cut the girl's shorts from her body. Kicking and still screaming, he held the pocket knife to her throat. "Calm down, and this won't hurt. If you kick me or hit me, I will kill you."

Anne calmed down. He removed her from the chair, and he tied her hands together and pushed her onto the bed and tied her hands to the corner of the bedpost. It was an old iron headboard, and the bed squeaked with every movement. With the knife still to her throat, he slowly took her soiled panties off and slid them down and off her legs, like he would a lover. He took the panties and placed them gently on the night stand adjacent to the bed. He then raped the helpless girl repeatedly. She cried silently the entire time, but she didn't fight because she was afraid to die. She did get a couple of nicks from the pocket knife that he continued to hold to her throat, but only because he got too excited a couple of times and couldn't control the knife properly.

When he had enough, he pulled his pants back up and got to work cleaning up the dead woman that was tied to the chair.

What scared Anne the most, out of everything she has seen, heard, and felt, was listening to the monster whistle while he cleaned up blood, teeth, and flesh off the floor.

"Just whistle while you work, feh feh feh feh few feh fewww, just hum along and join in song. It isn't really work, when you enjoy it this much, right?"

CHAPTER 17

Monday morning always seems to come too quickly, especially the further you get into fall and the days of riding the bike to work start coming to a close. It was raining this morning, so Jackson rode the bus. Mondays, he didn't mind riding the bus because he could get some extra sleep in.

Jackson barely got to his desk, and there was his buddy, John, standing in the entrance to his cubical. Big smile on his face.

"So, how did Saturday go? I wanted to call you yesterday morning but didn't know if you two would still be in bed, and I didn't want to ruin that. *Tell* me she spent the night, please tell me this, I'm married, and I have to live through you."

"It went okay, we went for a ride, got rained on, talked, and got to know each other. She had to go home early because she had her daughter. And I got the dreaded friend hug when I dropped her off."

"No no no, are you sure? Dang, man, I was pulling for you. What did you wear?"

"Dude, I don't think it was that bad. We'll do it again I think."

"So better question. What did she wear? Tell me it was a white shirt, and she was all wet from the rain."

"She looked sexier than I've ever seen her. It was a white tank top, but she didn't get wet, but I was drenched."

"Your luck sucks, man. If you tap that, you are my hero."

"Well, you may need to look for a new hero, my friend, because I don't think that will happen"

Jackson logged into his computer, wasn't even done opening his programs, and his IM started flashing on the bottom of his screen. It was Klaire.

"Hey, thanx for taking me on a bike ride this weekend, I thoroughly enjoyed it. Thanx for being a gentleman and not being a total pig. It was so nice to spend time with a guy who was actually interested in what I had to say for a change. Hopefully we can do something again soon. Maybe I should have you over and I can cook for you?"

"Just so we are clear, I was only listening to you because I want to get in your pants. Ha-ha Kidding!! Totally kidding."

"Maybe you are a pig. Lol."

"Yup, totally, not even sure I heard anything you said all day. ☺"

"Well, keep it up, and if you come over to my house, you may enjoy dessert…"

"Let me know when!! I love dessert!!"

"Well, I'll let you know what works, I gotta get to work. TTYL."

Jackson just sat there with thoughts of all the possibilities. *She wants me to come to her house. Now that sounds like a date for sure. How am I supposed to work after that? Maybe John will get a new hero?*

CHAPTER 18

Jackson arrived home around six-fifteen that night. A long day of work, lots of invoices processed, numbers still running through his head, but thoughts of Klaire were also on his mind. As he pulled his truck into his garage, after the three-fourth-mile trip from the bus parking lot to his home, he was so stuck in his own mind that he didn't even notice the black sedan parked directly in front of his house. He hit the door opener button, hopped out of the truck, and reached down to pet Raider, who was always happy as a pig in shit to see his master every time he returned. The black lab would hop up and down on his front legs, all excited, just waiting for some attention.

Still petting the dog, suddenly the dog's attitude changed, looked at the closed garage door, and started barking. A second later, he heard his doorbell go off from inside the house. He walked to the front of the garage and opened the door and looked at his front step where he could see one of the two officers that had stopped last week. He figured the other was further up on the porch ringing the bell. He guessed correctly.

"Officers? Got any more leads on the Wicked-Witch-of-the-West killing? Or were you just hoping to catch me in my towel again? Sorry to disappoint you, but I'm fully clothed today."

Sherriff Osborn spoke first, "Mr. Ackerman, we need you to come down to the Sherriff's office for some questions."

"Is this really needed? I have laundry to do, and I was hoping to take my dog for a walk. I honestly don't really care much about Roxy, or who killed her."

Detective Holmes said rather impatiently, "It is needed. And we have some new questions for you this time, and we need them to be recorded for the record this time."

"Holy hell, fine. Just let me drop my lunch box in the house. Am I driving myself, or riding with you?"

"Oh, you can ride with us. You remember what the backseat of a cop car is like, don't you? We ran your record. You've been in one a couple times before we see." The sheriff loved it when he was able to get a good dig in on someone.

Jackson did know the back seat of a cop car, but at least, this time he wasn't handcuffed. And he surely wasn't hog tied and shackled like the last time he was in a police cruiser. But for some reason, he was more uncomfortable this time.

As they pulled away from the curb, Jackson saw a familiar face jogging up the street, wearing a long loose Twins shirt and yoga pants, with earphones plugged into her ears. As they drove by, he saw her pull the earphones out of her ears and just stare at the backseat of the cop car and at Jackson. The surprise on her face was evident. As they drove away, Jackson strained his neck and was able to see her reach into her bra and pull out a cell phone and start punching numbers.

The Sherriff's "office" looked more like an interrogation room. It was decidedly smaller than the ones you see on TV, where they have multiple people grilling a perp. Walls were off-white, with yellow staining from all the cigarettes that had been smoked in there over all the years. The ever present one-way mirror was one of the two larger walls, adjacent from the door. Four metal folding chairs and a plastic table were all that adorned the room. Jackson was directed to the side facing the "mirror." The chair he sat in was bent, and only three of the legs touched the ground at once. He got up and tried the other one, which was slightly better.

The Iowan detective and the Minnesota Sherriff both sat opposite him, each with their notepads and pens. The detective also had a brown leather folder. It appeared to be the first time this folder had ever been used.

"Mr. Ackerman, we are going to record this conversation. After I start the tape recorder, I am going to ask you to list your full name and birthday, and we will go from there. Since the detective is out of state, I will be asking the questions, and he is only here as an observer for now. We have some paperwork filed with the judge here in town to grant him access to any prospective suspects/witnesses. But for now, you should only answer questions from me. I am going to read you your Miranda rights to get that out of the way."

He read Jackson his rights and turned the tape recorder on, told the recording device the current date, those who were in the room at the time, and why they were there. "Mr. Ackerman has been read his rights. Do you understand your rights as they have been read to you?"

"Yes."

"The reason for this interview is to discuss with Mr. Ackerman his whereabouts on the previous two weekends and to see if he has any involvement in the murder of Roxy Monroe or the murder of Brandy Thompson."

Jackson's heart dropped when he heard the second name. How could she be dead, who would want to hurt her? His sister was just with her Saturday!

"Did you say Brandy Thompson? She was murdered?"

"Yes, and guess where she was found?" the Sherriff asked.

"I'm going to guess by a mailbox in front of a certain detective who is sitting across the table from me."

"Yes, and I didn't appreciate it any more this time than I did last time," Detective Holmes said, clearly agitated.

"I can imagine. But this doesn't explain why I'm here. I haven't even seen her in years."

"Did you know Ms. Thompson was back in town?"

"Yes, but I…"

"So you knew she was in town, but you haven't seen her in years?"

"Ya, small towns here, you hear a lot of things. Doesn't mean I saw her, or was even planning on seeing her."

"Where were you this Saturday and Sunday?"

"Well, Saturday, I went for a ride with a friend, we stopped at the Dam Saloon for a while, and I took her back and dropped her off in Chatfield at her vehicle. I went home after that. Sunday, I spent the entire day in Chatfield Elementary at a volleyball tournament."

"Wasn't it raining Saturday? You are telling me that you went for a ride in the rain?"

"You know what they say, if you haven't ridden in the rain, you aren't a real biker. I ride in the rain a lot."

"Okay, I'm going to take it that you can prove that you were riding with someone, and that she would back up the fact that she was with you, and the volleyball alibi should be easy to prove true or false pretty easily. What did you do in between those two things? There is a lot of time missing."

"Well, I was home just after dark on Saturday because I took a long way home. Then I just sat on my couch and watched TV by myself, and I probably moved up to bed around twelve-thirty or so."

"Nobody stopped by, called, or texted to see if you wanted to go out? Is this a normal weekend for you? You don't go out with friends? You didn't go for a ride down across the border to see an old friend?"

"Nope, I'm pretty boring on weekends. If I'm not up north fishing, I either have my stepdaughter or just stick to home usually."

Detective Holmes had enough of being silent, he had a lot of questions, "You didn't go see Brandy and try to rekindle an old flame? Maybe got shot down?"

"Detective Holmes, you know you can't ask questions to this witness. Jackson, please don't answer that question." The sheriff scolded the visiting officer.

"Sorry. Won't happen again." The Iowan was clearly upset with not only himself for blurting that out, but also with the politics involved.

"So, Jackson, you say you knew Ms. Johnson was in town, and from people we've talked to, it is pretty common knowledge that she left you, and you were pretty upset about that. Are you sure you didn't go talk to her? Just to see if there was anything to rekindle?"

"I already told you I never saw her."

"I'm just curious. Why did her last couple text messages to her mother mention that she ran into you, and you wanted to get back together. She told you she wasn't interested, and that you were angry, and she was a little frightened of you."

"Again with text messages? I don't know what to tell you. I was home, never talked to her, didn't even know she was in town until Sunday. Someone doesn't like me or something, I don't know."

Detective Holmes couldn't control himself any longer. "Okay, enough with the bullshit, where is the other girl, is she still alive?"

"I think I may want a lawyer. We are done here. Take me home."

The two officers looked at each other, and each swore under their breath. They didn't have enough to arrest him, so they had to take him home. They did have enough to warrant having someone follow him for a while though.

They dropped Jackson off at home, and he was finally able to look at his cell phone, which had been vibrating inside his dress pants pocket constantly for the entire duration of the interview. Sixteen messages from his sister, three from Tami, and a missed call from a number he didn't recognize.

I better call Emily, she must be freaked out. I'm sure Tami called her as soon as she saw them taking me away and needed to know what was going on.

The phone rang once and was answered immediately, "What the Harry Hell is going on? You got arrested? Why were you in a police car, is this your only call? Did you do it? I won't tell. I just need to know."

"What, did I do it? Are you seriously asking me that? How do you know why they took me anyway?"

"Dude, small town, I work for the county. I know stuff before some of the crimes are committed. Lol."

"They think I killed these two ladies. If I were going to start killing people, it certainly wouldn't be someone that I liked! Did you know there is still someone missing? I wonder who that is. I bet it is someone I know, and they will try to pin that on me also."

"You don't know her. I met her last night for the first time. I'm pretty sure I was standing guard when they were taken. They were taken together from the after-bar party I was at I believe."

"What??!! Wow. Did you know that the last two dead people had text messages saying that I was bothering them, and that they were afraid of me? I need a lawyer."

"I know a few. I'll call you back in a bit, let me make some phone calls. *Don't* talk to anyone. *Anyone!*" Emily hung up as quickly as she answered her phone. She knew a lot of lawyers, just had to figure out which one owed her the biggest favor and could handle this.

Jackson grabbed his smokes and sat on his front porch, chain smoking and watching the car just down the block. Clearly a police officer. These guys pretty much suck at surveillance.

Jackson sent a text to Tami and just said, "I'm okay and home now." She replied saying she wanted to come over but was told it would be better if she didn't right now. Jackson could see the neighbors, peeking out of their windows from behind the curtains.

I may have to call these nosey neighbors as witnesses to confirm that I was home. You can't take a crap in this small town without everyone knowing what color it was.

CHAPTER 19

The rest of the week went by without anything major going on, so Friday night he went to pick up Haley after work. Her mom had moved her to Dover since their divorce, so he had to always go get her and bring her back. He was told it wasn't Camille's issue to worry about; she didn't even need to let her see him at all. He had no rights. She knew that Haley loved going with him though, and Camille liked going out with her boyfriend and not having to worry about getting a sitter.

Haley didn't know that Jackson smoked, and she would give him a lot of crap if she did know, so he had always hidden that from her. He wanted her to have a high opinion of him, and he didn't want that to change. He just couldn't quit that nasty habit. Sometimes, he had to wait until she fell asleep to sneak outside and have his lone smoke of the day.

They played hoops in the driveway when they got back to his place. It was a gravel driveway, so dribbling wasn't always very easy, but they played horse, so there wasn't a lot of dribbling anyway. He always had to shoot left-handed so that it was fair. She was actually left handed, so she argued that she was making her shots with her left hand, so he had to also. She was getting old enough now that he no longer was just allowing her to win, she still won about 80 percent of the time, but he wasn't letting her win, she was earning them.

They watched some TV, starting with some shows on the Disney Channel, and when that become too overbearing for Jackson, they surfed and came across some sumo wrestlers. Haley found this entertaining, and they would pretend they were sumo wrestlers in-between matches. Bumping bellies, backing up, and doing it again. It was hard on Jackson's knees because he had to half squat in order to get their bellies to be at the same height. They laughed and laughed. When it was over, they found a Lifetime movie and curled up together to watch it. All snuggled into her stepfather's arms, Haley looked up and said, "Do you think Uncle Chad is watching Lifetime right now? We should call and ask him." And she reached for the cell phone lying on the couch next to her.

"Oh, no, you don't. He would call and have my man card taken away. Don't ever tell anyone we watch Lifetime...like ever."

"Okay, I can keep a secret, you know that." And she fell asleep within minutes.

Jackson truly loved his time with this little girl. She was his best friend. If given the choice between anything else in the world, he would have probably chosen sitting on his couch watching Lifetime movie with his favorite person.

CHAPTER 20

Saturday morning and Haley was restless. Even hanging with her stepdad got old for an eleven-year-old.

"Can you call Sarah's mom and see if she can come over? I want to go to the swimming pool, I think it is the last weekend it is open for the summer."

"Sure, I'll call."

So he made the call, and Sarah's mother said she already had her swimsuit on and was waiting for the call. They must have planned it the week before at volleyball or something. She would bring her over, and they could both walk from there.

After the girls were gone, Jackson sat on his deck with the dog. The police car was still parked out front, but they couldn't see him from their vantage point. He sent Klaire a message on Facebook. It took a while, but she got back and said she was busy with her daughter, so she wasn't able to chat, but they were going to the bowling alley later, maybe they could accidentally run into each other there? That sounded good to him. He was trying to think of something for Haley and him to do later.

He set his phone down and started petting the dog when his phone started ringing. He saw it was Tami.

"Hello."

"Hey there, big stud. What are you doing right now?"

"I'm just sitting on the deck. Haley will be swimming for hours, so I'm just playing with the dog."

"Wanna play with me? I bet I'm more fun than a dog. I'm a block away, and I'm walking fast."

"I still have company out front, so go past the house and come in through the back yard so they don't see you."

"I'll be there in a couple minutes."

It was funny, when people hung up cell phones, there wasn't the old click sound that you used to get from the old land line phones. Wow, he was getting old, nobody has those anymore. Haley probably wouldn't even know what that was.

There was a small wooded area behind the house, and he looked up, and out of it walked this cute little thing. She had a tighter shirt on today that showed off her curves very well. It was a white top with a bright green stripe on each side running from her armpit down. Her yoga pants were black, and she looked pretty damn sexy coming out of the woods at him.

"Nobody saw me. I like this adventure stuff with you."

She walked up to him and grabbed his hand and led him into the house. Her hand was warm and soft, and he could feel what she wanted by the way she touched him. Once they got into the house, she faced him and put both hands on his chest. He was afraid she could tell that his heart was ready to beat right out of his chest.

"Did your sister tell you that I filed for divorce a couple days ago? I am moving out on the first of the month. You said, once I'm divorced, we were free to do as we wanted, right? Well…" She kicked off her little white walking shoes that she had on; she was now barefoot. She reached up and gave him a kiss on the cheek and hovered there with her face touching his. "I'll be upstairs in the bedroom if you want to join me."

She turned and walked up the stairs, turned and looked at him when she got to the top, as he stood at the bottom watching her perfect little ass as it moved up each step. Frozen, he didn't know what to do. Technically, she was still married, but she was getting divorced. She walked around the railing to his bedroom. Still contemplating what he should do next, her blouse floated down over the railing and landed at his feet. Yup, he had his mind made up, and it may not be the smartest thing he ever did, but he hadn't had sex in a very long time.

Jackson took two steps at a time, and by the time he reached his room, there was an extremely sexy and very naked woman lying on his bed. She motioned with one finger to come to her, and he did.

Not a word was spoken as she took his clothes off for him. She kissed his bare chest and pulled him down on top of her. Their mouths locked in an almost tribal passion. Each wanting the other more than anytime they could ever remember. There was more lust in that room at this moment than there had been the previous seven years combined.

He moved down and took ahold of her breasts, one hand on one and his mouth covering the other, sucking and licking her nipple, making it as erect as his shaft was. She moaned softly with anticipation. She could feel his manhood on the inside of her thigh and was eagerly awaiting it to be slid into her. As he came back up and kissed her neck, he maneuvered up and inserted his organ into her very wet opening. There was no awkwardness, and they seemed to fit together absolutely perfectly. With every thrust, their thirst for more grew.

Jackson was afraid that he wouldn't last very long, and he wanted to make a good impression. Normally, when he made love to a woman, he would warm her up, either with his fingers or his mouth, or both, and it would prolong the lovemaking and get her closer to climax before he got inside her. But this was not lovemaking, it was screwing. And he didn't even really care about her at the moment, and she didn't care about him either. They were both getting exactly what they wanted and needed. He was about to finish when she pushed him off of her, rolled him over on his back. This settled his blood flow a bit, and then she climbed on top of him.

"I want to finish with you at the same time."

And she kissed his mouth and then sat up, riding him like a saddle. They both moved their hips fast and perfectly together in motion. He had one hand on her hip and another on a breast, fondling it, tweaking her nipple, and pushing and pulling with the other on her hip. Both of her hands were buried in his chest, digging her nails into his pecs. They both climaxed together, her shaking and him with a low moaning noise that he had never made before, but he didn't care.

She fell off, onto the other side of the bed. They both laid there, completely exhausted, sweating, and breathing hard. Her chest was rising and falling, and he just watched it, admiring the perfect shape of each breast, the flatness of her stomach. The small scar from her cesarean was visible, but it looked good on her.

She was also checking him out. He was pretty chiseled. She knew that he had been working out since his divorce, and wow, it must have been working because his body was rock hard in all the right places. He had a couple small scars on his arm and one on his side. She was completely sexually satisfied for probably the first time in her life.

"Wow, that was…"

"Amazing," she finished his sentence.

"Yeah."

"Aren't you glad I stopped by? And don't worry. I'm on the pill. I should have probably told you that earlier, but I forgot."

"Holy crap, didn't even think of that!!"

"Well, I need to get going, things to do," and she rolled over and gave him another kiss and sat up and started to get dressed. "I'll text you later, and I'll let you know if I need help moving next week."

"Okay, we can use my truck."

She finished dressing, everything except for her blouse, which was still lying at the bottom of the stairs. She gave him a final kiss and walked out into the hall. She turned and said, "Please don't tell anyone about this. I'm not officially divorced, and I don't need him to hold this against me."

"Oh, okay. Mums the word."

She left him lying on the bed, completely naked. He heard the door close softly, and he got up to look out the back window just in time to see her disappear into the woods behind the house.

"What the fuck just happened here?" he wondered out loud. He smiled and started to get himself dressed again. "Some really awesome sex, that's what just happened. Damn!"

He walked down the stairs and outside. In the front of the house this time, making sure anyone coming from the swimming pool wouldn't be able to see him, and he had a cigarette. And he waved to the police officers sitting down the street. He saw one of them wave back, and immediately the other one smacked him. Jackson got a chuckle out of that, so he tried waving again. No return wave this time.

CHAPTER 21

L ater that evening, after Haley had returned from the pool, she wanted a nap. She wanted to go bowling but needed a nap first. She woke up and took a quick shower to get all the chlorine off her and out of her hair.

"Mom says if I don't shower after swimming, my hair will turn green. I actually would kind of like green hair. I think I could totally rock it."

"Well, I don't think you want that kind of green, and I don't believe I'm going to say this, but I agree with your mother, better wash it."

"Can we go early and get something to eat? You won't have to try and cook like normal!"

"Hey, I can cook just fine!"

"Really, what were you going to make me, is it frozen pizza or mac-n-cheese tonight?"

"I was gonna make... Hey want to go early and eat there? Ha-ha."

"Wow, great idea, wish I'd have thought of that one."

When she was done showering and getting ready, she pulled her still half-wet hair back into a pony, and she grabbed her stepfather's bowling ball and shoes and headed for the truck.

"Thanks, I might have forgotten and had to rent shoes."

"Ya, now you can afford to buy me some candy with the money I just save you."

They drove down to the alley, which was just across town. They pulled up, and the parking lot was completely packed. They walked in and asked about a lane.

"Sorry, man, no open bowling tonight, all lanes are reserved for some fiftieth birthday party."

So there was one small booth still open, so they decided they would at least order some food. The waitress brought them each a menu and a glass of ice water and said that she would be right back. As she was walking away, he noticed Klaire and her daughter walk in. Dang, that little girl looked just as cute as her momma did. She was going to be a heartbreaker when she grows up.

"Klaire, over here!"

"Wow, this place is slammed. I take it we won't be bowling?"

"No, some fiftieth birthday party. You are more than welcome to sit with us and eat though, we haven't ordered yet."

"Sounds like a decent enough back up plan," and she gave a sweet little smile. "And who is this young lady with you?"

"I'm Haley, nice to meet you."

"Nice to meet you also. I'm Klaire, and this is my little girl, Mandi. Say hi, Mandi." The girl only hid behind her mother's leg and didn't say a word. She must have been about four or five. "She's pretty shy."

Haley was checking Klaire out, "Klaire, are you a model? You are so pretty. I think you and my stepdad should date. You'd make cute babies, and I could have a sister and so could Mandi. My mom said she won't have another one of me, so I guess he is my only chance."

"Well...wow, thanks. No, I'm not a model, I actually work with Jackson."

"Oh, so this already is a date then, you must have asked him because he is pretty shy about asking pretty women out."

Jackson spoke up, "Okay, motor mouth, that's enough questions."

They ordered their food, and the kids ate. Haley loved little kids, so she had no problem playing with a younger child. They all laughed at how outspoken Haley was and how she seemingly enjoyed trying to embarrass her stepdad.

When everyone had completed their meal, Haley came up with a wonderful idea.

"Why don't you guys come over to our house, and we can watch a movie? Do you like Disney movies? I have all of them. I'm kind of spoiled, especially since the divorce. I pretty much get whatever I want."

"Well, I don't know, we should probably get home—" But Klaire was interrupted by Mandi.

"Do you have *Cinderella*?! I love *Cinderella*. I have a Cinderella dress at home, but I don't have the movie because I accidentally put it in the microwave and hit play. Did you know that you can't play a movie in a microwave?"

Klaire was so amazed that her daughter was actually talking and talking a *lot*. "Dang, who put a quarter in you? If it is okay with Jackson, we can stop for a while."

"Let me see, is it okay to have a gorgeous woman and her adorable child stop at my house? Hmmm. Check please!"

They got the bill paid, and the waitress was happy with her larger than average tip. Jackson seemed to leave bigger tips than most, especially when he was in a good mood.

Klaire followed Jackson, but Haley and Mandi insisted on riding in the same vehicle, so they both rode with Klaire since Mandi needed to be in her child seat still.

"Do you like my stepdad? I can tell he likes you. I think I like you too, and Mandi is so stinkin' cute too!!"

"I guess I am starting to like him, but we will have to see, we barely know each other."

"He's a great guy. I'll tell you that much. My mom's new boyfriend, I don't like him, so I think if you find a good guy, you should just stay with him."

"Okay, I'll keep that in mind. Ha."

They all arrived at the house, and the two officers who were just about to change shifts pulled back into their usual spot. They had sat outside the bowling alley the entire time, and one of them even went in to get them both coffees. They were happy that something was actually happening at their stake out.

None of the females even noticed the cops sitting just down the street in their unmarked car, but Jackson did.

Haley showed everyone in and went to her stack of movies. Here is *Cinderella*! She stuck it in the VCR and started it up.

"I think people only own VCRs so they can play old Disney movies," laughed Klaire.

"Okay, I'm going to sit here and, Mandi, you sit next to me, and your mom next to you then my stepdad." Haley had the seating all arranged on the couch, which was the only piece of furniture in the house. The couch was not comfy, but it worked.

Klaire leaned over and whispered in Jackson's ear, "I think your daughter wants us to hook up. She was putting a good word in for you in the car."

"Well, that makes three of us that want us to hook up, assuming you want to. Ha," Jackson joked.

"We'll see, but I do like where this is going," and she reached over and took his hand.

CHAPTER 22

Nobody knew who fell asleep first, but they all fell asleep before Cinderella's carriage turned back into a pumpkin. The two girls were snuggled together, and Klaire's head was on Jackson's shoulder. Klaire was the first one to wake up around 5:30 a.m., and it took her a bit to figure out where she was at. When she figured it out, she snuggled in closer with Jackson. He woke up enough to pull her in tighter, and they both fell back asleep for a while.

When they woke up again, they woke up to the smell of smoke. They both jumped and saw neither child on the couch with them. They ran to the kitchen to see Haley and Mandi making breakfast. Eggs, bacon, and some toast that looked like it was made in an incinerator.

"We made everyone breakfast!" Mandi exclaimed.

"We kinda burnt the toast though," explained Haley.

"That was nice of you two, wow, a lady could get used to this!"

"I'll get us all some plates and silverware. We'll have to eat on the floor or on the coffee table since we don't have a table here," Jackson said, half-embarrassed that he hadn't bothered to even buy a table or chairs in the eleven months since his divorce.

They made new toast and threw the burnt stuff out to the dog, who snarffed it down like it was lobster. They ate on the floor and giggled and laughed the rest of the morning. They were getting ready to leave when the doorbell rang.

Haley ran to the door and yelled "Mom's here," and she went back to playing with Mandi.

"What are you doing here? I was planning on running her up this afternoon since there was no volleyball today."

"We were at Frank's parent's house partying last night, so we just thought we would stop by and grab her on our way home," Camille explained. Clearly nursing a hangover. "We spent the night in the cabin, and it wasn't very comfortable out there. I hate that place."

"I thought she was going to spend the whole week with me anyway, what happened to that?" Jackson asked, remembering the conversation from the day Klaire had decided to go on a ride with him.

"You get enough time with her as it is, besides, her *real* dad wants her before school starts," Camille said with just enough bitchiness to show who had the upper hand in this conversation.

"That's good, but I could have run her over to him. It is just across town. You didn't need to stop in."

"Oh, I think I did need to stop to see what kind of things you have Haley doing." Camille snorted, like she knew something he didn't know that she knew about.

"What's that supposed to mean?" Jackson replied, clearly not understanding what she was getting at.

"Oh, you know, since you were arrested and still have a police stake out sitting outside. I don't know what you are into nowadays, or who this floozy that spent the night is, but I'm thinking you may not be spending as much time with Haley as you have been getting."

"*Mom*!! I'm not sure what a flew-see is, but Klaire is a nice person. She is just a friend, and I invited Mandi over to watch a movie, and we fell asleep. So if you are mad, you should be mad at me," spouted Haley, defending her stepdad.

"Whatever, let's go," huffed Camille.

"Love ya!!" Haley hugged her stepdad, "See you soon!!" and she headed out the door. "Remember our conversation from the car, Klaire! See you, Mandi, thanks for coming over!"

Jackson hurried to the door, "I wasn't arrested. I was questioned, there is a difference!!! Stupid small-town gossip."

He closed the door and turned to Klaire and Mandi.

"What is she talking about?" Klaire asked.

"A couple people I know were murdered recently, and the cops had to come ask me if I did it since I didn't like one of them, and I may have been engaged to the other one in a former life."

"Holy...wow. Um, well, we need to go. I don't need my little girl involved in any of this," Klaire nervously responded. She was a little scared and didn't know what to think.

"I didn't do it, in case you were worried. I was actually with you the day one of the murders happened. It was the day we went for a ride."

"Well, I wouldn't think you would, but I still don't need my little girl involved in this. Maybe our timing is just bad."

"Of course, I understand. Children should always come first. I hope we can pick it up again as soon as this is all straightened out. I know we don't know each other well, but from what I've learned so far, I am very interested in pursuing whatever it is we have started here," Jackson shared.

"I have actually really enjoyed your company as well. I didn't think I would, but there is something that draws me to you. We need to get going though. Thank you and Haley for a fun evening. Perhaps, we can do it again soon, if you get this...whatever it is cleared up," Klaire admitted, and she leaned in and gave Jackson a peck on his cheek and held her cheek close to his for a few seconds. "By the way, don't be telling all your buddies at work that you slept with me, even though it was just sleep. I don't like people talking about me and my personal life."

"I'm actually glad the night ended up like it did, with us just 'sleeping together' and nothing else. I want you to know that I'm not just after your body. I want all of you...even though...you have a body that just begs to be touched," Jackson admitted.

"We will have to see if you can have the rest, the body comes with it you know. Ha-ha-ha." Klaire blushed as she said that. She wasn't exactly used to bragging about her body. "On that note, we gotta go."

"C-ya later, Mandi!! Thank you for coming over and for making us breakfast."

"Bye, Jackson," Mandi said shyly. "Do you think I can borrow your *Cinderella* movie?"

"Mandi Jo! You don't ask people for things they own!" a shocked Klaire almost shouted.

"It's okay, you can borrow it, Mandi. I'm sure Haley wouldn't mind one bit. *Plus*, that way I know you will have to see me again," Jackson said to the little girl.

"Nice, Jackson Ackerman, use the cute little girl to get the mom," chuckled Klaire.

"Hey, what can I say, I enjoy seeing you two lovely ladies!!"

"Okay, we are outta here, see you later, we better leave before you try to give her something else."

They left with the movie, both seemingly happy, considering the shocking news that Jackson was somehow involved in a couple of murders.

The detectives wrote down what time everyone left the house. They had long since ran the plates on the vehicle so they knew who was driving each vehicle. But they were not the only ones paying attention to who was coming and going.

CHAPTER 23

The rest of the week went as normal as it could; the neighbor mowed Jackson's lawn like normal. Jackson took his dog for a walk every night and was getting Raider ready to walk Thursday evening after work. When he was hooking the dog up to his leash, he noticed something moving in the tree behind his house. He wasn't sure what it was, but he knew it wasn't the deer that normally roamed back there on occasion. He walked a couple steps to his truck, which was in the garage, and dug out one of his hunting knives. He snuck back over to the door to the back deck, and he saw someone coming out of the woods. Dressed all in black, clearly trying not to be seen.

When the person got right next to the door, Jackson said, "You pretty much suck at being sneaky."

The petite, little woman nearly fell over from being scared so badly.

"Jesus *balls*!!! Don't do that to a girl!!" shrieked Tami. "Nearly scared my tits off me!"

"We wouldn't want that. They are a nice asset to have." Jackson laughed. "What are you doing, trying to sneak into my house anyway?"

"I was thinking you would already be on your walk, and I was going to sneak into your bed and spend the night with you. I told my husband that I was staying at my parent's house, and I am moving out in two days."

"I can't have you spending the night here, what if someone else saw you sneaking up here, like I did?"

"I'll be legally separated as of tomorrow, so it shouldn't matter, unless you are embarrassed to be seen with me?" Tami said as shyly as he had ever heard her say anything.

"I just don't need more trouble is all I'm saying. I'm not embarrassed. Since you are here, I guess Raider here isn't getting walked tonight. Want to watch some TV or something?" Jackson unhooked the dog and put his radio collar back on him. He opened the door to the house and gestured for her to enter.

"I was hoping for the something part of that offer," and she walked past Jackson and dragged her hand across his chest and pulled him along with her.

She led him to the living room where she pulled the curtains closed and pushed him down onto the ugly couch that he hated so much. She reached over and hit the power button on the stereo system, tuned it to a soft rock station, and turned the sound on low. Tami did her best striptease act that she could do. Which wasn't too bad judging from the erection she could feel under Jackson's jeans, when she started grinding with him. He went to grab her and pull her closer to him, but she slapped his hand.

"No touching, until I say so," she commanded. "I need to torture you for a bit longer."

Jackson did as he was told; he wasn't sure he wanted to be in this strange relationship that was forming with this lady, but she was super hot, and she may have been the horniest woman he had ever met. He would go with it for now.

"I think you have had enough torture, now take your clothes off and show me what you got," Tami demanded.

Tami still had her underwear on but nothing else. Jackson slowly took his clothes off. When he was completely naked, he laid Tami down on the floor on her back and propped her legs up onto his shoulders. He had a little sneak show of his own for Tami, as he has dug into his jeans pocket and pulled out his hunting knife that he had grabbed earlier. As she was lying there nearly naked, completely vulnerable with her legs in the air, he slid the knife down her bare leg, starting near her knee on her left leg, which was on his right side. She had heard the rumors and seen the police pick him up, so she started to shake a little with true fear.

"Don't move, I don't want to hurt you," Jackson said in a deep, serious voice.

"Please don't hurt me!!" Tami said in a whimpering voice.

"Quite the opposite, I want to please you," Jackson said, still in his serious voice.

He reached the point between her legs that was calling to him. He took the knife and gently slid it under her eighty-dollar lacey underwear and sliced them all the way through and then again. He ripped them off and threw them over toward the stereo and threw the knife against the wall so that it stuck in the wood trim near the floor.

He went down on Tami, and using every trick in his book, he made that woman squirm and tense up and moan, twist, turn, and hold his head with one hand, as she pulled and pushed on her own breasts with the other. She had never felt such euphoria, and right before she thought she would explode, he pulled himself into her with his solidness, thrusting into her holiest of holies. He could feel her innards grabbing and pulling on his member, begging for it to keep the action up. It throbbed, and he could feel her legs wrapped around his bottom like a vise grip. There was no getting away from her until she was done with him. She leaned forward and buried her face into his chest, which was now dripping with perspiration as she was.

He couldn't hold back his excitement any longer, and at the very moment he exploded into her, he could feel her orgasm at the same time, making it an even better ejaculation.

They were both completely wiped out and were not able to move. He just laid on top of her for a while; his manhood was no longer solid as it was before. The blood slowly rushed back to the other parts of his body that needed it. He regained brain function and slid himself out of her and rolled over and laid on the carpet beside her. His knees completely scraped with carpet burn.

"I didn't even notice the carpet burn on my knees. That is going to hurt for a few days," Jackson said, still trying to regain his normal breathing.

"I think I have some on my back too," and Tami rolled over, and he could see a big red burn mark right around the area some ladies would have a tattoo.

"Nice tramp stamp," he laughed.

They decided to go up to the bedroom and lay there together with the fan blowing on them. There was central air, but the fan still felt good on their naked sweaty bodies, cooling them off, and soon they became chilled from the sweat and the cool air.

The two pulled the covers up over them, and she snuggled into his chest and began sucking on his chest. He flipped her over and stuck his head between her breasts and licked the sweat from between them. It was a sweet and salty taste; he moved to a nipple and ran his tongue over it repeatedly, causing it to become erect. Her breasts were firm and so was her ass, which he had cupped in one hand.

Wanting to repay him for earlier, she pushed him off and slowly kissed his chest and moved down, inch by inch, to his stomach, which was flat and muscular, not quite a perfect six pack but pretty good for someone his age. She finally made it down to his shaft, which she inserted into her mouth. She took almost the whole thing in, while keeping a grasp of the base as she worked it. Using her lips, tongue, the side of her face, she pleased him orally until she thought he was almost done. Then she turned around, still holding the base of his organ. She placed it inside of her, and she slid down onto it with all of her weight.

The ceiling was angled at the one side of the bedroom, which happened to have the bed butted up against. She put one hand on the slanted ceiling and leaned back and put the other one right square in the middle of his sternum. Riding him like a bronc at the rodeo, she had complete control of him. She watched as his toes curled in, and she knew she could probably do whatever she wanted to him at this moment, and he couldn't, or wouldn't, stop her.

Jackson thought to himself, *If we were filming this, we would be rich. People would pay a lot of money to watch porn this good.* Then he finished when she suddenly tickled him on the bottom of his sack. It was unexpected but extremely fulfilling.

He was so exhausted; he was asleep within minutes, and she was also, shortly after he was. Neither bothered to put anything back on; they didn't have the energy to.

When Jackson woke in the morning, he was alone; he hadn't seen or heard her get dressed and leave shortly before he had woken. She thought she was being sneaky and got out with nobody seeing her. But just as she was spotted coming into the house by Jackson, someone was there to see her sneaking out.

CHAPTER 24

S amantha had a rough week at work, which she always seemed to bring home with her. Living alone, you tend to bring your thoughts home with you, and they stay there. Monday, the cancer ward she works in lost a young boy from Atlanta to that damn *C* word. He was the cutest little boy, barely five years old. He was brought up to Mayo from Atlanta by his parents, who seemed to be the nicest people ever. All of them were very polite and appreciated everything that she would do for them. Little Xavier Allen Johnson had been receiving chemo here for around five months, but he was just too far along by the time he got there that there wasn't much hope for him. He had shown some signs of fighting the disease right away, but after the first month, everyone pretty much knew what the outcome was going to be.

Samantha helped the family with making the arrangements to get Xavier back home to Georgia so he could have the funeral. After working in this unit for years, it just becomes second nature to work with the airlines and funeral services. It was easier for her than it would be for the families to figure it all out on their own, so she gladly offered her help. Of course, the Johnsons were very apprecia-tive, as always. Southern charm even through the hard times. She was used to "MN nice," but this was something beyond that. This was true humbleness and gratefulness.

If Monday wasn't bad enough, Thursday afternoon, before she was getting ready to leave for a much needed four-day Labor Day weekend, the worst news of her career came from her doctor. Her favorite patient, Tayah, has passed away. Tayah and her parent's David and Brenda had become like family to Sam. Normally, she tried to not get involved in her patients' lives, for not only professional reasons but also because sometimes things like this happen, so she liked to keep her distance.

Tayah had come to visit Samantha's area as a beautiful little ten-year-old girl. Long-flowing blonde hair, blue eyes, perfect teeth, and what looked to be great physical shape. Sam knew she was into sports the moment she walked in. She could remember she had her basketball jersey on. She came in because she wasn't feeling very good, with a constant pain in her stomach, but not bad enough to make her sit out of any games. She was planning on going to her fourth grade basketball team's practice after her appointment. Samantha remembered how disappointed she looked when she walked out of the office that night, after her doctor had informed her that she wouldn't be able to play hoops for a while. The illness was nothing compared to her emotions about the fact that she couldn't play ball.

Sam and Tayah's parents had become good friends. They were from a nearby town, and after a few visits and phone calls to set up appointments, her mom friend requested her on Facebook. That was almost six years ago. Tayah had taken driver's training and was looking forward to getting her driver's license. Now…that wasn't going to happen. Her dreams of becoming a nurse no longer going to happen. Nothing was going to happen because…she was gone. Samantha was crushed.

Sam went home for the evening and sent a text message to Brenda letting her know that if she needed help with anything, to let her know, and that she was sorry for their loss, and how she was going to miss seeing Tayah.

She put her pj's on as soon as she got home, which consisted of an extra-large concert shirt that she commandeered from a super buff roadie at a Motley Crue concert a few years ago. He wasn't Nikki Sixx, but he did have one fine booty.

Curled up on her couch with a soft furry blanket, she cried herself to sleep. She always tried to keep up the image that nothing bothered her, but deep down, she was a softie. Anyone who knew her could see right through her and knew this, but she would never admit it.

The next morning was her first of four days off. She had planned on going to the river with some friends for the weekend, but she wasn't feeling up to it right now and decided to just lounge around in some sweatpants and sweatshirt, no bra or panties. Just relaxing. She looked in the mirror and saw that her eyes were still puffy and red from crying all night, and her makeup looked like she was going to a Halloween party, and she was some crazy zombie. *Omg*, look at how crazy her hair looked!!!

She was kind of hungry since she hadn't bothered to eat anything the night before, but she didn't want to cook.

"Let's see, Dairy Queen or Kwik Trip?" She just happened to live across the street from the ice cream shop and the gas station/convenience store. Both of which were bad for her hips and ass. "Hmm, ice cream at DQ, or ice cream and chocolate at KT? Kwik Trip it is!!"

Sam grabbed a hat out of her closet and washed her face off, so she at least looked somewhat human again.

"I hope nobody sees me this morning," and she headed out across the street to pick up her comfort food and calories.

CHAPTER 25

Since Jackson had a four-day weekend, he decided he would sleep in and make his way up to the cabin. Chad was going to meet him there, but he was going to work all day and head up right after that.

Jackson was in charge of the food for the weekend. So he grabbed his biggest cooler out of the garage and pulled it into the house. He looked inside his freezer above the fridge in the kitchen, and all he saw were frozen waffles, which were for Haley when she stayed. One hot pocket, which would not be a good meal for two grown men, two frozen Tombstone pizzas, and three ice cubes in an otherwise empty ice cube tray.

He grabbed the two frozen pizzas. They had a pizza oven at the cabin, a little rotating heater thing that looked more like a milkshake machine than an oven. "Okay, that's one meal. I'm through with Friday. Two and a half more days left."

Seeing the humor in only having three ice cubes, he grabbed the tray and emptied it into the cooler. "I guess I need to stop and get ice." He filled the ice tray with fresh water from the sink, along with the other two empty trays still sitting in the freezer.

Luckily, Jackson had another small cube freezer with meat in it. It was right outside the door of the kitchen, in the garage, so he slid the cooler over to the door and opened it. Deer steak sounds good; one package of those should feed the two of them, so he tossed one of those in the cooler. There was an opened box of Swan's chicken breasts sitting there, so he grabbed four of those. That looks like about all that will work out of here.

Back to the fridge, *Wow, I need to go grocery shopping*, Jackson thought as he stared at a refrigerator with a door completely full of condiments, a one-fourth gallon of milk, a twelve pack of Diet Dr. Pepper box, that contained two cans of pop, and a container of some sort of leftover food from his parent's house from the last time he was over there. *God, that had to be two months ago. I bet that is pretty good by now.*

Jackson grabbed the two cans of pop, ketchup, mustard, A-1 steak sauce, mayo, and what was left of his grandma's homemade strawberry jam. He threw all of that in the cooler.

Looking into his cooler and the lack of actual food in it, he said, "Pathetic, Jackson," as if there was someone there helping him pack. Of course, there wasn't. That may have been one of the only things he missed about being married to Camille; she was there to talk to most of the time. Now, he talked to himself, his dog, and once in a while, the deer hanging on the wall.

He already had the truck loaded with his fishing things that he needed. Most of his equipment was already there, but he always thought he needed to have a pole with when leaving for a fishing trip in the truck. He put the cooler and his bag of clothes in the back seat of his Ford F-150 and closed the third door. Everyone always said he needed a full four-door truck, but he couldn't afford a new vehicle since Camille got the last new vehicle that he may ever pay for. This black Ford better last him a while, and with his history of Ford trucks, he just hoped he would make it up fishing and back. Never know when this damn thing was going to bust a coil or something else expensive as hell.

He didn't like admitting that he couldn't afford anything, so he would tell people that he loved that old truck. Truth was, he couldn't wait until he could get a new Chevy because he was completely over owning a Ford.

Jackson said goodbye to Raider and backed out of the driveway, hitting the garage door button to close the door. The neighbor kid promised to feed and water the dog and even take him for a walk if he was bored. The kid was always bored, so he hoped he wouldn't wear his dog out walking him too much. He was fourteen and didn't seem to have many friends, but he seemed like a decent enough person, so Jackson didn't mind giving him some cash to look after his dog.

As Jackson pulled up to the stop sign at the end of the block, he reached back and grabbed one of the two cans of Diet Dr. Pepper out of the cooler and popped it open. He took a swig and placed it in the cup holder. He opened the console and pulled out his pack of smokes and punched the lighter which was just below the radio. Good thing about having an old truck is that they still have lighters installed in them.

The lighter popped out, indicating that it was hot and ready to set fire to something. He grabbed it and placed it to his cigarette and drew in. That first cigarette of the weekend was always the best. He was going to enjoy this one.

No sooner had he thought of how good the weekend was going to be and he noticed the light-brown Crown Victoria pull up behind him.

"Ahhh, *hell no!*" he said in an agitated tone that he rarely used.

Jackson slammed the truck in park and opened his door, leaving it open, and walked back to the "undercover" cops. He motioned for them to roll down the window.

"Are you fuckers going to follow me all the way up to the cabin and camp out in the campground with me? Did you bring a boat because I'm going fishing. Make sure you have sunscreen. You burn more easily on the water you know."

"Well, if that is where you are going, we may follow you, not sure yet. You should have given us a heads-up so we could have packed for the weekend," the driver of the car replied.

"Try to keep up," and Jackson walked back to his truck and took off.

Jackson got as far as Chatfield and figured that he better fuel up the gas hog and get the rest of the food for the weekend. He was glad to see that the truck still had some fuel in it, so it was only a bit over eighty dollars to fill the tank. *Geez, I can make it up and back on about twenty-five dollars on the bike, and this is only going to be enough to get there.* Jackson didn't like it when it was his turn to bring food.

After filling the truck, he walks into Kwik Trip and grabs one of those little basket things for putting groceries in. He always feels gay holding this little basket, like Dorothy in the *Wizard of Oz*. That reminded him of his sister, who was happy as shit that her ex's wife was offed, which reminded him of the two dork cops sitting outside, waiting for him to pick up some luncheon meat and bread.

Jackson grabbed two loaves of bread, a package of ham, and one of bologna, a package of hotdogs, a jar of peanut butter, and two packages of sliced cheese. He was halfway to the checkout when he remembered. *Pop!* He went back to the back part of the convenience store and grabbed a twelve pack of his Diet Dr. Pepper. Just as he was grabbing it, a truck driver walked out of the rest room and announced, "I wouldn't go in there for a while, damn truck stop burritos."

Jackson looked at the man and chuckled, "But they sure taste good, don't they?"

"Damn right, they do."

Jackson made his way to the checkout and paid for his food and gas. The attendant put everything in a couple of plastic bags, and he turned and looked in the other checkout line, and he saw someone he knew.

"Hey, Samantha!"

She didn't even want to turn around, she knew that voice anywhere. It had to be her friend Camille's ex-husband, Jackson Ackerman. The one man she did *not* want to have him see her like this. She turned, with her half-gallon of cookies-n-cream ice cream, three different candy bars, and a black coffee.

"Hey, Jackson, what are you doing here? Don't you work on Fridays either?"

"No, I work four ten-hour days. I'm heading up to the cabin for some fishing. What do you have planned for the day? Are you having an ice cream party? Lol."

"Ya, all by myself. It's been a long week."

"A good-looking woman like you, with no plans for a long weekend? Some lucky man would be in heaven to spend time with you."

"Ya, I'm hot, you can see my outfit right. I'm the poster child for sexy."

"Well...I have seen you look better, but you still make most women look bad, even in your sweatpants. The hat makes up for it. Gotta love a woman in a baseball cap. *That* is sexy!"

"Well, I better get home to my party." She couldn't get away quick enough; she was so embarrassed that he had seen her looking this bad.

"Hey, Sam, seriously though, you aren't going on any hot dates this weekend?"

They walked outside together, Jackson holding the door with his ass since his hands were full.

She could tell Jackson was wanting to flirt with her, but apparently, he kind of sucked at it. "Well, you know...if a good-looking guy would ever *ask* me out, I would maybe have a date for a long weekend...if you happen to know anyone who would want to put up with me."

Jackson was actually very surprised. Was she telling him that he needed to ask her out? He had always been attracted to Samantha since the first time he met her. He remembers right after he got married, Camille and he picked her up, and they all went to a street dance together. She looked like the girl next door but sexier. She wasn't flashy, but she definitely stood out in a crowd.

"Well, I'd ask you out now, but you already have a party going on, and I have fish to catch. I don't believe I have your number, but if it is okay with you, I can e-mail you on Tuesday when we get back to work and get that from you if you don't mind. I may know someone who would be interested in 'putting up with you' for a while." Jackson used his hands to signal air quotes, but it looked stupid since he had a twelve pack of pop in one hand and three bags of groceries in the other. To make things worse, he dropped one of the bags.

"Ha-ha-ha," Sam instantly burst out laughing. "Oh, Jackson, you still make me laugh. Yes, please e-mail me and let me know who this someone is." She winked and turned to walk away.

"Just warning you, he may not be that hot, but I've heard that he can make you laugh!" he yelled across the parking lot. "And don't worry, it was just my meat that I dropped, it will be okay."

Wow, that was dumb, he should learn to not say stupid things. *Why the hell am I nervous around her? I'm not nervous around anyone.*

He watched her hurry away; she surely should not wear sweat-pants, not with the bottom he knew that she possessed. She still looked good. He wouldn't kick her out of bed for eating crackers. Well, unless they were those Triscuit things, he'd kick her out just on principle. Those things were disgusting. Jackson thought about that again. Who was he kidding, he couldn't think of a single thing that would truly make him kick that lady out of his bed.

Jackson stuffed the food into the cooler and tried to not smash the bread, so he put that on top of his clothing bag. As he pulled out of the gas station, he saw the light brown-car pull out behind him.

CHAPTER 26

The cabin was cold and musty smelling, with a hint of the smell of bleach and cleaning solutions. How long had she been here anyway, a week, two, a month? Days all ran together. Why wasn't anyone out finding her? Surely her family would be worried; she normally talked to her mom every day. Her boyfriend must be worried sick too. Was this creep ever going to let her go? He barely fed her anything, and she was always sitting in her own urine. She had probably lost thirty pounds since being here, and since she was so tiny to start with, her health was deteriorating fast. She figured she would be dead in another week at this rate if he didn't kill her first. He had bound her and gagged her one day and blindfolded her and stuck her out back of the cabin for an entire day. She could hear other people but couldn't get their attention. He had moved her back inside after they had all left.

The sun was just starting to set when the door swung open. There he was; he looked like he was in a good mood.

"Well, good news!! Today is the last day you will have to be here. I'm getting you out of here because I have people coming here again, and we can't have them seeing you. That could get ugly. Before we get you out of here though, we need to go on a date."

She wasn't happy to hear those words. His version of going on a date was her being tied to the bed and him raping her. Usually with his penis, or fingers, but sometimes he wouldn't be able to get it up after doing it once or twice, so he would find whatever he could find and use that. She wasn't sure what was worse, but it all hurt. She was pretty much oblivious to the emotional pain by now, but the physical pain was horrendous. Her private area was so sore that it constantly throbbed, even when he was gone for the day; it just plain hurt. He had shoved the handle of the broom so far up inside her that she was pretty sure it had caused long-term damage. She just had to get through one more night, and he would let her go.

As he tied her up, he got down and smelled where she had urinated and took a deep whiff. "I'm going to miss that smell, not sure how I'm going to be able to get off without it now, but I'm sure I'll manage."

He only got off one time before he went looking for something else to use this time. He came back from outside with a funnel and more rope.

"Let's go for a ride! You are getting out of here!!"

Ann actually managed to smile a little at the thought of going home and leaving this nightmare behind her.

He put her in the back of his truck and closed the tonna cover that he had just purchased. She didn't know how far they had driven but estimated that it was about thirty to forty-five minutes. She was trying to keep track of time and anything she noticed as far as sounds, smells, anything that could lead the police back to this place. She was even trying to keep track of how many left and right turns he was making, but with her mind not working well from the malnutrition, she lost count and became confused, so she had given that up. Finally, the truck came to a stop, and she heard him get out. The truck was still running, but the cover to the bed of the truck opened, and he slid her out and leaned her up next to a mailbox post. Tied her up but not very well, she figured she could get those knots out as soon as he left. She sat there on the ground, dirty, and bloody from being raped, naked. He brought the funnel out and jammed it up inside her as hard as he could. The pain she had was excruciating, and she screamed out in pain. He put a rag in her mouth to shut her up. She was balling hysterically from the pain as he walked back to the truck to get something else.

He returned with two jugs of gasoline. The first, he started dumping into the funnel that was in her vagina, filling it with gas, then dumped the rest of it over her legs. The second jug was dumped over her head and her torso.

He put the two jugs back in the truck and walked back to her.

"I told you that you would get out of there today, but I'm afraid you won't make it back home. Asta Lavista, baby!" He thought he was pretty cool quoting that line from an old *Terminator* movie. He lit a wooden match and threw it at her, expecting her to burst into a fireball. The match went out when he threw it, and it got caught in the wind and didn't land anywhere near her.

"*Shit!* I better pick that up, my prints are on it. I almost messed up. Ha-ha. I figured I'd burn all my DNA that is on and in you, but I could have made it simple and left them a print."

He then took out a glove from his pocket and tried to light another one. It was much harder with a glove on, but he finally got it lit and dropped it closer to her, and she exploded in flames. He actually felt like he got blown back a little by the burst of energy from the fire, and his glove actually started on fire, but he quickly got that put out before he got burnt.

He quickly hopped back into his truck and took off, making sure not to spin out so the police would have a harder time figuring out which tire tracks were his on the highly used gravel road. Even if they do figure out what kind of tires he used, they were a very common tire.

He had just enough time to get back and clean up the cabin before anyone else showed up.

CHAPTER 27

Detective Holmes was just about to hit the sack for the night, but he thought that he would check his Match.com account one more time to see if he had anyone interested in him. He seriously had second thoughts about his profile picture of him in his police uniform. *Do girls still like a man in uniform?* Seems like they all want the bad-boy biker guy, drinking and smoking and showing that he don't have a care in the world. That was about as far away from him as you could get. He wasn't a church-going, bible-thumper, but he was about as straight laced and as boring as they came. Heck, it was barely what, ten-fifteen on a Friday night, and he was getting ready to go to bed alone again. Same thing that he had done damn near every night since he got out of the academy. Maybe he needed to start hitting the bars and trying to find a woman. Find one the old-fashion way since this online dating thing didn't seem to be working.

He looked through a few pictures and decided that it wasn't worth it, and he would just turn in for the night. He'd get up in the morning and mow the lawn as soon as the grass was dry enough, then head to the office to see where he could get with these murders and the missing lady.

That's when he noticed headlights turning from off his road onto the highway. Not that this was something out of the ordinary, but living in the country, he usually knew when someone drove by his house. He was trying to be more diligent about watching who drove by since dead ladies started showing up by his mailbox. He glanced in the direction of his mailbox, just to prove there wasn't another dead body there. Detective Holmes caught another light source out of the corner of his eye. This was more of a flickering than just a headlight. He got closer to the window and leaned onto the sill.

"*Holy fuck*, someone set something on fire down there!! Ohhh nooo *ohhh noooo*!!!" He instantly realized what it was, grabbed his cell phone, and a blanket. Calling 911 for a cop isn't exactly something that he ever wants to do, but what does he do? He needs to report it; he is a witness, and he needed the fire department. He knew it would be too late by the time they arrived, but they would need to come.

Racing down his driveway in nothing more than a pair of athletic shorts, he called 911 and told them he needed a firetruck and police. "*Now, God dammit, I need them right friggin now!*" The dispatcher didn't know if the detective was angry, or scared as he yelled into the phone at her. In truth, it was a little of both. He was angry that this perp kept choosing to drop dead people off at his house. Angry that he couldn't catch the guy and scared that this woman may still be alive as he raced toward her armed with just a blanket.

It was only around 150 yards from his front door to the end of the driveway, but it seemed like it was miles. It was surely the longest stretch he had ever run in his life. As he reached the burning pile leaning on his mailbox, he knew right away that it was a human. He attempted to put the figure out with his blanket, but it only caught on fire too and was of no use. All he could do is stand there and watch this lady burn to death. He had seen in movies where someone would shoot someone on fire to put them out of their misery. Not only was he not carrying his sidearm but that would really mess up the evidence. He didn't hear any more sounds, so he figured she had finally succumb to the flames. *Thank God.* Never thought he would want someone to die, but her suffering was finally over.

He was about 90 percent sure this person lying in front of him was Anne Passe, the missing girl who went missing with Brandy. The girl's boyfriend of three months hadn't even notified anyone that she was missing for three days. What a piece of shit that guy must be; he heard secondhand that he left the party they were at together with someone else that night. So he had an alibi, but it was still a pretty shady deal. He may have to pay that guy a visit again, but he was pretty sure he already knew who was doing this, and he lived right across the border in a little town called Preston. He got a bad feeling about that guy, and he just had to find one piece of hard evidence to nail that bastard's balls to the wall. As soon as this lady quit burning and smoldering, he was going to find that shred of evidence and go pay another visit to Mr. Jackson Ackerman. This time he would lead him away in cuffs. Maybe even call the press anonymously and get a little bit of PR time in, in case he decided to run for sheriff.

CHAPTER 28

Sundays at the cabin always seemed to come too fast. It didn't feel like they even were on the lake very much all weekend. Friday was mostly spent cleaning up around the cabin, mowing the weeds, and picking up all the small branches that had fallen during the thunderstorms during the last couple of weeks since he and his brother had been there. It was about one-thirty, and Jackson started bringing his bag of clothes and things out to his truck when he saw his brother coming up the dirt path. He had been out walking the dog.

"Hey dumb ass!! What are you doing? Aren't you staying another night? It is Labor Day weekend. You don't work tomorrow," Chad yelled at his little brother from a distance. He couldn't tell if he was pissed that his brother was leaving, or shocked.

"Oh, for fuck sake, I'm a dumb ass. Hahahaha, totally spaced it, thought it was a normal weekend. I guess my mind is on other things," Jackson replied, feeling like a total dork.

"What you got going on in the little brain of yours anyway? You thinking about some girl, or about all these women that you happen to know, who keep getting killed."

Jackson thought about it for a bit, "A little of both, I think. Mostly about these women being killed and the fact that our sister hasn't found me a lawyer yet, which she promised me she would get me."

"You better get on that!! Jeezus Christ, what are you waiting for? If she don't get you one, you find yourself one. You don't need to be caught up in all that shit. You better have one by Tuesday evening, or

I'm going to find you one myself," Chad said, slightly irritated that his younger brother was taking this so lightly.

"Ya, you are right. I'll get it done Tuesday morning," Jackson replied. "I'll get it done, don't worry."

"Well, I kinda worry about shit when my brother is the number one suspect in multiple homicides. Sorry for caring."

"Sorry, you are right. I guess I just keep thinking about why anyone would choose those particular women. I mean, Roxy, I get why someone would want to kill her. She was a dumb bitch. But Brandy…she was a good person, beautiful inside and out."

"Dude, don't beat yourself up, you didn't do it to her. You treated her like crap when you were dating, but that didn't kill her. You did mess that relationship up you know." Laughed the older sibling, "Sorry, but you did, she was a great girl."

"Salt…wound…rubbing…" Jackson started rubbing his shoulder hard, imitating his brother rubbing the salt into his still open wound.

"Jeezus Christ, it's been twenty years, time to get over it. You were young and dumb and full of cum. You messed up, get the fuck over it already," Chad said, a tad bit irritated.

"I'm over it, she just didn't deserve that."

"Nobody does. Except, maybe the bastard doing the killing," Chad ended the conversation with that as neither one of them knew what to say.

CHAPTER 29

It was Monday, Labor Day, so most people had the day off. A lot of people were doing their final camping trip of the season before school started the next day. A lot of adults were waking up hung over from the previous couple of days.

The campground was just starting to wake up, and Tami had been up for a while, getting breakfast ready for her two kids and her husband. They had not really been getting along very well the last six months, but they seemed to have made up, and the last week was actually very pleasant.

She had the picnic table set just perfect, like a scene from a magazine. There were pancakes with bacon, scrambled eggs, and even toast; all made over a campfire. She stood back before waking the family up to eat, admiring her work.

"Fuck, Martha Stewart, I'd like to see her do this without her stove."

She poked her head inside the camper and yelled in her best soothing, motherly voice. "Rise and shine, sleepyheads!! Breakfast is on the table, don't let it get cold… Randy, I made the bacon just the way you like it…since you gave me you know what, just how I like it last night."

Her husband lifted his head slightly off the orange, black, and tan thin camper mattress that never seemed to be able to keep any sort of sheets on it, gave his wife a smile, and stretched before getting out of bed.

Tami was the happiest she had been in a long time, and she was thinking that she needed to tell Jackson that she was going to stay with her husband and put an end to their little fling. She heard through Jackson's sister, who worked just across the hall from her at the courthouse, that he was interested in some girl he worked with anyway. But on the other hand, why quit something so good; he is probably the reason her marriage was so good right now. She was less on edge after some amazing sex and would come home in a good mood and not yell at her husband, which put him in a better mood. Heck, this affair may actually be essential to her being able to stay with her husband. *I'm keeping him and just let him keep thinking I'm leaving Randy.*

The family sat down in the calm September air to eat their meal. There wasn't much talking, just a lot of clinking of forks on the metal plates that they used while camping. The kids ate like their parents have been starving them for a week; teenage boys seemed to be bottomless pits. The older one, who was the spitting image of his dad, was getting to be tall now; his brown hair was getting longer. Ever since he saw a couple pictures of his father's mullet back in high school, he had been growing it out. It was shaggy and looked pretty bad according to every adult who took time to notice it.

The junior of the two kids was short and resembled his mother's side. Tami had been seriously worried, hoped, and even prayed that he did not turn out to look like his father. Considering the fact that he was indeed not her husband spawn but a former boss, who had promised her a promotion if she slept with him. She never did get a promotion, or even a raise. She got him off, and all she got was some really bad extra-marital sex, a case of the crabs, and a baby. Tami was more afraid of her son looking like his blood father, mostly because she didn't want to have to look at any resemblance to his troll looking face for the rest of her life. So the fact that he was just short was just fine.

Tami was the first to finish as she barely ate anything, and her husband could tell she was ready to go for her morning walk. So he said, "Hun, get going on your walk. The boys and I will handle cleaning up, then when you get back, we can go to the pool for a bit before packing up for home."

"Aww, thank you, guys!! I won't be gone long, just need to get a little burn in to work off that pancake I just had. Later!!"

*****

Tami took off on her walking route; there was a trail system that went out into the woods. The trails branched off multiple different ways, but after coming to this campground for years, she had it down to a science and knew what route was the most beneficial to her burning calories and also which one led past the most campers that would have the most men sitting outside on her return route. She usually got a whistle or two as she passed, depending on how many of the wives were around at the time. She enjoyed the attention and always wore something to make the guys look but also enough to cover up, so she didn't look like a slut.

She set off on her walk, moving at a brisk pace, but not enough to be considered a power walk. As she started up the first hill in the woods, she could feel the burn in her calves and her ass muscles. She thought of Jackson and how he had worked a couple of her muscles that she forgot she had, and she thought that she would need to work on those the next time she was in the gym.

CHAPTER 30

It was just getting to be daylight when he got to the spot that he had selected the day before. Two days of surveillance and a lot of walking and he had the perfect little ambush site. This trail was pretty busy the first day of the weekend and a little less on Sunday as some of the wanna-be athletes couldn't get their lazy asses out of bed, probably because they hit the sauce a little too hard the previous evening. This morning, there were even less people than the day before. The die hards were still out; most of them were on the path early before most people were even up, making it difficult for him to get to and into his hiding spot.

One issue he had to face was that these people who ran and walked these trails were very familiar with them, and if he changed the landscape to create a makeshift blind, to hide out in, they would notice and become wary. So he had to find something natural that would work.

The place the he picked out was a little water runway that he could lay down in and see his prey as they climbed the hill. Then as they crested the hill and began to descend, the trail angled off just slightly to the left so that he would have time to get up and make the five steps to the trail quickly enough that he could catch her. He had practiced this the afternoon before, and he was very happy with this set up.

Dressed in full camo, with face paint and everything, he lay in wait. There had already been a few runners and walkers go by him, and nobody had notice him yet. The morning dew pretty much had him soaked from head to toe. He hadn't planned for that since he was doing his scouting for a spot in the fall afternoon and not the morning. It was a cool sixty-degree morning, which normally would not be cold, but he was wet, and so he was cold. He cursed himself for not thinking about the dew. He had been hunting his whole life and knew that it would be wet in the morning, but in his haste to put this plan together, it was a detail that was overlooked.

As he lay there shivering, he started to get angry. He was having a hard time staying still since he was shivering. He was contemplating giving up and heading home empty-handed. But his deer-hunting self convinced himself to stick it out just a little bit longer. His experience taught him that when he would give up and think nothing was coming in to be shot and he would get up to leave early, that is when the big buck would step out, and he would scare it away, and he would never see it again. This was the same thing; he can't spook his victim away. He *had* to stick it out.

His thoughts were running wild, and his patience was about to end when he saw movement on the trail below… *Holy hell! It is her!*

The predator immediately forgot about being cold; he forgot about being wet; his adrenaline was through the roof.

Tami came over the hill and started down the hill. She never noticed the man hidden just off the trail who was there to cause her harm. She was in the perfect position; nobody was ahead on the trail, and nobody was coming up behind her to spoil the trap. He thought to himself, right before he sprung, *Damn, I'm a genius, this is working out so great!*

He leapt to his feet and went to sprint the few steps that were needed, and his foot slipped out from beneath him, and he landed right on his face in the mud. His face actually made a loud thump as it hit with all of his body's weight.

Tami heard the thump and stopped her walk and turned to see a camo clad man lying face down in the waterway. She screamed and took off running down the path. Her hair, which was put up into a bun caught a branch and fell out and was getting in her face as she ran on the uneven terrain.

The hunter quickly got up, muttering and swearing as he started the pursuit of the lady. "Fuck, fuck fuck *fuck*!!" he said, louder than he should have as he was trying to *not* be noticed or heard by anyone.

Tami started slipping on her way down the hill as it was a little bit rocky in this area. She wasn't really a runner, but right now, she wished she had taken it up; some green monster was after her and gaining ground. She was too concentrated on running and getting away to scream anymore, and she didn't have enough breath to do that anyway. As she reached the bottom of the hill, there was a path that led back to the campground. It wasn't her normal route, but she just wanted to get away and thought this would be quicker.

He noticed her changing her course, and he headed through the woods to where she would end up. Like a good defensive back that he was while playing on his high school football team, he knew that he needed to take a good angle, and that he could catch her.

Tami never saw him coming as she was hit with a shoulder in her ribs, knocking what wind she had left in her body out of her. Landing on top of her, he quickly covered her mouth, and using his weight, tied her up as quickly as he could, using the extra sock that he had in his pocket to stuff in her mouth to keep her quiet.

Leaning in really close to her ear, he whispered, "Thank you for making me run. I thoroughly enjoyed that."

CHAPTER 31

Monday afternoon and Samantha was just crawling out of bed. It was a Netflix weekend; she binge-watched every movie that had to do with cancer that she could think of: *Stepmom*, *The Bucket List*, *My Sister's Keeper*, and about ten others that made her cry and laugh. She even watched *Forrest Gump* again because his mother "got the cancer," and "she died on a Tuesday."

She was a sucker for movies and quotes. *Forrest Gump* just had so many one liners, and she needed something a little lighter.

She hadn't changed all weekend, but she did manage to make two more trips over to Kwik Trip for more coffee, a bag of chips, and a pack of cigarettes.

She was sitting on her back step, smoking her second smoke of the day, and she looked at her left hand, holding the smoldering tobacco and said out loud, "I work in a goddamn cancer unit, and here I sit, smoking a cigarette, wow."

She finished up outside and decided to go in and maybe clean up a little bit; her apartment was a pigsty, and she actually smelled pretty bad. Well, it was a pigsty to her anyway; a lot of people would just call it normal. She had it cleaned up and spotless in seventeen minutes.

She walked into her bedroom and stripped down to just her underwear and put her clothes in the laundry hamper. She decided to pull up Facebook before getting into the shower. She hadn't been on it all weekend, and she wanted to see if Jackson had any pictures of fish, or his adventures posted. He was usually pretty good at posting things. She had been secretly following him since his divorce. She found his posts funny, and she enjoyed his smile for some reason. His teeth were not perfect, but they were nice, and in the pictures that he was smiling in, it always gave her a sense that the world was still a good place and that there is happiness in it. She saw a lot of sadness at her job, and his smile brought her peace.

She didn't even need to search for Jackson's name; there he was, very first posting that she saw holding up a twenty-inch bass, next to that picture was a picture of his brother, Chad's nineteen-inch bass, and the caption above them was, "That's right, ladies. Mine is bigger." She immediately hit the "like" button.

Nice, Jackson, I hope I get to see how big it truly is, and she let her left hand that was holding her phone down by her side, and she closed her eyes and ran her right hand along the curves of her breasts and down the left side of her stomach, very slowly and softly. She ran her index finger across the top of her panties, just underneath but not too far down.

Samantha opened her eyes quickly and looked into the mirror. *He isn't going to want to touch this nasty stinky body, get in the shower, girl, just in case he happens to stop in unexpectedly on his way home.* She reached in and turned the shower on to let it warm up. She turned around and looked back into the mirror.

"Do I really want this man, who was married to my friend... yes, yes I do," and she smiled from ear to ear and removed the rest of her clothing and stepped into the shower.

CHAPTER 32

Since Jackson was pretty much already packed up for the ride home a day early, it didn't take him long to get his things together and back into the truck.

"Can't wait to hit the traffic in the cities, holiday weekend, it is going to sa-uck!"

Chad was lugging his bag of clothes out of the door, and one of the handles was stuck on the door handle, pulling on his bag only made him more upset until he figured out what the holdup was. "Ya, maybe I should have let you leave yesterday. You would probably be home about two hours quicker than you will be today."

"It's okay, I get 93X radio station the whole time, so I'll just jam and wave one finger at people as I pass them. Wish I got the good stations back home. Angry music keeps me mellow."

"You're an odd one, that's for sure. Say, don't serial killers listen to hard rock?"

"*Hey now*!!"

"What, too soon? Ha-ha, have a safe trip. I need to walk the dog before we take off."

"Okay, you too, maybe I'll see you in traffic, ha."

Chad snatched up his dog and put the leash on him and started out down a dirt path. The dog pulling on the chord, but Chad had complete control. He had some of the strongest hands on him that Jackson had ever seen. That eighty-pound lab was no match for his strength.

Without turning around, Chad yelled one last thing to his little brother, "Get a lawyer tomorrow!!"

Jackson hopped in his pickup, turned the ignition switch, adjust the volume, as it was never loud enough. Disturbed's "Down with the Sickness" had just started to play. "*Sweet!!*" And he rolled out of the campground, singing along.

Jackson drove around the north shoreline of the lake and turned south. It wasn't long before he hit traffic. About seven miles to be exact, forty-five mph. He thought to himself, *This is going to be a long ass ride home if I already hit traffic.*

Every now and then, he would see a couple of guys out riding their motorcycles, and he wished that he was on his now. It was not only a beautiful sunny fall morning and a gorgeous day for a ride, but it was so much easier to pass people on the bike. He reached over and turned the music down as it was commercials playing, and he started thinking about the women in his life, and how he had actually been doing pretty well lately. He had been having a sexual relationship with Tami, who was leaving her husband, but really, where was that ever going to go? Jackson was usually a very committed guy, who hadn't cheated on anyone since...since Brandy. He had promised himself that he would never ever cheat on another woman because he saw what it did to her and to him. The guilt was overwhelming for him. He just couldn't ever go through that ever again.

Tami was still married, so she was actually cheating since she was still married, but that didn't make Jackson a cheater, did it? His views on marriage had changed quite a bit in the last couple of years, but dang it, this was still wrong.

Jackson decided then and there that he was going to end it with Tami; he wanted no part in this relationship. Besides, if she would cheat on her husband like that, what would make him think she wouldn't eventually do it to him also? Yup, it was over. Besides, he had Klaire, who seemed interested in him, and now Samantha... Samantha. He would have never guessed in a million years that she would have any interest in him. From what he knew of her, he couldn't remember her ever having a boyfriend. Was she really good at keeping her relationships a secret, or did she actually not normally date?

Jackson's head was spinning, but the wheels on his truck didn't seem to be; he had been on the road for two hours now, and he wasn't even close to being halfway home, like he normally would be, in lighter traffic. More time to think.

Klaire was interested but didn't want anything to do with him until he got this thing cleared up with the murders. She was absolutely beautiful and fun to hang out with. Her daughter and Haley got along great. He really wanted to see where this would go, but he also didn't want to possibly put her in danger. *Crap! Am I putting her in danger??*

The thought hadn't even occurred to Jackson that anyone in his life could be in danger. He had been thinking that the cops would eventually catch the creep killing people, and he would move on with life as normal. The police were not catching the guy though, will this guy just stop, or what was his motive?

The brown car that had been hanging out with him all weekend was about fifteen cars back, having a hard time keeping up to him even though he wasn't even going the speed limit. They were really lucky Jackson wasn't on his bike; they would never keep up to him.

Just then his cell phone vibrated. Jackson pulled his phone out of his pocket and saw he had received a text message from Klaire. "Hey, how was your weekend trip? I saw on FB that you caught some fish. Are you home yet?"

"It was a good weekend. We caught and ate a few fish, nothing too excessive though, nothing to bring home to eat. I am still on the road, may be another couple hours with this traffic."

"If you want to meet me in Rochester, we could go out to eat together. I am child free until tomorrow, and I know that I told you that I need to stay clear of you until this whole murder thing is over, but..."

"You can't get me out of your mind."

"Something like that yes. Lol."

"I'll text you when I am close. Where would you like to meet?"

"Do you want to hit Red Lobster? I have a craving for their stuffed mushrooms."

"Sounds awesome, I'll see you in a while."

Jackson couldn't help but smile. The next hour and forty-five minutes seemed to fly by as he slowly crept along in traffic. He completely forgot about the brown car that was following him and all about the person who was trying to frame him for murder. He had a date with Klaire, and that is all that mattered at the moment.

CHAPTER 33

The cabin was dark; her hands were tied very tightly behind Tami, and she was still gagged with a sock in her mouth. Her mouth was extremely dry; she was sweating profusely, not because it was hot in the cabin, but she was scared out of her mind. She knew there was someone killing women that were in Jackson's life, but how many people even knew that she was in his life? Was Jackson actually the killer? Was she having an affair with a serial killer?

The door opened and there stood her attacker; he was too skinny to be Jackson, so she knew right away that it wasn't Jackson. She thought she recognized him but couldn't place him. He walked over to her and leaned in really close to her, almost touching her neck. She could feel his breath on her skin.

As he leaned into this woman that he had tied up, he could see her skin glistening with perspiration. She had very nice skin actually, and even though she had loose-fitting sweats on, with the ropes, they made her clothing more form fitting, and her clothing accentuated her body's curves. As his face got closer to her neck, he could smell the fear oozing out of her through her glands. Fear has a special kind of smell that regular sweat doesn't have. He found it strangely erotic, and he instantly became erect.

"Jackson Ackerman sure does have some beautiful women that have been and are involved with him. I don't know why I started with that ugly whore and didn't go straight for these hotties." The killer spoke out loud as if he were giving Tami a compliment.

Tami could see that the floor was covered in plastic under her chair, so she knew this was not going to end well; him being so close

114

to her made her panic even more, and her breathing picked up, and she was having a hard time catching her breath with the gag in her mouth. Her chest was heaving as much as the ropes would allow. She was starting to hyperventilate to the point that she felt like she would pass out.

"Don't you be passing out on me!!! You need to be awake for this!!" and he slapped her, and she actually calmed her breathing a little bit.

He took out his knife and started cutting. Not the ropes that bound the helpless woman. Not into her flesh either. He cut her clothes off her, and they hung in strands, held only by the ropes that were holding her to the chair. Her breasts were bare, and he could see most of her pubic hair, what little she hadn't shaved off.

"Ahh, a nice little landing strip shaved for me I see. I like a woman who grooms everywhere. Perhaps, I should bring my big old plane down the runway and into your hangar?" And he dropped the knife down onto the floor and reached down and undid his pants, pulled his boxers down, exposing himself to her.

Tami thought that, *Maybe this guy just wants to rape me and will let me go? Maybe he won't kill me.* Maybe she could live to see her kids and her husband again. She could do just about anything to stay alive, she thought. His penis looked to be of average size, but she really didn't want to be so close to it and definitely didn't want it inside her.

"I'd really love to give it to you, but I'm afraid we don't have the time, and I don't want to leave any more evidence than I have to. So I'll just have to go home and wack it later to the thought of having you...the things I do and have sacrificed for my cause...tis a shame."

The killer walked over to the table, where he had Tami's cell phone laying. He was surprised that she took her cell phone with her as she walked, but then, most people always have their cell within reach of them, *especially* when they are hiding something from their significant other.

He found the app for the camera and took a picture of her naked breasts, careful as to not show any ropes that were still binding her. He then took a picture of her pubic hair, quickly deleted it, and tried again. Three more times, he took pictures and deleted each one. He wasn't able to get a picture that didn't include a rope.

"Let's see how he likes this?"

He scrolled through her contact list but wasn't able to find Jackson's name anywhere. He looked and looked but wasn't able to find his first or last name anywhere.

"Where is his number!!" he screamed at the helpless woman. "I know you have it, where is it?!" He ripped the tape off her mouth and pulled the sock out of her mouth. "*Answer me!* Where is Jackson's number!?"

As he ripped the tape off, her skin instantly burned, but him pulling the sock out of her mouth was a relief, so they almost offset.

"It's…it's under…it's under his sister's name, with a…with a two behind it," she cried, tears falling down her face. "Emily2."

He found it almost immediately, clicked to add the picture, and typed. "Thinking of you," and hit the send button.

"I don't know if anyone else in the world, other than the three of us know what you two had going on. I doubt those bozo cops who sit outside his house even knew. But I have been watching, so I know."

Hanging on the wall near the door was his trusted machete; he grabbed it and walked over to her. She still had tears streaming down her cheeks; he leaned down, licked her left nipple, which was on his right, tasting her sweat. His manhood still fully erect, cupping her right bosom with his left hand. He licked his lips and kissed her on the mouth. She tried to bite him but wasn't quick enough. She wanted to spit at him, but her mouth was still too dry to have enough saliva to muster up and spit.

Still cupping her breast, he swung the death knife at her neck, almost completely severing her head, but some flesh held it from falling to the floor. The vertebrae were cut all the way through, and her head flipped over onto her right shoulder. He took his hand off her and swung again, this time removing her head from her now-lifeless corpse.

Tami's head landed on the floor, face up, with her eyes still open. Staring at him, like she was still alive and thinking about what just happened. Blood pumped from her neck, squirting everywhere for a couple of seconds, and then just oozed from her hole at the top of her body. Blood ran down onto her breasts, completely covering one, and forking at the peak of her other like a river splitting around a big rock.

The executioner stood there, admiring his handy work. Still with his pants half down, his little soldier still standing at attention. Blood had splattered him on his face, and he wiped it off with his hand. He didn't remember ever being this turned on in his entire life. He watched the blood continue to drain onto her chest and started to pool around where what was left of her underwear were and the chair was.

His hand still bloody, he grabbed himself and pleasured himself right there. He couldn't wait any longer. He was careful not to blow his load onto her body, even though he really wanted to. It only took a couple of seconds.

He went outside to the water hydrant and cleaned himself up a little bit before the real cleanup began.

CHAPTER 34

Jackson pulled into the Red Lobster parking lot, and he got out of the truck. Five hours in the truck had his body aching. He was stretching out and trying to get the blood flowing back to his body when he saw Klaire walking toward him. She had been waiting in her vehicle for him to arrive.

"Are you ready for some seafood?"

"Yup, I ate quite a bit of fish this weekend, but I'm in the mood for some lobster."

"Oh, dang it, I'm sorry. I wasn't thinking that you were fishing all weekend and then I invite you to eat more fish."

"Oh, no worries, anytime I can go out to eat lobster. I'm a fan of that. Anytime, I can eat lobster with an extremely sexy woman… Ya, sign me up for that!"

"Well, I don't know about the 'extremely sexy woman' part, but they do have lobster here." Klaire laughed and used her fingers to simulate air quotes around the "extremely sexy woman" part. She knew that she wasn't ugly, but she very rarely felt sexy, except when she was around Jackson. The way he looked at her and talked to her made her feel good about herself. It was hard for her to explain to herself. He didn't look lustfully or creepy at her, but she could tell that he really did believe she was beautiful.

"I hope you don't mind, but I called ahead, so we shouldn't have to wait," Jackson said as they were walking toward the door. "I had some time to look up their number on my way."

"You shouldn't be on your phone while driving, that is dangerous," Klaire said, and she gave him a gentle nudge with her elbow.

"Isn't that why you are attracted to me because I live on the edge?"

They were seated almost immediately, and they both knew what they wanted, so the waitress wasn't at their table very long.

"I thought you were going to wait until I am clear of all of this murder business before we reconnected?"

"I know I said that, but I'm not sure I can do that. I know you haven't killed anyone, and I do want to see where this will lead us. I will probably keep Mandi away for a little bit, but when I don't have her, I may try spending some time with you."

"I am perfectly okay with that!"

They continued with small talk about their girls and stuff happening at work. When they had finished eating, they got up and left. Jackson paid the bill, with a slight protest from Klaire, but she let him pay.

They walked out to the parking lot, and Jackson walked her to her vehicle.

"Thank you for a nice meal, and for paying, you didn't have to do that. I invited you."

"One thing my father taught me is that the man always pays for meals. Yes, it may be a little bit sexist, but I believe a little bit of chivalry should still exist."

She reached out and took his right hand with her left hand and held it. Using this, he used it to pull her closer to him so that they were chest to chest, looking into each other's eyes. Nothing more was said; he just leaned in to give her a kiss, and she met him halfway. As their lips met for the first time, he could feel how soft and caressing her lips were. It was like they were meant to be tangled together. It was unlike any kiss he had ever felt. This kiss had passion in it that he had never felt. Normally, when he kissed a woman, it was mostly a feeling of lust, and his need to have sex was driving it. This was more like a feeling of being embraced by a warm ocean of caring and just a sense of belonging to each other.

They slowly released their hold of each other's lips and just stood there, inches apart, both still with their eyes closed, taking in the moment.

"Wow," Klaire sighed, barely audible. She didn't mean for it to be heard, but he did hear her, and he smiled sheepishly.

"I better get going. I still have to unpack and make sure my neighbor kid fed the dog and do some laundry before I go to work in the morning."

Klaire just nodded her head that she understood; she didn't dare say anything because she was afraid that she would blurt out that she loved him, and it was way too early to be saying that. Her heart was still all a flutter. She ran her hand down Jackson's cheek and turned slowly to her car door.

"I'll see you at work tomorrow," Jackson said, and he turned to head to his truck.

As he got into his truck and started the engine, he looked in the mirror and thought to himself. *I need to eat more lobster, must be something in it.* He laughed to himself as he headed out of the parking lot and to the highway, where he still had about forty-five minutes on the road ahead of him.

Jackson's phone buzzed, notifying him that he received a text message from Tami. He didn't bother opening it.

CHAPTER 35

Detective Holmes received a call from the office Tuesday morning, about seven-thirty. The school bus driver whose route took him past the officer's country residence noticed something leaning against the mailbox at the end of his driveway. The chief of police was on his way there, and he wasn't happy with his lead detective.

When the chief arrived, he tore into Holmes, "Are you *any* closer to catching this asshat than you were three weeks ago?"

"No, sir, but I have some good news and some bad news."

"Start with the good news. I need some of that."

"After the last person showed up here, I set a trail camera up to see if I could catch this guy in the act."

"That is fantastic news, Detective, let's look at those pictures!"

"Here is where the bad news comes into play… He must have noticed the camera because it is gone."

"Wow. You, incompetent bastard, you can't even hide a surveillance camera good enough that someone doesn't notice it?"

"Sorry, sir."

"You have until the weekend to come up with some solid evidence, or I'm pulling you from the case. And cover that lady up. We just had a whole bus load of school kids on their way to school see a naked dead lady, holding her cell phone to her head, which is in her *lap*, outside one of our officer's houses. The school board is going to have my ass in a sling over this. And you are just snoring away in your house while this guy keeps leaving you packages?"

"I'm on it, sir. Just waiting for the lab team to get here so I don't ruin any evidence that may be on or near the body."

"The FBI will be here in a couple hours since this is now officially a serial killer. Be nice to be able to actually hand them over some evidence."

The crime scene investigators pulled up in their black van, two of them hopped out, one of them still eating an egg McMuffin.

"You stopped at McDonald's on the way out? Seriously?" Detective Holmes inquired rather pissy.

"Did she come back to life? We figured we had three minutes to stop. Calm down, we'll be done in a jiffy."

"Start with the phone. I need to get into that as soon as I can."

"Roger dodger," replied the shorter of the two investigators, the one who had already finished his breakfast.

After all the pictures were taken and paperwork filled out, it was close to an hour and a half before they got the cell phone to the detective. He was told that he needed to wear gloves in order to handle it, and he better not do anything stupid with it because they were going to stand there and watch him.

He grabbed the phone and went directly to the text messages. There were quite a few that were not read yet, so he went through and read them. They had already identified the body, so they knew who she was. A majority of the texts were from her husband's cell phone. The last text she sent was to Emily2. It was a picture of her breasts accompanied by the words "Thinking of you." But it wasn't the last text in the message string. It was replied to with "Nice. We should really talk soon."

CHAPTER 36

Tuesday morning and Jackson was on his way to work. He rode his bike since he was planning on leaving early. He had a list of lawyers that he planned on calling in the morning and was hoping to meet with one of them later in the day. He figured any lawyer worth his salt would push a divorce or some minor boring regular case to help defend against a murder rap.

He parked his motorcycle in the parking ramp and started walking to the door when his cell rang. "Who the hell is calling me this early?"

He pulled the cell out of his pocket, and it was his sister. "Hey, what's up, sis?"

"I got you a lawyer, and she wants to meet you today. She is from Preston, but she works for a firm out of Rochester, something, something, and something."

"Ya, I've seen their commercials. Isn't their tag line, 'We are really something!'"

"Smart ass!!"

"I was beginning to think you weren't going to come through for me. I actually took the afternoon off to go find my own lawyer."

"Hey, these things take time, you just can't pull out a phone book and pick the first one you see. I asked around, even talked to a couple judges that I know, and they both came up with this lady as their first choice."

"I'm going to guess that she is expensive as hell then if everyone thinks she is so good."

"Well…she isn't exactly cheap, but I bet my good-looking brother can sweet talk her into a decent price, maybe a little bit of bow chicca bow wow might help too. She is single!" Emily teased.

"Ya, when she finds out that women in my life are starting to turn up with no heads, I'm sure she will want to hop right on my magic pony," Jackson replied, with a little sarcasm in his voice.

"Go see her today. I'll text you her number and address. She is expecting you, so just head over any time today. She said she would drop whatever she is doing to meet with you. And…I bet she would ride the pony. I've heard she like guys like you…ha-ha."

"What the hell does that mean? Guys like me?"

"You will see, gotta go. I have to leave for work in a half hour, gotta get pretty. By the way, who the hell is already at work at six-twenty in the morning?"

"Us lucky ones, who only work four days a week! Later, sis, and thanks."

Jackson got to his desk, and a few minutes after he sat down, his buddy, John, strolled over and grabbed some stale chips that someone left out in the aisle from Friday and started munching on them, and he took a seat on Jackson's file cabinet.

"So, we both know my life if boring."

"Ya, did you do anything fun with the family this weekend?"

"Hell, no, I mowed the lawn, and we went to Menards and got a new playground set for the kids. Put that thing up all goddamn weekend. Instructions say two to four hours construction time. Must be if you actually own a construction crew cause it took me two-and-half frickin' days!"

"Wow, that is pretty exciting," Jackson chuckled a little bit.

"Enough about me!! Did you bang anyone, or kill anyone this weekend? Please tell me you banged Klaire, please?"

"Well, I went fishing with my brother, so I didn't have time to kill anyone, maybe a few fish. Ha, but I did squeeze in dinner date with Klaire. *Don't* tell anyone, we want to keep it on the down low. You know how people talk here."

"Of course, I know how people talk here, look what we are doing right now!" John laughed, "So…did you…you know," and he made a motion with his hips and hands like he was dry humping a sack of potatoes.

"No man, we had a nice meal…and we kissed when we got to the parking lot."

"Did you feel boobs, grab her ass?" John seemed to be getting excited and short of breath.

"No, man, we are taking it slow, but it was a pretty good kiss, man."

"You are the man!! I can't believe you made out with Hot Klaire!"

"You, I can't believe it either! I hope this whole murder thing that seems to keep trying to have me involved in it doesn't screw it up because…damn, man, she is fine."

"If you get any nudes, would you show me? I've been married to the same woman for years, and I haven't seen a hot naked woman in a long, long time…excluding my wife, of course."

"Oh, of course." Jackson laughed because he knew that even John didn't find his wife attractive; he just liked that she would have sex with him on a fairly regular basis.

"So, this murder thing, you have any idea why someone would want to pin them on you?"

"*No* idea. And if I was going on a murdering spree, I surely wouldn't be killing the people he has chosen. Well, maybe the first one, she was an evil witch."

"Probably a chick doing it, mad that you won't sleep with her, or stopped sleeping with her. If you have a woman killing people to sleep with you…that may be more impressive than if you do end up hooking up with Hot Klaire…okay, no, but maybe a close second," John smiled and walked back to his desk, leaving Jackson to get his work done.

Jackson had most of his work done by nine, but he figured he better hang out for a little longer to save some of his precious paid time off. He googled the name of the lawyer that his sister had texted him. No wonder she couldn't remember the name of the firm, it was Messner, Laimer & Winehieser. Jackson thought that maybe they should have used their first names instead of their last names.

Around nine-twenty-three, he decided that he had enough, and he was going to head over to this lawyer's office. He put his out of office notification on his e-mail, shut down his computer, and clocked out of the day. He had already told his supervisor that he was leaving early for personal reasons; he thought that she had a pretty good idea why since she was always up on the latest gossip and news.

CHAPTER 37

M essmer, Laimer & Winehieser's office building was locked up tighter than a drum when Jackson arrived. The door had the office hours posted on it, and it said 10:00 a.m. would be the time they opened.

"Dang it. I could have stayed at work for another half an hour and saved the PTO!" Jackson caught himself saying this out loud. He walked over to a nearby bench that was on the sidewalk and lit a cigarette while he waited. He was on his second smoke when the cute little receptionist arrived, fumbling with her keys and trying to not drop her purse. She hurried up and unlocked the door and flipped the lights on. Jackson gave her a couple minutes to get settled in before he walked in.

The receptionist was professionally dressed, wearing a gray jacket with a matching skirt; she had nylons on, making it look like her legs were darker than her natural skin tone was. Not a ton of makeup but some bright red lipstick.

"Hello, may I help you?"

"Yes, my name is Jackson Ackerman. Ms. Laimer is expecting me to stop in today. I don't have an appointment, was told to just come in."

"Okay, if you can please have a seat, Mr. Ackerman, I will see if she is available."

Jackson took a seat, and he looked through the old magazines that were laid out neatly on the coffee table in front of him. He selected a *National Geographic* book, mostly to see if they still had the African ladies with naked boobs that they all used to giggle over as youngsters. He wasn't really turned on by these pictures, just curious to see if they still did that. Many days in the library back in elementary school, they would snicker and be dumb about those pictures.

To Jackson's amusement, there was a picture of a native African lady about three quarters of the way through. He laughed to himself and went to put the magazine down.

"Mr. Ackerman? Ms. Laimer is ready for you now, please follow me."

The receptionist led him down a short hallway and held the door for him. Jackson stared at the young lady's ass the whole way and wished the hallway was a little bit longer.

"Thank you," Jackson said as he went through the door.

The lady inside the office was not nearly as cute as the one who just led him to that office. Inside was a very large lady, not fat at all, but about six foot four, with some manly features. She has on almost the identical thing as the receptionist, minus the lipstick...or any makeup actually. She was not a pretty lady, but she had a smile for Jackson the moment she looked up from her desk.

"Jackson! Your sister says you may have some legal issues that could possibly use my help? I don't get many murder cases around here, so I told her I'd take it. I owe your sister a solid, and I haven't done any pro bono cases at all this year yet, so guess what. Not only will I take this job, but it is also free for you."

"Are you serious? Wow, thank you, I appreciate it more than you can imagine. Must have been a serious solid my sis did for you."

"I don't get out a whole lot with my job, and she...well, to be blunt, she helped me get laid."

"Holy hell! Ha-ha-ha wasn't expecting that." Jackson laughed.

"Sorry, I can be a little too blunt sometimes."

"No worries, just wasn't expecting it."

"So, let's sit down and talk about what is happening. I kinda got the low down from Emily, but I want to hear it from you, in case she missed something."

They sat for a couple hours discussing the last couple of month's activities. Jackson didn't know what to do since he wasn't the one doing the killings, so he just told her what he knew.

"Now, it sounds like this killer kind of has a pattern, other than the one random girl who you didn't know, he is killing every other weekend."

"You know, I hadn't thought about that. I guess he is. Because I'm either up at the cabin, or out doing something on my own, without Haley, of course I'm not allowed to have her anymore, as long as this stuff is going on."

"Well, if he sticks to this pattern, someone is due to show up dead…today, I would think. Since yesterday was a holiday, he probably took an extra day too. So I would almost put money on some sort of law enforcement to be contacting you."

"Well, I'm in luck because I not only have my brother as an alibi for most of the weekend, another friend for supper last night, but two police officers, who are sitting outside in a brown car. You can go see them if you would like. They suck at not being seen."

"Stay here. I need to see this," and Ms. Laimer walked out of the room and right outside onto the sidewalk. She looked around, saw what she wanted to see, and came back in. "Brown car, about two parking spots behind, what I am assuming is your motorcycle?"

"Yup, that is them, Tweedle Dee and Tweedle Dumb."

"Well, we can use that if we need to. Who knows, maybe the police will do their job and actually catch the real guy. Until then, do not talk to them, and if they try to get you to talk, tell them you want your lawyer and call me immediately," she handed Jackson her card.

"So, I'll be talking to you real soon I bet!" Jackson got up and left.

CHAPTER 38

I t was just barely after noon, and Jackson had the day off, and he was already on his motorcycle. He decided that even though he loved riding, that he didn't really want to go on a day trip in his dress clothes, so he rode toward home and pulled into the Fillmore County Courthouse parking lot.

Jackson walked up the steps and back to his sister's office, which was on the main floor. He walked past Tami's work area, but he didn't notice her over there. He didn't notice anyone actually.

"Hey, sis, what's up? Kind of dead around here, where is everyone?"

"Hi, poor choice of words. Let's go outside. I'm not sure you should be here," Emily spoke in a somber tone.

They walked down the stairs and to the back side of the courthouse. They both lit cigarettes, and Emily spoke first. "Tami's dead."

"What? Seriously? Son of a...," Jackson didn't know what to say.

"Word on the street is that you were boning her, and her husband is pissed at you."

"Why is he mad at me? They were getting a divorce."

"If they were, he didn't have any idea about it, just found out that you two had something going on, and he thinks you did it."

"Why does everyone keep thinking I am killing people? What the hell is going on?"

"Well, even I didn't know you two were doing the dirty deed, and I know more than most people. But come to think of it, she had been asking more about you than normal."

"I told her that I wouldn't touch her until she was divorced. She said that she was filing and that you knew all about it!"

"Nope, don't know a damn thing about that. She must have been lying to you to get you into bed. Kinda sounds like something a guy would do, kinda proud of her actually."

"Ya, well, be proud of her because it may get your brother killed by her husband."

"I wouldn't worry about him, the police though, they may be a little scarier. I hear they have some evidence against you."

"*How* do you know this stuff?"

"I work in a courthouse, there is more gossip here than anywhere else in the county. People can't keep their mouths shut."

"Good thing I got myself a lawyer, I guess."

"Yes, how did that go? Did she give you the family rate?"

"No charge, she said you got her laid, so she is taking me on for free. I hope she isn't expecting any other sort of payment because I'm not going there. You said she liked 'guys like me.'" Jackson made air quotes with his fingers.

"Yup, guys like you, you know male. She would do anything with a penis. She isn't picky. You know Aaron who works as the overnight custodian? That's who I set her up with."

"Damn!! That dude has more acne than the local middle school. He only has eight fingers too, right?"

"He only needed two from what I hear. Ha-ha-ha."

"Gross."

"I better get back to work, my break is over," as she snuffed out the remainder of her cigarette and put it in the butt bucket by the door.

"Later."

Jackson walked around the building and got on his bike and rode it the couple blocks to his house.

He pulled up, and there was a squad car and an unmarked vehicle, but clearly, it was a state-owned vehicle with Iowa plates on it parked in his driveway. They were both parked in the middle of his driveway, so he wasn't able to pull in to get into his garage, so Jackson pulled onto the grass and parked on the sidewalk.

Detective Homes and Chief Osborn both got out of their vehicles and walked up to Jackson.

"We need to talk, Mr. Ackerman," Detective Holms began.

"You can talk to my lawyer," was the reply.

"We need to know where you were this weekend," Chief Osborn added.

"Well, you don't need my lawyer for that!" Jackson waved to the two officers in the brown car parked right down the street. He waved for them to come on over and join them. "Come on down, boys, you are needed!"

"Listen, a lady you know was killed, again. We need to know where you were," the detective repeated what the chief already said.

"You must not have heard me, you have my alibi. They are walking right down the street and are employed by our county. You guys assigned them to me. I can't believe you don't talk to each other. If you had, you could quit wasting my time."

The two undercover officers showed up on the lawn, and Holmes asked, "Can you both vouch for Mr. Ackerman for the entire weekend? Was there at any time that you didn't have eyes on him for longer than an hour's time?"

"Sir, the only time that we did not have actual eyes on him was when he was inside a building that we were watching the exits on. That plus, we were five hours north of here, so even if we did lose him for an hour, he didn't have time to do anything down in this part of the state, or Iowa, as it would have taken too long for him to get here."

The other officer chimed in, "He did catch a couple nice fish, and we did witness what we believed to be a first kiss with a very pretty young lady. We have it all documented in our logs if you would like to verify."

"Thank you both. I believe we can take you two off babysitting duty now. Please go home and take a shower, and maybe a nap. You both look like hell," the chief told his men.

"Thank you, sir."

"Yes, thank you."

The detective seemed a little bit miffed that his lead suspect now had an airtight alibi. "So, now that we pretty much know this isn't you doing this. I have a couple questions. Do we still need your lawyer to ask them?"

"Let's see what they are, and I'll tell you."

"Okay, you know how we keep having text messages saying things like the victims are afraid of you, or following you."

"Yup."

"Well, this time, it looks like you were sent a text, and you replied to it."

"Yes, I did reply to a text message last night. Anything beyond that, and you will need to speak to my lawyer."

"Fair enough."

"Have a good day, gentlemen, I'm going in to call a couple of people and warn them that they may be in danger. That pretty lady that I just had a first kiss with last night, and I may even warn my ex-wife, along with my family." Jackson turned and walked to the house, then he paused and turned back around, "Please find this guy soon. All of our lives will be better if you do. If I think of anything, I'll call you."

CHAPTER 39

Samantha had a busy morning; it was now almost time for her to go home, and she finally had time to pull up her e-mail to send Jackson an e-mail to chat with him a little. She held out a hope that he would stop by Monday night on his way home, but he hadn't. Why would he, they weren't dating, and all they did was flirt a little. But she still hoped. She typed just a short e-mail to him, and before hitting send, she noticed that his out-of-office reply was on. That was one good thing about Mayo's e-mail, if you pulled up an e-mail and put their name in it, it would tell you if they were out of the office. This just saved her from sending an e-mail and wondering why he didn't reply. She did wonder why he had today off though.

She decided to try and send him a message on Facebook.

Hey, you aren't at work today? What's up with that?

It didn't take too long, and Jackson replied to her.

I was there for a few hours before I had to go meet with my lawyer, then I had cops at my house when I got home. Fun day!

I heard you were in the middle of a murder controversy, do I need to be scared of you? Ha-ha.

Yes, I am. No, you don't need to be scared of me, but it seems that people I know are starting to show up dead, so please be careful.

Oh, don't worry, I'm a big girl. I can take care of myself.

☺ *Good, I'd hate to see anything happen to you.*

Say, not to change the subject, but I was wondering…if you aren't too busy killing people this weekend…if you would like to go to a Buckcherry concert with me. I have an extra ticket, and I really want to see them.

I'm "Sorry," I'd have to be "Lit Up" to go stand "Next to You" because you are kind of a "Crazy Bitch."

I see what you did there, using their song titles. But is it really a no, or would you go with me?

Sorry, I had to do that. Yes, I will, go, they are in La Crosse on Saturday night, right?

Yes

Okay, want me to pick you up?

I'll meet you at your house, if that is okay.

Works for me!!

Cool, try to stay out of jail until then! I need to get back to work. TTYL.

Jackson couldn't believe he just made a date with someone when he was starting a relationship with Klaire. *It isn't really a date,* he told himself, *just going to a concert with a friend. Crap, I'm turning into a whore. I don't want to be like that.*

He walked outside to pet Raider and talk to him. The dog didn't seem to understand anything Jackson said to him, but he did enjoy being the center of his owner's attention.

CHAPTER 40

J ackson spent the rest of the week taking turns chatting with Samantha and Klaire. Trying to keep the conversations straight was getting harder and harder for him. He wasn't going to be able to keep this up for very long. Friday night, he was going to a movie with Klaire. There was a movie that just came out that was supposed to be a real tear-jerker, and Klaire wanted to see it and spend time with Jackson.

Jackson rode his motorcycle to Rochester and met her in the parking lot of the theater. Jackson bought their tickets, and they went to stand in line to get some popcorn. The two were so engrossed in each other's company, neither one of them saw it coming. Jackson was attacked from the side, nearly knocking him off his feet.

"Haley! What on earth are you doing here? What a nice surprise. You almost knocked me on my ass, but it is great to see you!"

"Sorry, I was just so excited to see you that I just ran and didn't slow down. I needed to hug you."

"Well, I love that you wanted a hug so bad, I've missed you."

"I've missed you also. Hi Klaire, so nice to see you again!" Haley released her stepfather and gave Klaire a quick hug.

"So nice to see you too. I wasn't expecting to see you. This date just keeps getting better. Now I wish that I would have brought Mandi with. She would have loved to see you. She keeps asking when she gets to see you again."

"Well, Mom won't let me go to Jackson's house until this murder thing is all cleared up. She thinks he is mixed up in something bad, and that he could get me hurt," Haley said in a sad tone, clearly showing that she missed her stepdad.

"What movie are you going to see? Mom, Frank, and I are seeing the ultra-sappy movie with that super sexy man in it. I can't remember his name, but he is cute. Mom wants him to jump her bones."

"Haley!! You shouldn't be telling people that, that was our secret!" Jackson knew that voice anywhere; it was Camille.

He turned to see his ex, walking up behind him, with her boy toy in tow.

Klaire paid her no attention and kept talking with Haley, "That is what we are seeing too. I hear it is supposed to be good."

"Jackson will cry, he is a softy, hope you brought some Kleenex. He'll say it is allergies or something, but don't let him fool you. He will be crying."

"Okay, Haley, like your mom said, don't be telling people that, that is our secret," and he chuckled, slightly embarrassed. He was supposed to be a manly man; of all people, he didn't want Klaire to know that.

"I can verify that, he will cry. He likes to act all tough, but yup, he is a softy," Camille added.

"Only girls cry during a movie," Frank chimed in.

"Hey, watch it, Frank, he may have a big heart, but he can still kick your pussy ass!!" Haley spouted and took a couple steps toward her mother's boyfriend.

"Haley, you don't talk that way," Jackson grabbed her and gave her another hug as she stood still giving Frank a death look. Her stepdad kissed the top of her head. He leaned down and whispered into her ear. "I would totally kick his pussy ass, wouldn't I?" Haley just shook her head in agreement.

"Well then, let's order, the guy is waiting," Klaire interrupted in an attempt to change the mood and subject.

"Let's go, Haley," Camille said, in a slightly miffed tone, giving Frank a dirty look. She clearly didn't want to see him get his ass kicked in a theater, or anywhere for that fact. She did hate that Jackson was always taking the high road though. Just once she wished he would fight for her, or show that he cared. He always just tried to avoid a fight. When they were married, he would have ripped Frank's head off. Since the day she cheated, it was as if he just turned off all his feelings for her. It drove her nuts when she thought about it.

"Did you see the look he got from her?" Klaire said to Jackson in a hushed voice.

"At least, it was directed at him. I've had that directed at me for many years. She actually scares the shit out of me," Jackson admitted.

"Do I scare the shit out of you?" Klaire asked sheepishly and batted her eyes and turned slightly away shyly.

"You terrify me but in a whole different way."

"I do? I'm not scary like her, am I?"

"No, but it scares me that I could fall for you, and I'm scared that you will break my heart."

"If you give me your heart, Jackson, I will protect it," and she grabbed his hand and gave him a peck on the cheek.

"Excuse me, folks, we have people waiting, can I take your order please?" interrupted the pimple-faced teenage boy working the snack area.

The couple ordered what they wanted and made their way to the theater that was showing their movie. They walked in and sat near the back of the theater. Jackson didn't want his ex watching him. The thought of that just made him uneasy.

Jackson pretty much had the popcorn devoured by the time the commercials and previews were over. He set his bucket down. Klaire still had some of her peanut M&M's left, and she was slowly eating them. The main feature started, and Jackson reached over and grabbed her hand. His hands were slightly clammy, with a nervous sweat, but she took it in her hand anyway.

Klaire let go of his hand for a moment, folded up the rest of her M&Ms and reached down and put them into her purse. She lifted the arm on the shared seat so she could slide closer to him. She wrapped one arm around his bicep and retook his hand with her other hand. She tucked her leg underneath her on the seat and leaned into Jackson.

"There, now we can watch the movie. I'm all comfy now," and she smiled at him and went back to watching the movie.

The movie was very good, and it would have been pretty emotional, causing Jackson to tear up, but he was more preoccupied with the lovely woman who was clinging to his arm. Her hair smelled like berries, and she had some perfume on that was very pleasant to smell. It wasn't strong, just enough to let you know that she had it on. Her makeup was flawless; she didn't wear a lot. She didn't need a lot. She had five piercings in her left ear, the only ear that he could see at the moment, one metallic dangly earing, a small silver hoop and a silver stud with a tiny diamond in it in her lobe, and another small hoop and a plain silver stud on the top of her ear. He wanted to nibble on it, but he held back that urge.

Klaire turned slightly and whispered, "Are you staring at me?"

"I wouldn't say staring, more of just admiring the scenery."

"Is that what I am, scenery?"

"I don't like labels, let's just say that I am enjoying the movie, and I couldn't even tell you what is going on."

"Pay attention, you hornball, there may be a quiz later."

Jackson went back to watching the movie. During one of the more mushier parts, he happened to look down to where Haley and her mom and Frank were sitting, and he thought he saw a little head peak up and look back in their direction. Haley was checking up on him to make sure his date was going as well as she hoped it was.

Jackson leaned in and whispered into Klaire's ear. "I think you are right. I may have a quiz after the movie, but it won't be about the movie, it will be about how our date is going. I just saw Haley's head peak up over her chair to see how we are doing."

"She did that earlier, too, when you were examining my ear," Klaire said back and gave his bicep a little squeeze. "See, you need to behave, she is watching."

The movie got over, and they left their seats. Haley and her mom were ahead of them, and Camille seems to be holding onto her shoulder to keep her moving and not go back and talk to her stepdad.

By the time they got to the parking lot, they were nowhere to be seen. Jackson and Klaire walked to her vehicle. The Yamaha was parked right next to it.

"Why don't you ride a Harley, like everyone else?"

"Because I like to ride my bike, not fix it."

"Ha, okay, fair enough."

"That, and it was half the price, and I can't really afford a Harley right now."

"Well, I am going home, are you going to follow me on your bike, or ride with me?"

"I didn't know that I was going home with you tonight."

"You were hoping though, right?"

"Yes, I surely was. I just don't want to rush you into anything."

"Listen, your buddy, John, at work. You two must have been talking."

"What did he say? I told him to not say anything because everyone there gossips, and I didn't want you to get scared off."

"Well, you must have told him that we hadn't had sex yet because he actually made a board, where you pick a date. Closest to the exact date wins the pot."

"Holy shit, are you serious? Did anyone put any money into it? Who bets on that sort of thing?"

"There were over fifty people signed up when I left work today. Twenty dollars per pick, and some people put in more than one day. So, there is over a grand in there."

"Holy Helen, what is wrong with people?"

"Well...I put my twenty dollars on tonight."

"You did? You got in on the board? Isn't that cheating, how did John allow that?"

"I made the lady who sits next to me do it and promise to not tell anyone, and I get the money. I did promise her I'd refund her, her own personal entry fee, and double it so she isn't totally losing."

"So you want to have sex with me for the money?"

"No, you silly man. I want to have sex with you because I am extremely attracted to you, and I need to have your cock inside me. The money is just so nobody else makes it off the two of us. I'll give it to you if you want."

"I think having sex with you will be payment enough, I'll follow you."

"I'm not sure I can even wait. If your daughter wasn't in that theater, I would have went down on you during the show. I've wanted you for a long long time now. I've had a crush on you for about a year now. You are the hot guy at the office, you know."

"So the hot chick and the hot guy are hooking up, perfect!"

Jackson pulled her close and kissed her passionately; he held her ass with one hand and her back with the other. He pulled her close enough so that she could feel his manhood was erect. Her breasts were smashed against his chest. They were both very turned on and wanted to rip each other's clothes off right there.

A car pulled up and rolled down the window. "Really, Jackson, get a room." It was Camille. She rolled the window back up and started to drive away. The two were still locked in each other's embrace, and they looked in the back window, and there was Haley, smiling from ear to ear with the biggest grin he had ever seen on her face. She gave them two thumbs up, which made them both laugh.

"Okay, let's go to my house. Don't get picked up for speeding with that stiffy in your pants. You may get arrested for concealing a deadly weapon."

CHAPTER 41

Jackson had to leave early in the morning because the dog needed to be fed; he kissed Klaire good-bye and told her that she should come down and watch football with him on Sunday. It was opening day next Saturday, and may be the last Sunday that he could watch football all day. Hunting takes priority, and that started in seven days from today.

He got home, and he was relieved to not have his two shadows following him anymore. Raider was happy to see him and was more interested in getting petted than the food that Jackson put in his bowl. He got a little extra attention since Jackson was in such a good mood this morning. It isn't every day that you wake up with the hot chick from the office. He was surprised to learn that he was considered the hot guy at the office. But then he got to thinking of it, and there really weren't many good-looking men that worked in his office, most were nearing retirement, and the younger ones were nerdy. There was really only one other man who would be in the running, and he was married, so he probably got knocked down a bit for that.

He had to get ready for the concert tonight. He wasn't sure how that was going to go. He thought that Samantha was interested, but now that he was involved with Klaire, he couldn't lead her on.

"Raider buddy, I go almost a year with not a single lady, even a bad-looking one, showing any interest. Now, in the last couple months, I have three at the same time. One of them is dead now but still two very attractive, super awesome ladies. What do I do?"

His dog just looked at him and cocked his head to the side as if asking a question back to him.

"It's okay, Raid, I don't have the answer either."

CHAPTER 42

Samantha showed up early; Jackson was ready, of course, because he liked to be early too. She had some really short jean shorts on and a very tight tank top that showed off her curves. He kept trying to read the name of the band on the shirt but kept getting distracted by her cleavage.

"Damn, Sam, you are going to catch a cold in that outfit."

"I was hoping to catch a rock star actually. Do you think I have a chance?"

"If he is male, then absolutely. Better than average I'd say."

"Thanks, I figured I better show off my boobs since my face isn't too much to look at."

"Are you kidding? Your face would be enough, without seeing how smoking hot the rest of you is."

"Jackson Ackerman, you need to stop flirting with me. I hear you have a girlfriend."

"So you know about that? I was wondering how I was going to tell you that. I didn't know if you were serious with our flirting the other day. If I wasn't involved, I would so be interested in dating you."

"To be honest, I was a little let down when I talked to Camille this morning, and she mentioned it. But once she told me who it was, I completely understand. She used to date one of my other friends. She is super nice, and that lady is hot. If I was a dude, I'd want to do her too."

"So are we still going to the concert? As friends?"

"Hell ya, I can't be walking around looking all hot and shit like this without some protection. Ha-ha." Samantha laughed, mostly because she really didn't think she was pretty at all, but she did feel rather sexy today for some reason.

"I got your back, girl. Let's go sit on the deck and smoke quick, and then we can take off."

"Sounds like a plan."

"I'm grabbing a pop. I have beer if you want one?"

"Grab me one please. They are like eight bucks at the venue."

CHAPTER 43

It was nearly 2:00 a.m. when Jackson and Samantha got back to his house. Both of their ears were ringing still from the concert. They we both still pretty jacked up from the excitement. They had gotten to go backstage at the Lacrosse Center somehow. Mostly because the security guard knew Samantha and had a crush on her since high school.

Hellyeah was the warm up band, which was a surprise to both of them because it was supposed to be a local band that was up and coming, but they cancelled at the last minute, and Hellyeah happened to be on their way through from Chicago to Minneapolis; so they agreed to fill in.

Once backstage, Samantha caught the eye of Vinnie Paul, the drummer, and he invited her over to hang out with them. He was in a good mood and didn't have his usual roadies with him and asked if Sam and Jackson would help him out. So Jackson was in charge of making sure Vinnie had enough sticks, in case he broke one, or if he dropped one, Jackson needed to rush in behind him and replace it. He was needed twice. Sam, well, he had something special for her.

Vinnie is a master drummer and known throughout the world as one of the best; he and his brother Dimebag Darrell had formed the famous heavy metal band Pantera earlier in his career. His current bandmates had challenged him to do one of their songs while getting a lap dance. Vinnie asked if Sam was interested in performing this for him. Samantha agreed immediately.

So near the end of their set, he called Sam out and announced that she would be giving him a lap dance during their hit song,

"Alcohaulin Ass." She performed like a high-end stripper, made him mess up a couple times. The crowd loved it, and so did the band.

After their set, and while Buchcherry was playing, Samantha was doing shots with the band backstage and watching the rest of the show. Jackson had a blast just taking it all in. A once in a lifetime experience.

*****

Jackson pulled into his driveway, and they were still both singing at the top of their lungs. They decided to stay up a little longer, and Samantha had a couple more of the beers that Jackson kept in his fridge.

They were sitting on the back deck, talking about everything. The lap dance came up, and Sam said, "That dance I did for Vinny, if you ever break up with your lady friend, you call me. I would love to reenact that for you."

"It's a deal! You have to wear that same outfit though, so it is authentic."

"Oh, honey, if you play your cards right, this outfit may not even be in play by the end of it."

"I better get to bed before this goes too far," Jackson said, not wanting to ruin what he had going with Klaire but knowing that things were getting a little too much for him. "Are you okay to drive home, or do you want to crash on the couch?"

"I'm okay. I haven't had much to drink in the last couple hours, just half of this beer."

He walked her out to her car, and he gave her a hug. "That was an epic night, my friend."

"Yes, it was, we will have to hit another concert soon."

"Sounds good, drive safe," and Jackson turned to go back in his house and hit the sack.

Samantha got in her ride and turned the switch, nothing, she tried again. Nothing. She opened the door and yelled, "Hey, my car don't start!"

"Just come in and sleep on the couch. I'll have my neighbor look at it in the morning."

"Are you sure? You won't get in trouble?"

"Only if you don't sleep on the couch, which I can't believe I am saying this, but you need to."

"Don't worry. I wouldn't want you cheating on me if we ever do date, so I'm glad you insist." Samantha was actually impressed. Nobody that she ever really wanted had turned her down. She was super horny though, but she would keep her pants on…this time.

CHAPTER 44

There was a banging on the door early Sunday morning. Well, it seemed like it was early; it was actually eleven. The door opened up and in walked Haley and her mother. Samantha was still asleep on the couch, and she woke up and was rubbing her eyes. Jackson had heard the pounding and came down in an old pair of gym shorts.

"Haley, what on earth are you doing here?" He walked over and gave her a hug.

"She insisted on watching the first week of football with you because she knows that you will be in the woods most likely the rest of the year. We were on the way to my parents, so to shut her up, we are dropping her off until after the Raiders game," Camille said, in a pissy voice.

"Ya, you get to watch the Vikings with me, and I get to watch the Raiders with you!" Haley chirped.

"What are you doing here, Samantha? I thought you were going to a concert last night," Camille asked.

"We did. Jackson went with me. We got back pretty late, and my car didn't start."

They heard a noise and saw a SUV pull up to the curb. They all strained to see who it was.

"It's Klaire!!" screamed Haley. "Oh, and Mandi is here too!!" Haley ran outside to greet them. She led them in the house.

"Wow, full house, Jackson, didn't know you were having a party. I would have brought balloons," Klaire said. Klaire was dressed in some form-fitting jeans with sparkles on the back pockets, had her hair pulled up under a Vikings baseball cap, with a pony pulled through the back of it. She had on an old retro Fran Tarkington jersey that was cut down a little to show a hint of cleavage but not skanky looking. "Hi, Samantha, what are you doing here?"

"Oh, it isn't what it may look like. Jackson and I went to the concert in LaCrosse last night, and my car didn't start when we got back. Don't worry, I slept on the couch. We are just friends."

"I'll actually vouch for them. She was still sleeping when we got here. And they have known each other a long time. There is no way she could be interested in him," Camille snorted.

"Okay, then, let's see if we can get your car running. Let's check it out. Camille, do you know you can get in trouble for leaving your dog in the car alone with the windows up?"

"Oh, funny man. Frank isn't a dog, but he does obey pretty well, unlike you."

The caravan of people ushered out the door, except the two little girls, who went upstairs to play in the toy room.

Samantha popped her hood and tried the ignition for the fun of it. It didn't start. Jackson looked in and saw that the battery had been disconnected.

"Someone didn't want you to leave last night. This was done on purpose, no way this just happens on its own."

"But who? And why?"

He hooked the cables back up and slammed the hood down. "Try it now, bet it starts."

She turned the key, and the engine roared to life.

"Well, glad it wasn't anything else that would have cost me money. Probably some kids playing a joke. Okay, time for me to leave you to your football. Thanks for the couch, Jackson, catch you all later."

"We'll be back after the second game this afternoon to get Haley. Don't think that this is going to keep happening, this is a onetime thing," Camille turned and got in her car also.

"Guess that just leaves the two of us and the girls and some football! This could be a perfect day."

"Well, it would be better if I didn't pull up to the guy who I just started dating's house, and his ex-wife is there, *and* some good-looking lady spent the night with him. You are lucky I actually trust you."

"I am lucky," Jackson said and smiled, grabbed her and kissed her. "Let's go in. I need to shower before the game and get some food started. You can a…join me in the shower if you want."

"Both of our girls are here, you know we can't do that!!"

"I had to offer, never know."

"Now you know, no sex while the kiddos are awake and running around."

"Dang it."

"Get in the shower. I'll look around and see what we can make for food. I am kind of handy in the kitchen."

"Hot damn, beautiful, *and* you can cook?? I don't know who will be more excited, myself or Haley."

CHAPTER 45

Thursday night and Jackson got home from work and was looking forward to the upcoming opening day of deer season, just a day and a half away now. He changed his clothes as soon as he got home and grabbed his bow out of the garage. He hadn't shot his bow in over a month, so he figured he better shoot a little to make sure it was still on.

Jackson walked out his back door on to his deck. He had a target, in the shape of a deer about twenty yards from his deck. It was in the back corner of his lot, with no houses or anything other than some bushes behind it. He could also shoot at it from the front of his house if he wanted longer shots, but he wasn't planning on that tonight.

He knocked his first arrow, took aim, made sure that his form was perfect, and looked through the peep sight at the yardage pins that helped him gauge where the arrow would end up. He selected his twenty-yard pin, put it right on the target where the deer's heart would be, and he touched the trigger to let the arrow fly.

Ffwack!! That was one of the best sounds there was to a bow hunter. The sound the arrow made as it flew through the air and hit its intended target. The shot was absolutely perfect.

Jackson looked over at Raider, who was watching him, "Still got it!"

He took two more shots before going to retrieve his arrows. He was getting pretty good, and he found that if he shot more than three arrows at a time, he ended up ruining arrows because they hit each other. Although he thought of himself as a pretty good shot, he had been invited to a 3D archery shooting contest earlier in the spring.

One of his friends picked him up and took him. He came in second to last, out of thirty entrants. The one person that he did beat broke his bowstring halfway through and couldn't finish. That was pretty humbling for him.

After Jackson had shot six rounds of three at his fake deer, he decided that was good enough. So he put his bow back in its case and put it in the back seat of his truck. The arrows had their broad heads attached, and it was ready to rock for Saturday morning.

He went back in the house and down to the basement to where he stored his hunting equipment. He had three tubs of things that ranged from clothing, knives, calls, scents, and cover-up scents. He pulled out his favorite backpack, (he has three) and he started filling it up.

Buck grunt, knife, small rope for dragging deer, doe bleat, cover-up scent, doe-in-heat scent, warm gloves, extra knife, because you can never have enough knives, and toilet paper. Toilet paper was always essential because it sucks to have to use your socks in emergency situations.

He dug into his clothing pile. Scent controlling pants and long-sleeve shirt, camo socks, boots, hat, facemask. All his clothing had to match and was Mossyoak brand. Patterns mattered to him. He took out his light jacket. It was supposed to be warm, and he didn't want to get all sweated up and let the deer be able to smell him. Jackson was as anal about scent control as his ex-wife was about her house being spotless.

Jackson stood there and thought, *What am I forgetting?* and he pondered that question while looking at the tubs of clothing and equipment. *Bug spray!* During early season hunting, he always has to put up with the mosquitoes. He dug through his belongings until he came up with his earth-scented bug spray, made especially for hunters. Of course, it cost twice as much, and the can was half the size as normal bug spray, but hunters pay for stuff and don't care what the price is.

He brought everything upstairs and put it by the door, so he was ready to go Saturday morning. His license was in his wallet, so he was set. Now he just had to wait until the season opened.

CHAPTER 46

Friday night, Klaire didn't have her daughter and was excited to be able to spend the night alone with Jackson for the first time. She got off work and went home quick to freshen up and pack a few things for the overnight. She knew that it wouldn't be a late night, and that she would probably be getting out of bed alone since he would be off early in the morning to head to his tree in the woods.

She drove to Jackson's house in Preston; she had some classic rock station on, and she was enjoying the ride, the windows down and singing at the top of her lungs. She was in one of the best moods that she could remember. There is nothing like being in a new relationship to help put you in a good frame of mind. She had plenty of people ask her out over the last couple years, but either they were too self-absorbed, or they only wanted one thing from her and wouldn't want to actually be in a relationship. Jackson seemed to be different. She hoped he was different.

Klaire pulled into Jackson's driveway, kind of off to one side so that he would be able to pull his truck out of the garage in the morning without having to move her vehicle.

She was barely out of her car when she saw Raider come running around the side of the house to greet her. She still wasn't very familiar with Jackson's dog, and she pulled her knee up and put one hand down to make sure he wasn't going to jump up on her.

Jackson had seen her pull in and was now standing on the front porch. "He won't jump up on you," he said. "I trained him to not do that. I hate that when dogs jump up on you."

"Good, I am not a fan of that either," Klaire admitted. She reached down and petted the black lab on the head a little. "Good boy...he is a boy, right?"

"Ha, yeah, he is. Now are you going to spend the whole night paying attention to my dog, or am I going to get any?"

"Oh, you will probably get more attention than you can handle, but you need to be patient. I hope you aren't premature and can wait." She trailed off, making it clear that she wanted him to make love to her, not just have sex with her.

Klaire left the dog and walked over to Jackson, wrapped her arms around him, and gave him a kiss. "What do you have in mind for our night together?" she asked.

"I was actually thinking. I have to be up early. We should just go to bed now," he said jokingly. He received a swift punch to the gut. It wasn't a hard punch, but he played it off like she knocked the wind out of him.

"I may be as close to a sure thing tonight as you will ever get, but I'm not *that* easy! Let's at least watch a movie or something."

"I've actually prepared a meal for us, it is ready. All we have to do is dish up, and we can eat. It is the first time I've ever made this, so if it sucks, I'll make you a frozen burrito or something."

"You cooked? What on earth did you make? Please tell me it isn't hotdogs."

"I know that you don't eat a whole lot of meat, so I decided that I would make you a vegetarian lasagna roll up. It has spinach in it, and I added mushrooms because I like them."

"*Damn*, I'm actually impressed and was totally not expecting this," Klaire said, amazed.

"Well, don't get used to it, normally I need meat in my meal, so I'm actually kinda impressed with myself. It actually looks like it turned out too!"

They went in and ate. They had to sit on the couch and used the coffee table as their table. Jackson found a movie on Lifetime and told a little white lie that he didn't even know there was such a channel; he usually just watched sports and sitcoms.

They finished eating, and Klaire picked up his plate and fork and his glass of water. She took them along with hers to the kitchen.

"You cooked means I have dish duty."

He got up and followed her to the kitchen and watched her as she filled the sink with soapy water, and she washed their dishes, and she dug around in the cupboards and found some old cool whip containers to put the leftover food into. She filled two of them and handed them to Jackson, who placed them in the refrigerator.

Klaire placed the casserole dish into the water and started to wash it. Jackson snuck in behind her and wrapped his arms around her waist. He placed his hands on her stomach. Her stomach was firm, and he could tell that she worked out. Of course, he already knew that, but he still loved that she was so fit. He kissed her neck gently, and she jumped a little because his hands on her stomach tickled a little bit. That coupled with the tingly feeling she got when he kissed her neck. She instantly had goosebumps all over her body. After her initial shudder, she eased back into him, and she knew that she was helpless to this man.

"You better just let that one soak," he whispered into her ear softly, as he continued to nibble on her earlobe.

She turned her head enough so that she could reach his mouth, and they locked in a kiss that made them both feel excited. She turned around and pulled him closer to him. She could tell that he was already erect as his member was pressed into her. She could feel her own sexual area becoming increasingly wet.

She took his hand and stepped out of his embrace. He had kind of a confused look on his face and just looked at her like what is going on. "I want to do this right, come upstairs with me. Make love to me, Jackson Ackerman. Make me yours."

He didn't say anything just followed her up the stairs. He stared at her perfectly shaped ass as they climbed the stairs. It was pretty easy since she was two steps in front of him, so it was literally right in front of him. He couldn't help it, so he reached up and grabbed it. "Damn, you have to have the nicest ass that I have ever seen."

"Thank you, but I'd rather have you like me for my personality."

"A personality will only go so far, but an ass like this...damn, this here will get you anything you want in life," Jackson kidded.

"Well, right now, this ass wants you."

"See, it is working already." He led her to his bedroom and turned her around before they got to the bed.

She reached down and pulled his T-shirt up, and he lifted his hands above his head, and she pulled it off. He did the same with her blouse, dragging his pinky fingers along her ribcage as he went, causing her to shiver and get the goosebumps again. He almost had her blouse off, and she stopped him.

"Wait, wait, my earring is caught." She grabbed her ear and untangled the blouse and earring and helped him finish taking off her shirt.

They both grabbed each other's jeans, and they unbuttoned them at the same time. She took hold of the sides of his jeans, while he slid his hand underneath hers and forced them down over her bottom as he felt her backside. She finished pulling off his pants, while he pushed her down onto the bed so he could finish pulling hers off. They were tighter and took a little more finesse to get off.

Jackson admired her body, tone everywhere, with a tan. He still couldn't believe he was here with her and thought that he may be in a dream. A really good dream.

Klaire clamped her hand on the waistline of his underwear and pulled him to her. He couldn't wait, so he helped pull them off and went right to work on hers. While he was doing that, she reached around and unhooked her bra for him, which he slowly took off her.

Jackson couldn't remember his manhood ever feeling as hard as it currently was; it was almost painful how hard he was but in a good way. He lay down so he was on top of her, and they began kissing. Softly at first, then a little harder. This was not lust that they were engaging in; it was something different, almost a respect for each other. Jackson couldn't quite explain it. He never had this with any other woman and certainly not with his ex-wife.

Both of their hands were in constant motion, sliding across each other's bodies, grabbing and pulling, sliding to the next part, and fondling some more. Jackson worked his way down to her breasts. Her nipples were erect. He thought to himself that they were the absolute perfect size, and he ran his tongue over her nipple and sucked on her breasts. Back up and kissing her, and she slipped her tongue into his mouth, and he met it with his.

Jackson slowly slid into her, and she almost buckled with the pleasure that it gave her. She grabbed his ass and pulled him so that he was all the way inside her.

The two made love for what seemed like forever, but in real time was only about twenty minutes. They came simultaneously, and it was almost a religious experience for the both of them. Her sex organ clamping down on him like a vise, causing him to explode into her, only making her tighten down on him even more.

They just lay there together, both breathing hard, but not wanting to move and lose the experience. He was still inside of her, and he looked deep into her eyes, and he swore he could see her soul. She seemed to be looking into his also.

Neither one of them knew what to say, so he finally rolled off of her, and they lay next to each other, and she curled up into him and pulled a blanket over herself and up to his waist.

It was still early in the evening, and it wasn't even dark yet, but the two stayed in bed together for the rest of the night, making love one more time before falling asleep in each other's arms.

CHAPTER 47

The morning came earlier than Jackson wanted it to. He had been in bed extremely early, but he found it hard to leave this beautiful person alone in his bed. He finally got the courage to get up and out of bed. He slipped downstairs and took a quick shower and put his hunting clothes on. He went back upstairs to say goodbye to Klaire. He leaned into her and kissed her on the lips and whispered, "I need to get going. There is a big buck out there, and he is not going to wait."

"Okay," he heard in a sleepy sweet voice.

"You are welcome to stay as long as you want. I probably won't be back until about an hour after dark tonight."

"I think I will stay the day. I need to wash the casserole dish still," and she gave a tired smile. "I will probably take a walk along the river on the trail too. I love this time of year."

"Me too." He kissed her again, "I'll be thinking about you all day and probably be distracted, and the big boy will walk right by me."

"Shoot him this morning, so I get you more this fall."

"I'll try. See you later."

"Bye…I'm going back to sleep, while you are out there sitting in a tree. Good luck."

Jackson went down the stairs and retrieved the rest of his hunting apparel and got in the truck. He started it, opened the garage door, and backed out, trying to not hit Klaire's SUV.

He drove the twenty-five minutes to where he hunted and got out and snuck into his stand. He had sprayed himself down with scent killer before leaving the truck. He walked through the field and into the woods in the darkness, to where his tree stand was. He tied his bow to the string below his tree stand and climbed up the ladder. Once there, he hung his backpack on the hanger and pulled his bow up to him. He knocked an arrow and got his release ready. He hung his bow on the bow hanger, so it was within reach and ready to fire if and when a deer came by. Now all he had to do was wait. First, wait for it to get to be legal shooting time since he was always early and was there twenty-five minutes before he could even shoot. Then hopefully the big buck that he had been seeing on his trail cams would come by. He didn't consider himself a trophy hunter, but he definitely had high standards. Small bucks walked; big bucks got an arrow behind their shoulder.

CHAPTER 48

He walked in through the garage, dropped a large piece of steak for the dog as he walked by him. The door was unlocked, and he eased it open. He actually took the time to wipe his feet on the rug as he entered the kitchen. He had never actually been in this house, but he kind of had a good idea of how it was laid out from different stories that he had heard.

Up the stairs, he slowly went. He kept his feet to the outsides of the steps, nearest the wall as he could get them. He knew in these older homes that stairs had a tendency to creak when you step on them. It probably took him five minutes to ascend the staircase of twenty-one steps. He snuck around the railing just enough to peer into the bedroom. The door was wide open, and he saw her lying there.

He carefully approached her. She was lying completely still in the bed; her breathing was shallow, and she already looked like she was dead. So calm, so perfect. This woman was not wearing anything that he could tell, and one breast was poking out from under the covers that she had covering the rest of her. He could smell the scent of recent sex in the air.

The killer leaned down close enough to be able to smell her hair. It was intoxicating to him. He noticed that his pants were now tighter, and he was hard. He wondered how this prick kept getting such beautiful women when he had struggled most of his life to maybe get one. He did have one now though, so he was on his way. Jackson was much older and had more time to acquire more, give him time and maybe he would also.

He just stood and stared at Klaire sleeping in the bed, his penis was hard, and he wanted to touch himself so badly. But he had to kill her. He looked around for something to use, but the room was almost completely empty. Most likely, a result of his ex taking most of his possessions. He wasn't able to find anything that seemed like it would work to kill her with, or to tie her up with. He could use the sheets, but he would have to wake her up beforehand, and that could not turn out well.

He decided to just take advantage of the situation, and he unzipped his pants and removed his glove and began touching himself. With his gloved hand, he gently pulled on the sheet that was covering her other breast, and she didn't stir, so he pulled it down to her waist, exposing her stomach. It didn't take the pervert very long, and he was able to climax. He shot it into the glove that he had removed. He really wanted to shoot it onto her stomach but knew better.

He stuffed the glove into his pocket and zipped back up. He backed out of the room and eased back down the stairs and out the door. Raider wasn't quite as nice this time; he had gobbled up the steak and wasn't distracted. He growled and barked, and it actually scared the guy. The dog could smell fear, and he attacked, biting the man's arm as he tried to get away from the dog. He kicked the dog free from his arm, and he took off on a dead sprint, hurdled off the back deck and into the woods. He couldn't hear the dog behind him, so eventually he stopped and hid behind a tree. He saw a light come on in the upstairs bedroom and a woman wrapped in a bed sheet peering out into the darkness. He heard the window open and heard her call to the dog, who started barking again in his direction. "What is it, boy? Is someone out there? I've got a gun, and I know how to use it!" she yelled.

He knew that he couldn't be seen where he was, so he sat tight until the light flipped back off. It was starting to get light out, so he crept away and back to his vehicle.

CHAPTER 49

Saturday morning and Haley was already missing her stepfather. She was awake way earlier than normal. She knew what he was doing, and she wished she could be sitting with him in the tree. It was opening day, and she was never allowed to go opening morning, but the next weekend she was always with him. She sat alone in front of the TV in her mother's condo, watching deer hunting shows. Primo's "The Truth about Hunting," then "North American Whitetail." She didn't normally watch these shows, but it made her feel more connected to Jackson at the moment.

Camille woke up, clearly nursing a hangover; she was on her way to get herself a glass of water. She wore a very short silk nightgown with lace straps. Her pink silky robe was hanging open with the ties drooping down to the floor.

"What on earth are you doing up? And why are you watching that crap?" Camille snorted.

"Just missing Jackson this morning is all, Mom. Do you think I can go out with him hunting next weekend, like we always do?"

"Absolutely not! I don't want you hanging around him anymore. Maybe he will kill you next. Who knows if he is the one killing all those women!"

"Mom, seriously. You know very well that he isn't the one. You just want him out of our lives. You can't make me stop loving him," Haley said very sternly.

"Whatever, my head hurts. I'm going back to bed."

"Is Frank out hunting this morning too, Mom?"

"Probably. Why don't you go out with him?"

"Mom, Frank? Sorry, but he isn't exactly Mr. Funman," Haley said irritated.

"You need to give him a chance. You will never know how fun he is, unless you give him a chance."

"I'll try, but I'm not promising anything."

Camille filled her glass of ice water in the refrigerator door and walked back to her bed. She stopped in the bathroom quick and grabbed a couple Advil to help with her symptoms.

Haley, still sitting on the couch, yelled back over her shoulder at her mother, who was already in her room. "By the way, I heard you and Frank again last night when you got home. First of all, ewww. Second of all, try to keep it down. I don't need to be scarred any more than you have already scarred me."

She just heard the door close and didn't receive a response.

CHAPTER **50**

Another weekend sitting alone in her home. Samantha had a lot of fun with Jackson Ackerman when they went to the concert together. More fun than she had had in many years. Why did she have such bad timing? She couldn't blame Jackson for dating Klaire. She was stunning and actually a good person. That didn't stop her from being jealous. Even when he was married to one of her best friends, she was jealous of Camille. Samantha never let him know that she was interested in him because she wouldn't do that to one of her friends. She had kind of forgotten about him, until that day she saw him on his motorcycle. Dang, he looked good on that bike.

Sam stepped outside to have a smoke. Her thoughts were of who was out there for her. She sat and pulled up her Facebook page and scrolled through her list of friends. Too bad, there wasn't a sort option to filter out only the single men.

"Nope, nope, nope, nope, ahh nope, maybe but he lives in Colorado now, nope, married, nope, nope, Jackson is a for sure, nope, married, gay, nope."

How pathetic was she, sitting looking for a man on Facebook. She was going out tonight and was going to find herself someone!!

She got up and went back in the house and got ready for a night on the town. Maybe she would call Camille and see what she was doing. She knew she wasn't attracted to her new man, so she didn't have to worry about anything there.

She called up Camille and found out she already had plans but was welcome to join her. So she drove and met her at the bar she was already at, and they drank and looked at men all night. Nobody really peaked her interest, but Camille certainly enjoyed herself. You wouldn't have known that she lived with someone.

All night, Camille was dancing with some guy, or sitting on someone's lap. It only made Samantha feel bad for Jackson, and how she used to do that to him, and he had no idea. She thought that her new guy wouldn't have a clue about how she really acted either.

Samantha had enough of the Camille show and drove herself home early.

CHAPTER 51

Jackson got home around midnight that night. He had shot a huge buck, right before the last of legal shooting light. Even though he made a good shot on it, he still had to track it a little way, and by the time he got it and himself out of the woods, it was getting late. He went over to his parents' house and had his father help him hang it up in his shed for the night, and he would cut the deer up the next day. It was cold enough that the meat wouldn't spoil, so it was okay to let it hang.

He had called Klaire already, so she was expecting him to be late. He walked in the door to the smell of a really nice meal.

"It may be late, but my man needs to eat," she said with a smile.

"So, I'm your man officially?" he asked.

"I don't just sleep with everyone, you know!! I am not that type of girl. So, yes, you are now my man. And I'm your woman."

"I am good with that," and he gave her a hug and a kiss.

He sat down and ate the steak and potatoes and gravy that she had prepared for him. It tasted so good; he didn't really eat much other than some granola bars that he had packed in his backpack at the last second. When he had finished, she looked at him and knew that the meal was to his liking.

"Now go take a shower. I don't want any deer guts or whatever coming to bed with us."

"Yes, mam."

"And please don't take too long. I want to see you a little bit before you fall asleep."

"I'm hoping I get to see a whole lot of you if you know what I mean."

"Pretty sure we can arrange something."

Jackson was off to the shower; he threw his clothing directly into the washing machine and hopped into the shower. He would wash his hunting clothes in the morning since he didn't have to go out into the woods.

He was just finishing up with washing his hair, when he heard the shower curtain being pulled back. Klaire entered the shower with him, wearing nothing but a smile.

"I didn't see any kids out there running around, now move over a little so I can get some of that warm water on me too."

They took turns rubbing soap all over each other and then rinsing it off. Jackson knew she had a smoking body, but here, in the light of the shower, he could really see how amazing she was. They made love in the warm stream of water and finished right before the hot water tank ran empty and the water got cold.

Jackson got out of the shower first, then he helped Klaire out and wrapped a towel around her.

"That was pretty cool," he said. "I didn't expect that at all."

"Just because I don't sleep around doesn't mean I'm some boring old prude in the sex department. I may have some other tricks up my sleeve, but I can't let you see them all the first weekend," she said and found another towel and wrapped up her hair.

They went up to bed, and neither one of them bothered putting any clothes on, just dropped their towels, and got under the covers. She did brush her hair quick, so it wasn't a rat's nest in the morning. Jackson just sat and watched her as she brushed her hair.

Jackson told her the whole story about the deer that he shot. She figured she would probably be hearing that same story with a few different twists, many times in the coming weeks, as he would certainly tell everyone he knew about it.

They finally turned the light off and snuggled in with each other. They made love a second time and fell asleep quickly afterward.

*****

The guy in the tree in the woods had a pretty good show. He had watched them take off their towels, and as she brushed her hair, breasts exposed above the covers the whole time. He was afraid to pleasure himself because he thought he may fall out of the tree since he had to hold the binoculars with one hand. He couldn't afford that to happen and possibly get caught. He was getting pretty tired; he had been waiting for Jackson's truck to pull back into the driveway for hours before he climbed to his perch.

After he was sure they were asleep and he didn't see any movement from any of the neighbors, he climbed down and walked inside the tree line to where his vehicle was parked. His truck was also black, and it was average looking, not too new and not too old. He could afford something nicer but preferred to not have it stick out. New vehicles tended to draw more attention, he thought.

Time for him to go home to his woman and wake her up. After watching Klaire, he was extremely horny and was going home to pretend he was giving it to her, instead of his girlfriend.

CHAPTER 52

Jackson took pictures of his buck before cutting it up and taking the head to the taxidermist. He tried to take a few in the dark the night before, but they didn't really turn out. He sent pictures to his family members and to Haley.

His parents skipped Sunday services at the local Lutheran Church that morning. They knew Jackson would need help cutting up his deer, and Mrs. Ackerman had already been at the church five of the last seven days for one thing or another.

Klaire went with Jackson and met his parents for the first time. They were surprised to see a female with him. He hadn't brought a woman by since he was married. They didn't even know he was dating anyone.

Jackson's father got caught looking at Klaire's ass. He didn't even know he was doing it, until he received a slap on the backside of his head. It wasn't a hard slap, but he definitely knew why he got it.

"Fine-looking young lady friend you have there, Jackson."

"Dad, just keep your hands to yourself, you are a married man," Jackson teased. "If you need something to do, go grab a knife."

The two men cut up the deer and put the quarters into the spare refrigerator that was in the garage. Meanwhile, the ladies were busy in the kitchen. Jackson's mom was impressed that Klaire seemed to know her way around the kitchen and wasn't afraid to dig in and help.

"You two been seeing each other very long?" Mrs. Ackerman asked.

"Not too long officially, but we have been flirting for a while now. This whole thing with women dying around here has me moving slow and cautiously. I didn't want to get my little girl involved in that mess."

"Oh my, you have a little girl?! How old is she? When do we get to meet her? Oh goodie, another grandchild to spoil!" Mrs. Ackerman was already planning a wedding in her head and more grandbabies.

"I'm sure you will meet her pretty soon, her and Haley sure hit it off. She is five going on thirty-seven." Klaire was glad that Jackson's parents seemed to be pretty inviting into their circle.

"You know Jackson loves that little Haley like she is his own. If that witch ever took her away from him, it would break his heart."

"Sounds like she is trying to put a stop to that. He hasn't got to see her much lately, but I think Haley will keep that avenue open, she seems to really love spending time with him."

"That girl, she isn't afraid of her mother. Most people are afraid of her. I know she scares the bejeezuz out of me. I just pray for her though, everyone needs someone to pray for them. I'll be adding you to my prayer list now."

"Thank you, that is very nice of you," and Klaire went across the kitchen and gave her a hug.

"Don't let my husband see you hugging me, or he'll want one, too, and I'm afraid, I can't compete with you, my pretty little thing."

"Oh, I don't know there, Mrs. Ackerman. It looks like you still have what it takes. You know, Jackson didn't even really introduce us. I don't even know your names."

"Oh dear, I'm so sorry. I am Mary, and his dad is Richard, but everyone calls him Dick."

"Very nice to meet you, Mary, I'm Klaire."

"Klaire Ackerman has a nice ring to it, doesn't it?"

"Oh gosh, don't be marrying us off quite yet." Klaire paused, "Klaire Ackerman, hmm," she thought about the thought of one day changing her last name. It was a pleasant thought.

Mary Ackerman saw the young lady thinking about it and just smiled and went back to getting Sunday lunch ready for the table. She liked this new girlfriend and hoped that Jackson wouldn't mess it up.

CHAPTER 53

etective Holmes was sitting on his couch, files, paperwork, and crime scene photos spread out across the entire room. He was at his wits end trying to figure out who was doing these murders. The one common thread in all of these women was Jackson Ackerman, but he was about 95 percent sure that he wasn't the one doing them. His alibis always seems to be pretty solid, and his last alibi was almost impossible to discredit, as he had two officers following him the entire time of the last murder.

But why was someone seemingly trying to frame him? Were they actually trying to frame him and forgot that in order to frame someone successfully that he had to actually be able to put them at the murder scene at the time it happened? Maybe they were just trying to hurt him? That didn't make much sense since Roxy was the first person that was killed, and Jackson clearly didn't give two shits about her.

They had to be trying to frame him.

"Okay, think, Holmes!! Who would want him out of the picture?" he said out loud.

He wrote notes on a piece of scratch paper:

Possible motives, he underlined this at the top of the page.

Underneath that, he wrote,

Love triangle? Triangles?

Gay lover? He crossed that off immediately. He saw all of the lovely women who Jackson had been with, and he was more certain that Jackson was not gay than he was that he wasn't the murderer.

Drug deal gone bad? That was scratched off too. He didn't see any signs that Jackson was a dealer; he appeared to be living pretty modestly.

It has to be someone who just plain doesn't like him, or wants to be him. Someone who is envious. Jackson didn't have much, so it has to be about a woman.

Holmes sat and looked at pictures, ran different scenarios through his head. None of them made sense. He decided that he needed a sit down with Jackson to pick his brain. He may know something he couldn't come up with. He was officially no longer on the case, and he had to turn in all of the evidence and files on Monday morning. Which means he needed to do it today. He got in his car and called the Sherriff in Minnesota, who would need to go with him.

"Meet me at Ackerman's place in a half hour."

CHAPTER 54

Jackson and Klaire made it back to his house around two-thirty, just in time to watch the Raiders game. They played the Bronco's this week, so they were on national TV again. Klaire decided she would stay until halftime before she had to leave and get her daughter.

They were just settling in on the ugly couch when through the window they noticed the police arrive.

"What in the hairy hell do they want now?" Jackson said irritated.

"Maybe they caught the guy and came to tell you?"

"I doubt it. They couldn't catch a cold," Jackson said sarcastically. Klaire giggled a little bit.

Jackson got up and opened the door.

"Mr. Ackerman, we need your help," the Iowa detective admitted. "We are no further to catching this guy than when we started this whole mess. I would like to see if you can help us by maybe giving us some info that we aren't thinking of. Would you be willing to help us out?"

"Can this wait until after the Raiders play? They are actually on TV this week."

"We would prefer to get started right away if you would please. I don't really have time to wait anymore. I basically have today to catch this guy before the Feds take over."

The detective seems down and actually looked kind of pitiful. Jackson could see that the man was stressed and doubting his abilities.

"Well, I will help you. Only because a couple of those ladies were close to me, and I owe it to them, not to you."

"Thank you for your cooperation," Sherriff Osborn said.

"Sure, come on in, I guess," Jackson said to the officers. He turned to Klaire, "You may just want to take off, you don't need to hear all of the details of this crap." He gave her a kiss.

Klaire headed up the stairs to gather her things and leave. She was disappointed; she was looking forward to sitting on the couch with her man for a couple hours. She did want all this business with girls getting killed over with though, so she was willing to forgo a little cuddle time to help get that resolved.

Jackson let the two officers have a seat on the couch, and he stepped outside quick and grabbed a folding lawn chair to sit on.

The officers grilled Jackson for three hours, asked him about almost every relationship he had ever had. There were not many to list, and the only one he had a serious relationship with was still alive. The three of them decided that they needed to maybe start watching Camille closer; she was the most likely to be the next target. That… or Klaire. That wasn't a very good thing for Jackson to think about, and it almost made him sick to his stomach.

"Detective, I watch a lot of TV, and I have seen where the killer a lot of times goes to the funeral of his victims. Have you had people at all of these funerals?" Jackson inquired.

"I have personally been at all of them. I sat in the back of the church each time and scanned the people. I stood at the funeral homes and watched to see if the same people went to all of them. I took pictures. Most of these people knew a lot of the same people, except for the one lady that you did not know," the detective answered.

Sherriff Osborn butted in, "Detective, do you have the pictures? Maybe we can have Jackson take a look at them and see if he sees someone who sticks out? Someone who probably wouldn't normally be there."

"That is a good idea. I have everything in my car outside, let me get them!" The detective's voice had more enthusiasm than it had previously.

He left and returned with some photo albums. One for each of the funerals. Jackson took the most recent one, from Tami's funeral.

He noticed the neat and organized fashion that it was put together. There were pictures of the family, her husband and children, her parents. Being from a small town, Jackson new most of the people in the pictures. There was his sister, Emily, in a couple pictures.

He then took the second and third albums. He knew quite a few people in both Roxy and Brandy's albums. Again, he saw Emily in a few pictures again.

The last album he looked at, he didn't know a single person, except for once again, his little sister, Emily. He didn't bring attention to this as he didn't want her to have to answer questions, so he kept that to himself.

"Well, I didn't really notice anyone out of place, guess that only happens on TV?" Jackson said.

"Okay, thank you for your input. I'm not sure we learned anything, but we can't say we didn't try," the detective stated in a more dejected voice.

The officers both stood and actually shook Jackson's hand, and they left.

Jackson stood on the porch and watched them leave. He lit a cigarette up and as soon as he finished it, he dug his cellphone out of his pocket. He pulled up his contact list and found who he wanted and hit dial.

She picked up on the second ring. "What now, don't tell me someone else died!!"

"No, not yet. I just spent the last few hours with the police though, and I noticed something from all of the pictures they showed me."

"Okay, what did you notice?"

"I noticed that my sister was at every single funeral. You were the only person who has attended each funeral. Isn't that kind of strange?"

"Do you know what is even stranger, Jax?"

"What would that be?"

"That you were not at any of them."

Jackson didn't know exactly what to say. He had been intimate with one of those ladies just days before, and he didn't go to hers, and he had a five-year relationship and was planning on marrying one of them, and he didn't go to hers either.

"I, ah, I didn't want to be a distraction. I was the lead suspect in their murder investigation. I have more respect than that for Brandy. Even if I wasn't the main suspect, if I showed up at her funeral, all the talk would have been about me and not her. I didn't want that. And Tami, well, her husband wouldn't have liked it much if I would have showed up. She told me she filed for divorce!! That obviously wasn't true."

"You should have been at Brandy's. Even her parents asked me where you were. They know that you still loved her, and that you could never kill her. You were just being selfish!" scolded Emily.

"Ya, maybe I was."

"I know you have this tough guy image that you think you need to uphold. Biker, hunter, nothing bothers you. But it is okay to show you're vulnerable every now and then too. You need to grieve, brother. I know you are hurting, you need to let that shit out, man. You are going to burst."

"Speaking of bursting, I just did that a couple of times last night. You need to meet Klaire, she is wonderful. Mom and Dad met her this morning."

"Way to change the subject. But hold on here. You brought a woman to meet the parents? You don't do that kind of shit? I haven't even met her yet! What the hell, bro?"

"You will meet her I'm sure. I really like this one. It isn't just sex. We actually connect and enjoy being with each other. Even with Camille, it was mostly about sex. Well, until the end, when she was still having it, and I wasn't. Ha."

"You actually sound happy, maybe you aren't grieving?"

"Oh, I still need to work that shit out in my head, but Klaire is a pretty nice distraction."

"Okay, I need to meet this distraction. What is she doing tomorrow? I need to meet her," Emily pushed.

"Not going to happen, she has her daughter, and she just started preschool, so she is on a strict schedule. It will have to be a weekend."

"Okay, I'll meet her on Friday then I guess. Set it up. Not even kidding. I can't believe she met Mary and Dick before me!"

"I'll see what we can work out. Don't you scare this one away!! You may be a little too much for her to handle so soon in my relationship. Ha-ha-ha," Jackson teased.

"Okay, stay safe, love ya."

"Love you too, girl, watch out for crazy men trying to cut off your head."

"Speaking of head, I am being called, apparently I have to give it now."

"Holy shit, didn't need to know that!! Bye," and Jackson hung up.

CHAPTER 55

The week flew by; Jackson called his lawyer and let her know that he did meet with the police and told her what they talked about. She didn't seem to have any issues with that, but she said if they come by again, to give her a call, and she would come over. Just to protect him in case something went wrong. She reminded him that she was doing it for free, so he didn't have to worry about her charges.

Jackson and Klaire instant messaged each other pretty much all day long while at work and then texted each other until they both went to sleep. Jackson was going to have her meet his sister Friday night. They were all coming over to grill out. Jackson's brother, Chad, was even coming down, and the two of them were going hunting in the morning. Jackson still had a doe tag, and Chad had both a buck and a doe tag so he could shoot whatever he wanted. Chad wasn't as picky as Jackson, so as long as it was a decent buck, he would shoot it.

Friday came and Jackson spent the majority of the day out riding along the Root River, down to the Mississippi and along its banks. Down one side on the Minnesota/Iowa side of the river and crossed the river and back up the Wisconsin side. He loved riding the river roads this time of year. The fall air was refreshing, and the leaves had all changed and were shades of red, orange, brown, yellow, and mixtures of those colors. Every now and then, there would be a gathering of leaves on the road, if nobody had driven by there in a little while, and Jackson would barrel through them, making them fly all over in a whirlwind. Jackson always felt like a little kid when he did that. He remembered doing that on his bicycle when he was younger but not going nearly as fast.

He headed back to his house and arrived around five. He got the grill all cleaned up. He wasn't home for long and his sister showed up. She only had to go four blocks from work at the courthouse. She lit two cigarettes, one for her and one for Jackson. She handed the first to Jackson before lighting her own.

"I thought your old man was coming too?"

"He should be here any minute. He was working down in southern Iowa this week, but he got rained out today. He stopped at the casino for a little while since he was early. He told me he made some cash playing blackjack."

"Good, call him and tell him to stop at the liquor store before he gets here. I only have like three beers left. I don't keep many on hand you know, not being a drinker anymore."

"Actually, I stopped over on my lunch break, you only have one left." Emily chuckled and shyly covered her mouth.

"Drinking on county time? What the hell? Couldn't you get fired?"

"Dude, you've met my boss. The guy is drunk by ten-thirty every morning."

"Oh ya, don't think he will turn you in."

They finished smoking and headed into the house. Emily pulled out her phone and called her boyfriend.

"Hey, Dan, can you pick up something at the liquor store? Jackson only has one." She opened the fridge and grabbed the last remaining beer bottle, twisted off the top. "Make that no beer here. He said you should just pay since you won money at the casino."

Jackson couldn't hear what was being said on the other end of the line, but he had a pretty good idea.

"Sorry, I told him, didn't know it was a secret. Plus, not like he will be drinking it. Just get it and some smokes and get your cute butt over here. I haven't seen it all week. And I'm out of beer and smokes now, so I need those too."

She hung up the phone and turned to Jackson. "He was actually at the liquor store already and checking out. It is like he could read our minds."

They washed their hands and started prepping all the meat. Deer steak and some hamburgers were sitting in the cake pans ready to be thrown on the grill when everyone arrived. They washed and wrapped the potatoes in tinfoil.

They threw the meat in the fridge for the time being and carried the stack of potatoes out, lit the grill, and threw them on.

Dan showed up with his arms loaded down with a case of beer in each hand and a ten-pound bag of ice under one arm.

"Future brother-in-law, I have two questions for you. Number one, where is your cooler? And two, more importantly, where is this hot new piece of ass that your sister is telling me about?"

"The cooler is right in front of the truck, in the garage, on the shelf. That hot piece had to work until five, so she will be here in about half hour. I wouldn't call her that to her face, she may punch you in the nuts."

"I'm not afraid of her, but I *am* afraid of your sister. Plus, if I said that to your woman, I wouldn't have to worry about her punching me in the nuts. That is, unless she knows they are in a Ziploc baggie in your sister's purse."

They both laughed, and Emily just gave them both a dirty look.

It wasn't long before Chad showed up. They were out back playing with Raider when he walked out of the garage onto the deck. The dog immediately left the Frisbee and ran to Chad. Chad was almost knocked over by the black lab.

"Dang, you would think he was your dog, as excited as he gets every time you show up," Jackson said to his older brother, kind of miffed that his own dog seemed to prefer his brother.

"What can I say, you have a smart dog," as he hastily and energetically rubbed and petted the dog who was wild about him being there. "Wassup, Em, Dan. So, where is the beer? It's been a long week at work, had to fire two dumbasses this morning, and I already did their buddy on Monday. They were drinking on their lunch breaks."

Emily looked at Jackson, "The nerve of some people." And she and Jackson burst out laughing.

Dan and Chad just looked at each other, knowing that they obviously must have missed out on something. Emily and Jackson had always had that bond they shared, and a lot of inside jokes were told between them.

"Sis, you are fired!" and they all started laughing, as the other two immediately knew what they were talking about.

They didn't even notice the beautiful blonde lady standing in the doorway, holding hands with a five-year-old. The little girl was looking shy because she didn't see anyone she knew. Then she spotted Jackson.

"Jackson!!!" she screamed and ran to him and hugged him.

Emily and Chad both smiled when they saw the little girl run to their brother and hug him. Kids just always seemed to love him and always wanted to be near him. Most likely because he was just a big kid himself.

Dan was not watching the little girl, like the others were. He was staring at the lady that brought her. She had a short little jean skirt on that accentuated her long, tan, very toned legs. A white spaghetti strapped blouse, with a lacey trim on the bottom that showed just a little bit of her stomach.

"Who is this beauty, Jackson?" Dan managed to get out, trying not to drool into his beer.

Emily walked over to where her purse was laying and picked it up. Everyone was wondering what she was doing. She turned to her boyfriend and gave him a stern look. "Dan!!" and she punched her purse as hard as she could. "Quit drooling!"

Dan made a motion like he had just been punched in the balls and bent over like he was in pain. This brought laughter from everyone except Mandi, who didn't understand the reference.

"She has your balls in her purse, don't she?" Klaire laughed. "I already like her."

Mandi wasn't old enough to catch the humor and said, "What kind of balls, can we play fetch with Raider with those balls?"

This brought even more laughter. Chad actually spit his beer out of his mouth as he was just taking a sip.

"*Nooo*," cried Dan.

"You don't want to touch those balls, hun, but there is a ball in the garage that you can grab and play with Raider if you want,"

Jackson said, trying to make sure she didn't think they were making fun of her.

"Okay", and she ran to get the ball, and the dog must have known what she was up to as he followed her, hopping up and down on his front paws showing his excitement.

Jackson walked over to Klaire and embraced and kissed her. "Everyone, this is Klaire. The little bundle of fun running around with the dog is Mandi. Klaire, this is my brother, Chad, my sister, Emily, and her horny boyfriend, Dan."

Everyone said hi at the same time.

They grilled and ate. They sat around, and all the adults, other than Jackson, enjoyed some malted beverages. Jackson and Mandi had pop, which made Mandi hyper. She ran with the dog for hours. She finally crashed hard from her sugar rush, and she curled up on her mother's lap around ten. She wasn't there long before she was out.

Klaire held her daughter tight and kissed the top of her head. "Poor thing, this is well after her bedtime, and normally, she doesn't get pop this late in the day. She is going to sleep well."

"I can put her on the couch if you want me to. I got a blanket and a pillow out for her."

"Okay, I got her, you sit here, I'll be back out in a few minutes."

Klaire got up slowly while still holding Mandi. She had obviously done that a time or two before in her life. She carried her in the house to lay her down for the night.

As soon as she shut the door and was inside the house, Dan spoke first, "Dude, not only is she friggin hot as hell, she seems like she is fun and fairly smart. She has to be younger than me also. What is she doing with your old broke ass?"

"I don't know or care why she is with you. All I need to know is does she have an older sister who is single?" Chad broke in.

"If I liked women, pretty sure that one could give me a big old lesbian boner. Why can't I be that hot?" Emily pouted.

"Sounds like you all approve of her?" Jackson chuckled.

"What will Haley say about her and the little one? I know how much she means to you. She won't be jealous, will she?" Dan inquired.

"Haley loves them both. She actually told us that she thought we would make cute kids together," Jackson smirked.

"I wouldn't doubt that but mostly because of her genes, not yours," Chad chided.

"Well, I hate to be a poor host, but two of us have to be up early to hunt in the morning. Besides, I still have to have some sex before I go to sleep," Jackson said as he stood to go inside.

As he was reaching for the door, Klaire opened the door to come back out. "Oh, are you coming in?"

"Yes, we need to get to bed if we are going hunting in the morning."

"Okay. It was so fun to meet you all. We will have to get together again soon," Klaire said in a sincere voice. "I'm glad Jackson's family is fun and not all stuck up."

"We will do this again soon," Emily replied.

"Good night, nice to meet you," Dan said as he grabbed the cooler on his way out the door. "Jax, we'll bring the cooler back next time."

"*Whoaaa* there!" shouted Chad. He stopped the cooler with his foot and opened it up and grabbed a couple beers. "I'm not going home until Sunday, and I'm guessing there isn't anything in the fridge here."

With that, Emily and Dan left, and the other three went back into the house. Chad had an air mattress that he brought with; he took it up to the spare bedroom on the second floor and blew it up with his little portable air compressor. There was a pillow and blanket laying there neatly, waiting for him, so he threw that on the inflated mattress and was asleep quickly.

Jackson could hear his brother snoring before he was even in bed. He always snored loudly when he had a couple drinks in him.

The two lovers helped each other undress in the light before turning the light off and started kissing each other, and she pushed him onto the bed. She was working her way down his chest, kissing it gently. Jackson was aroused and was oblivious to everything else, other than this beautiful young lady who he was going to make love to. Then she stopped.

"I'm sorry, I can't do this," Klaire said, slightly frustrated. "I can hear your brother snoring, and it feels like he is in the same room with us."

Jackson quickly got up and went over and turned his oscillating fan on high. "Better?"

"Much! Now get your sexy butt back here."

They made love to each other. When they were done, they just lay next to each other, not saying a word. Looking into each other's eyes, both knowing well that they were each in love with each other. Both of them too reserved to actually say it out loud. They could both sense how the other felt about them and ready to respond with "I love you too," but both were too stubborn to be the first to say it.

They fell asleep, still facing each other, still holding hands with one hand, and the other tucked under their lover.

CHAPTER 56

Morning came early for both Jackson and Chad. Jackson, being the scent-free freak that he was, was in the shower and ready to go. Freshly washed hunting clothes, washed in his special hunting clothes wash soap.

Chad rolled off his air mattress, which was now half flattened, but he hadn't noticed until now because he had been in such a deep sleep. The plug had apparently popped about halfway out, causing a slow leak. He didn't shower, didn't brush his teeth or anything. Just put on his hunting clothing and went and got into the truck.

The two were off and down the road, well before light. They didn't say a word until they reached their destination.

"How long you planning on sitting?"

Chad replied, "I can only sit for a few hours, and I get antsy. I'll probably sit until around nine to nine-thirty, and then I'll get down and slowly stalk my way to you."

"Sounds good to me. Good luck. Text me if you get something and need help. I'll leave the keys in the gas tank if you beat me back here."

"Okay, sounds like a plan. Don't shoot my buck. I want to actually hunt a little this year."

And they were both off, going to their separate stands, on opposite ends of the property that they grew up hunting on. It wasn't much for actual woods but enough to where it held deer, and the neighbors didn't hunt, and their land was full of woods. Jackson was going to sit on a field edge this morning, overlooking a corn field. Chad was going deeper into the woods to sit in the stand that his little brother had shot his monster buck from a week ago. They had a couple more really good deer on trail cams that Chad would be more than happy to take with his bow today.

Back home at Jackson's house, the door had not been locked behind the boys when they left. It opened and in crept evil.

Before entering, he threw a steak to the dog, and when it went for the free meal, he slipped a small noose made of wire around the dog's neck. He choked the dog out and killed him by hanging him by the top shelf in the garage. The dog didn't suffer as long as he had hoped. The dog bit him a week ago, and he hadn't forgotten that. The dog deserved to die.

Up the stairs it went, making sure to not make any noise. The master bedroom was cooler than the rest of the house, and a fan could be heard turning slowly in the corner. A nightlight was behind the fan, and it gave off a huge shadow on the wall above the bed of the turning fan.

He had been here a week ago and didn't have the right equipment to do the job. This time he was ready. He had never used it before on someone who was sleeping and hoped he was doing it correctly. He took out the bottle and put some on his rag and immediately put it over the sleeping beauty's mouth and nose. She never woke up.

He held it there for quite a while before taking it off. He had read that chloroform could actually kill if used in too high of a dose. He didn't want that because that would mess up his plan. He checked to see if she was still alive by pulling the covers down, exposing her naked breasts. He put his ear down to her chest and listened for her heart. He heard it right away but left his face there for a moment, to enjoy her soft skin. He ran his tongue over one of her nipples and fondled them for a second.

Then he got back to work. He threw the covers off to reveal that she was completely nude. He tied her hands together, then her feet together at the ankle. He used a small white rope that he had brought with him. He used to use it for dragging deer out of the woods, but he found it was also very useful when binding someone up.

He hefted her up over his shoulder and carried her down the stairs and laid her on the kitchen floor. He walked out into the garage and opened the garage door. He walked to the street, and he backed his truck into the garage quickly, making sure that nobody was watching. He closed the garage door.

He went back into the house and picked her up again and brought her out to the truck. He placed her into the back seat of his extended cab truck. Her skin was covered with goosebumps from the cool morning air. He ran his hands over her naked skin, feeling the fine hair on her standing up, trying to catch some warmth and warm her body.

He went back inside to find a blanket to cover her up. He walked into the living room and found a blanket. The problem was, there was a small human using it. All curled up, sleeping hard. She was actually very cute, he thought. He wasn't going to disturb her and was not going to hurt a child.

He decided to go up the stairs to find a different blanket. He ended up just taking the comforter off the bed. He needed to get the hell out of there before anyone noticed him.

Before he left, he made sure to leave something for Jackson, and he took a little something for himself.

He opened the garage door and he drove off, leaving it open.

CHAPTER 57

J ackson always kept his cell phone on silent, but it would vibrate when it got both a text message or if someone called him. He was sitting in his tree stand, watching a couple of turkeys mill around in the field. He had received a text earlier from his brother that he hadn't seen a thing yet. His pocket vibrated, and Jackson removed one of his camo gloves and took the phone from his pocket. He didn't recognize the number but decided to answer it anyway. It was too early for telemarketers.

"Hello."

"Jackson Ackerman?" came the voice on the other end. It sounded vaguely familiar.

"Yes, who is this?"

"This is Sherriff Osborn. Can I ask you where you are right now?"

"I'm out hunting, like I am almost every Saturday in the fall. Why?"

"Well, I'm at your house. I think you should get here as quickly as you can."

"Oh my god! What happened? Is Klaire okay, how about Mandi? Tell me they are all right!"

"Well, I think we should discuss this in person. We will be at your house. Please come right away, drive safe and not too fast."

"I'll be there as quick as I can. Can't promise that I'm not going to speed though."

"Understandable, be safe though and don't endanger anyone else on the way."

"On my way!"

Jackson hung up and called his brother.

"We need to go now! Meet you at the truck. Hurry!! I'll explain later, just get down from the tree and bust ass back to the truck."

He hung up a second time and began climbing down the tree as fast as he could. Chad was in the safer ladder stand, but Jackson's stand today had screw in steps and wasn't as safe when it comes to getting into and out of the stand. The steps were metal spikes about six inches in length that were hand screwed into the tree. They could be slippery, especially when it was wet or icy out.

He didn't bother to tie his bow and pack to the string and lower them to the ground. He threw one of the backpack straps over his right shoulder and held the bow in the other hand. He did manage to quickly pull the arrow out of the bow and place it into the quiver, so he was just holding the bow in his hand.

Halfway down the steps, he slipped and fell. The strap of the backpack that wasn't over his shoulder caught on a step and stopped Jackson's fall in a heartbeat. He slammed into one of the steps that were previously below him, jabbing into his chest. It didn't puncture him, but it ripped his jacket and shirt and gave him a heck of a scratch on the left side of his rib cage.

He was hanging upside down now and in what should have been a decent amount of pain, but he just righted himself, pulled the backpack off the step above him and climbed down the rest of the way. He was amazed that he never did drop his bow.

Jackson was on a dead sprint back to his truck. It was a difficult run through the first field, which was still holding the beans. Luckily, the ground in this field was pretty sandy, and the crops never did very well there, so they were not as tall as the soybeans normally get. Once he reached the gate of the next field, he had a much easier time running through the cut hay field to his truck. He remembered thinking that he wished someone could be timing him, as he was certain that he would have surpassed his personal best forty time.

He finally reached the truck and didn't see his brother anywhere in sight, so he took the time and put his bow away in its case.

Still no brother in sight.

He hopped in and started the truck and took off in the direction of where he should be coming from halfway across the field, he spotted him walking through the bean field. They got to the gate at almost the same time.

"Hurry up!! *Let's go!!*"

Chad quickened his steps and hopped in, not bothering to put anything away. He closed the door, and the truck was already moving. As he stuffed his bow and pack over into the rear seat of the truck, he asked, "So what the hell is going on?"

"Cops called! They are at my house and won't tell me what is going on! We have to get there!"

"Okay, sorry I took so long. I didn't understand how urgent it was," Chad said with a hint of being sorry in his voice, "*How* the hell did you get to the truck and back to the gate so fast in the truck? I wasn't moving that slow."

"I channeled my inner Usain Bolt. I'm guessing I could have beat him in the one-hundred-meter dash, and I had a twenty-pound backpack and my bow in one hand."

They went through the landowner's farmhouse driveway faster than they had ever gone; they were both very conscious of being respectful to him and his land. Neither gave it a second thought though.

Onto the highway and down the road they went. The old truck wasn't as fast as some of the old cars they had as boys, but it topped out at around 113 mph. Chad didn't say a word about the speed, and he was actually fairly calm for traveling at over 100 mph. They had both spent their youth driving much faster than that.

Normally, it was about a thirty to thirty-five-minute drive back to Jackson's house, but they made it in nineteen minutes. They passed car after car, and at one point, passed six cars and a semi in a single pass. There were not any close calls that really endangered anyone, other than if someone in another car would have decided they wanted to pass and didn't see the truck coming from behind them like a dog on fire.

The two brothers came up the street to see probably twenty squad cars, two fire trucks, and an ambulance sitting in front of and down the street on both sides of Jackson's house. The street was blocked off so Jackson jumped the curb and drove across his neighbor's lawn onto his and parked on the side lawn, facing the side of the garage. Multiple police officers instinctively drew their weapons and were ready for whatever was going to happen with these madmen driving so erratically.

The Sherriff saw who it was and yelled for everyone to relax and stand down. He walked up to the truck and greeted Jackson.

"Jackson, I can't let you go in the house quite yet, but I can tell you what we do know so far."

Jackson walked quickly over to the front of the garage, where the door was open. From there, he could see his best friend for the last eight years, hanging from a wire.

"Holy fuck, can I cut him down? Let me cut him down. He don't deserve to be hanging there like that for the whole world to see," Jackson pleaded, clearly showing his empathy for his dog.

"Jackson, we have to process the scene."

The Sherriff was cut off midsentence by Chad, "Cut the fucking dog down now!"

Sherriff Osborn motioned for one of the men taking in evidence in the garage to do so. "Take him down carefully and without contaminating the evidence. Show the animal some respect though."

"How are the girls!? Klaire and Mandi! Where are they?!" Jackson demanded to know.

"Well, Mandi is in the house right now with one of our social workers and a detective. They are trying to tell if she can help them. We don't know where Klaire is. We didn't even know her name until just a few minutes ago. The little girl just calls her Mom, she kept saying."

"So someone came and took Klaire out of my house? Did they hurt Mandi at all?"

"Mandi is fine. She didn't even know her mom was missing until we showed up at the door. A neighbor saw the dog and called it in to us."

Chad just sat back and took it all in. Why was this happening to his little brother? He didn't have any enemies. He kept looking at the poor dog, whom he was very fond of himself. All he could think about is that his brother's new girlfriend, that little girl's mother…may have the same fate as the black lab lying motionless in the garage. Poor Mandi, probably scared out of her mind, with all those officers who she didn't know around her asking her questions.

Jackson didn't know what to do. He decided that Mandi needed him, so he walked into the house.

"*Jackson!!*" screamed the little one, as she ran to embrace Jackson. "They say some bad man may have taken my mommy. I didn't see anyone. Is it my fault I didn't see anyone?"

"No, honey, you didn't do anything wrong at all. I think you are being very brave, talking with all these people that you don't know."

"I wish I knew where my mommy was. She said we could walk up to the park today and go down the curly slide. Can we still do that? Maybe Mom will join us?"

"We will have to see what all happens today. I can't promise you that we will today, but we will someday, okay?"

"Okay."

Mandi clutched Jackson tight around his neck as he held her close to him. He didn't have any answers for her. Hell, he didn't have any answers for himself.

He just stood there, holding her, with his brother by his side. The three of them felt like they were the only people there, not saying a word, just being there. All the while, police personnel were scrambling around, trying to find clues. Time seemed to stand still for them but went quickly for everyone else in the room.

Jackson could feel his leg starting to vibrate. He set Mandi down and grabbed his phone out of his pocket. Maybe it was Klaire calling to tell him she was safe, maybe it was the guy with some demands for him. It was neither and really not what he was expecting, even on a day like today.

"Jackson, I just woke up, and I can't find Mom. I went to her room, thinking maybe she had another hangover or something, but she wasn't in there, and I found a bunch of blood on the floor. I'm scared," Haley said, clearly scared and not sure what to do.

"I'll be right there!! I'm going to have the cops come, and they will beat me there. Go to the neighbor's house and don't come out until you see a cop car show up, okay?!" Jackson was actually fairly calm on the surface, and with his words, even though his skin was crawling, and he wanted to punch someone right at that moment. "Call me back when you get locked inside the neighbor's house. I'm on my way."

"Okay, hurry, I don't know what is going on."

"I'm on my way and so are the cops, see you in a bit! Bye, love ya!"

"Bye, love you too," Haley said and she hung up her phone.

Jackson looked at Mandi and said in as cheery of a voice as he could muster, "You remember my brother, Chad? Maybe he can take you to the park for a while? I have to go get Haley. Would that be okay if Chad took you to the park?"

"Would he go down the curly slide with me?" Mandi asked.

"I sure would," Chad replied.

"Okay, we can do that. Are you bringing Haley to see me? I like her. We have fun together."

"I will if I can. I'll see you later, okay?"

"Okay."

Jackson turned from the little girl as Chad took her hand to lead her outside.

"Sherriff Osborn!! Let's go!! You need to call the Dover police right away!!" Jackson yelled and everyone turned to look at him.

"What? We have work to do here." The Sherriff looked puzzled. "What is in Dover?"

"Let's go, you have enough people here. We are wasting time!!"

They both took off; the Sherriff's car was stuck in the driveway with a bunch of cars blocking it in. "Let's ride with the state patrol, his car is free. Sergeant!!"

They hopped into the Minnesota State Patrol squad car with the Sergeant who owned the car. For the first time in his life, the Sherriff got in the back, and he let Jackson sit in the front seat to navigate.

"To Dover as fast as you can. You need to send people to my ex-wife's house right away, my stepdaughter found blood on the floor, and her mom missing. Get them on the radio, and I'll give them the address."

The patrolman called in to the dispatcher, and Jackson gave her the address. As soon as they gave it to the dispatcher, they heard over the radio the bulletin go out with the address. They said a bunch of code numbers that Jackson didn't understand, but they sure got attention as multiple cars responded that they were in route.

Jackson was impressed with the state patrolman's driving skills as he flew through town and down the highway. He never felt uneasy or that the car was out of control, even though they were exceeding 100 mph. The squad car handled a lot better than his old Ford truck did at similar speeds.

The three men pulled onto the block where Camille resided. They could barely get to the condo because the street was packed with police cars, both marked and unmarked, city police, state police, and even a couple neighboring town police had responded. They ended up parking the car only four houses down, somehow weaving between cars to get as close as they could.

Jackson was out the car door as soon as the car came to a stop. He was stopped three car lengths later by an officer guarding the perimeter. Sherriff Osborne caught up with him and told the officers forming a barricade to let them pass, and they did.

They reached the front door of the condo, and the Chief of Police from Dover stepped out and stopped them.

"Sherriff Osborn, let me give you an update on what we know so far."

Jackson couldn't wait, "Where is Haley? Is she okay?!"

"There was nobody in the residence when we arrived here, but we did find a significant amount of blood in the master bedroom," the chief continued, like he hadn't heard Jackson at all.

Jackson was immediately on the phone calling Haley; it only rang once, and she picked up, "I see you. I'll be right out Jackson." And she hung up.

Seconds later, an officer was escorting the girl toward them.

"*Haley!* Are you all right?" Jackson ran and hugged her.

"I'm okay, but I'm scared. There was a lot of blood, and I don't know where Mom is," the girl explained.

The Chief asked, "When was the last time you saw your mother?"

"Last night before I went to bed, her and Frank were going out for the night, probably around eight to eight-thirty they left. I went to bed around ten and they were not home yet, but that is normal."

"So, technically both of them are missing?" Sherriff Osborn added.

"Her car is in the garage, so we will put a BOLO out on his vehicle." The chief said, "Let me get that going, and I'll be right back."

The chief walked away and spoke to a couple of deputies standing at the end of the driveway. They both took off after the conversation. The chief came back to the group made up of the little girl, her ex-stepfather, a Minnesota State Trooper and the Sherriff of Fillmore County. He pulled the Sherriff aside and asked point blank, "Sherriff, we currently have that man's ex-wife," he nodded discreetly toward Jackson, "and her boyfriend missing, with a large amount of blood. Normally, we look at the ex right away as one of the prime suspects. Is it a good idea to have him standing in our crime scene, where we may have to prove he may have been the perp."

"I understand your concern, Chief. Do you happen to know where I just came from, and how I got here so quickly? I was at Mr. Ackerman's home, where his own girlfriend was taken from early this morning. Whoever took her, left her little girl sleeping, just like here. I was standing next to Jackson when that little girl," he nodded toward Haley "called him. I saw the absolute fright in his eyes when he thought she was in danger. He wasn't faking that."

"He could be a psychopath and really good at faking?"

"I don't believe it. I've been talking to him for a while now, and I think I know how this man ticks, and he isn't our perp. His dog was hanging by a wire in his garage this morning when he got home for Christ's sake. A man doesn't kill his own dog like that."

"Jeezuz, who are we looking at for all this then?"

"I'm not sure, but whoever it is, is one twisted fuck," the Sherriff said.

Jackson saw the two black SUVs pull up, four people hurriedly got out of both vehicles, all dressing in black, the six men all in suits, white shirts all with a black tie but one who didn't have one on. The two women wore black suit coats and black shirts, with white collared shirts under their coats.

"Looks like the Feds are here gentlemen. You may be losing your command."

"How the hell did they get here so quickly?" asked the chief.

"They are usually closer than you think, and they have been watching this case closely," the Sherriff informed him.

As the group of agents reached the group of locals, the head man spoke up. "Gentlemen and ma'am," looking directly at Haley when he said that. Haley was currently clutching her ex-stepfather's shirt with both hands, cowering behind him as much as she could in an effort to not be seen. "We are with the Federal Bureau of Investigation. I'm Agent Dulfino, and this is my team. Who is in charge of this crime scene?"

"I am Chief of Police Seldon, good to meet you," and he held out his hand and shook the agent's hand.

"We are going to take this over, but we are not going to exclude you and your team. We do need you to have all of your men stop what they are doing inside and step out, so we can look things over. We will be talking with each of them to find out if anything was removed or altered upon entry of the residence. Can you help get them out now please?" Agent Dulfino ordered, more than asked.

"Yes, sir," said Chief Seldon, and he turned and went inside to remove everyone.

"I am going to assume that you are Jackson Ackerman and the little beauty behind you is Haley?"

"Yes," Jackson answered and held out his hand and also shook the agent's hand.

"Haley, if it is all right with you, I am going to have you go with one of my female agents, and she is going to ask you a bunch of questions. We want to find your mother as soon as possible, and you may know things, or have seen things that you don't even realize you know."

"Okay," Haley shyly answered from behind Jackson's leg.

"Mr. Ackerman, I would like to ask you questions, and Sherriff, I will have you work with my team, and you can fill them in on what you know so far from the previous girls, and both of these incidents this morning."

The agent seems to not only be able to take charge, but he gave the impression that he probably already knew everything the Sherriff knew, even though he had never talked to him.

Two members of the FBI spoke with the Sherriff and Agent Dulfino took Jackson for a walk down the sidewalk. One of the female agents took Haley off, and they walked over toward the park that was a half a block away, and they each took a seat in a swing. The remaining four agents walked into the house, each carrying a case of tools and crime scene necessities. They each pulled latex gloves on as they stepped inside the door. The local officers were filing out, and they had the place to themselves.

CHAPTER 58

Everything was kind of cloudy, and the room smelled like bleach and cleaners. She was still too drowsy to open her eyes, but she could tell that she didn't have any clothes on, just like how she fell asleep, but she clearly was not lying in Jackson's comfy bedroom under his soft comforter. She felt cold and could feel that she was sitting upright on a wooden chair, and she was bound with some kind of a rope. She was slowly gaining consciousness and felt the cold plastic under her feet. She curled her toes to verify that it was actual plastic that she felt.

Suddenly, she was awake. Klaire was frightened, and she made a gasp as she finally was able to open her eyes. She was indeed tied up in a chair, in an unknown place, naked as hell.

"Welcome back to the land of the living…or whatever the hell this is," she heard from beside her.

It was a female's voice, and it sounded vaguely familiar. It sounded like, *OMG*, it was Camille, Jackson's ex! She was strapped to a matching wooden chair, but she was clothed in some short shorts and a nice blouse. She looked like she was ready to hit the bar scene, minus the tie downs.

"I wasn't sure if you were hurt and dying or drugged. I could see you breathing, so I figured you were drugged," Camille continued.

"What the fuck? Where are we? How did you get here?" Klaire wanted to know everything right now. She had so many questions.

"I'm guessing similar to how you got here," and Camille nodded her head so as to show her new roommate the gash in the side of her head, complete with a good amount of dried blood. "Only I got smacked in the head, not drugged nicely like you did.

"Looks like it hurts."

"It is getting better, probably looks worse than it is. As for the where the fuck are we question you asked. I do know that one. We are in my boyfriend's family's cabin. I've spent a few nights here, on that uncomfortable as hell bed over there," Camille said, with a lot of distain in her voice.

"But why are you here?"

"Dude is the guy who's been killing everyone I think! I was thinking for sure it was Jackson. Here I was thinking all this time that I had once slept with a serial killer...looks like I was actually right, just not who I thought it was," Camille laughed a little as she said this.

"Well, I still haven't, thank God. Is he going to kill us both?" Klaire inquired. "I mean, why would he kill you? You are his girlfriend."

"He has to be crazy. All I can think of."

The door to the small cabin opened, and there stood Frank, holding his favorite machete. He thought that him making an entrance like that, with the big blade, would have an effect on the women, like in the movies when the killer always showed up in the doorway with the light to his back, holding the scary-looking machete. He walked over and took a seat on the bed. As he sat, he pulled up the comforter in his hands.

"Notice anything familiar? I wrapped you in this, so you didn't freeze. Pretty thoughtful of me, wasn't it?"

"Ya, now why don't you be even more thoughtful and let the two of us go?" Klaire replied.

"Now what fun would that be? I do know that I will be keeping this here blanket on this bed here from now on though, as a reminder of our night," Frank boasted.

"Why the fuck am I tied up here, Frank? I thought you loved me?" Camille asked.

"Well, you see at first, I started doing this for you because I do love you, and I know how much that bastard ex-husband of yours hurt you, and I wanted to hurt him back. Then, I kinda got to liking what I was doing, and nobody is off limits."

"You are one sick, demented fuck, Frank," Camille bitched.

"Oh shocker, hun, you haven't noticed all the different sexual things we've been doing together? I thought you would probably get off, just having me tie you up! Speaking of that, who wants to go first on top of my new bedspread?"

"She can. I don't want you touching me. Only Jackson can touch me," Klaire said.

"Oh, well, that won't happen again. I have plans for Mr. Jackson Ackerman. He won't be pleasing anyone else." Frank stared admirably at his machete and ran his fingers along the blade, making it appear that he planned on using it on Jackson.

Camille had enough, "Frank, just let me go, and we will forget any of this happened."

"Oh, we need someone to join us before I let anyone go. He has to tell me what he wants to do before we can do anything."

Klaire was a little confused. She still wasn't thinking completely clear from being drugged, "But how will he know where to look. He doesn't know who is doing all this?"

"Oh, I left him a clue. He is a smart boy. He will figure it out."

CHAPTER 59

Everyone finally got done talking with everyone else, and Jackson and Haley were reunited. Sherriff Osborne walked up to them and asked Jackson what he wanted to do.

"Well, I'd like for you to catch this son-of-a-bitch," was his reply.

"I'm sorry, I should have been more specific. By the way, that *is* my plan. What I meant was, Would you like a ride home? Where is Haley going to go, and what do we do with Klaire's daughter?" the officer asked.

"Wait...I'm confused," Haley said "Why are we worried about where Mandi is going?"

"We haven't been able to tell you yet. When you called, the good Sherriff and I were at my house. Someone took Klaire last night also and left Mandi sleeping on the couch."

"I think I'm going to be sick," exclaimed Haley.

"And they killed Raider and hung him in the garage," Jackson said in a somber tone, trying to hold back his own tears.

Haley ran over to a nearby bush and actually did get sick. Jackson followed her to console her. The Sherriff went to a nearby squad car and popped the trunk and grabbed a clean towel out of it. He walked back to them and handed it to the girl, who was still on her knees, dry heaving now, with her stepfather holding her hair back.

"I'm sorry, Haley. I just kind of blurted that all out, and I know it is a lot to take in right now." Jackson felt horrible, but he didn't know of a way to soften it for his little girl.

"Why would they kill our dog? And Klaire is like your soul-mate!! She has to be all right!! She just has to!! Poor Raider. Does Uncle Chad know? He loved Raider like his own dog too."

"He was with me. We both saw him hanging. He made the cops cut him down. He won't show anyone that he is hurting, you know him. But I know he was as heartbroken as us."

"I don't mean to be a dick here, Jackson, but I need to get to work. Would you like a ride back with us, or would you like to stay a while and figure things out? I can have someone else bring you back to Preston if you like," Sherriff Osborne inquired.

"No, let's go now. As far as Mandi goes, her grandparents live in Chatfield, maybe see if you can have someone contact them, and they can meet us at my house and pick her up. They will need to be notified about what has happened to Klaire also."

"I'll actually call the town cop in Chatfield, I'm sure he knows them. I'll send them over and fill them in and ask them to stop down and get the girl. It is better to tell people this news in person, not that it makes it easier, but phone calls are too impersonal."

They walked over to the same car that they arrived in. The Trooper was waiting for them. They all got in, this time Jackson in the rear seat with Haley. They didn't put their seatbelts on, and Haley sat as close to Jackson as she could get, and he held her tighter than he had ever held anyone before.

The trooper only looked in his rearview mirror once the entire way back to Preston because the sight almost brought a tear to his eyes, and he couldn't be crying while on the job. It would make him look like a pussy, and Minnesota State patrolmen were not pussies. He would cry later on at home, alone, where nobody would know.

CHAPTER 60

"Excuse me…Frank, is it?" Klaire spoke toward her captor.

"Yes, it is Frank. What can I do for you?"

"I've been naked for almost twenty-four hours now. Can I perhaps have some clothing?"

"I don't think so. I like how you look naked. You are one of the sexiest women that I've ever seen, and I have you naked. Here. In my cabin."

"Frank, you goddamn pig!!" yelled Camille.

Frank got up and walked over to the two women; he eyeballed Klaire up and down. "Hey Camille, did you notice how I didn't cover her breasts with any rope so I have a good view of them? Beautiful, aren't they?"

Klaire was clearly cold. She has goosebumps, and her nipples were fully erect and even a little firmer than normal, as her body contracted and tried to keep the heat in. She didn't have a scratch on her body, and she looked like she was there under her own free will if you didn't see the tightened ropes that were holding her in place.

Frank reached down and fondled her breasts. "Do you remember last night when I was licking your nipples and holding your breasts in my hand? You liked that, didn't you?"

"I had no idea you touched me like that, you asshole, stop touching me!!" Klaire screamed at him.

"Stop touching her, Frank!! I'm your woman, you don't be touching others!" shrieked Camille.

"Oh, I've touched most of them, my dear."

"You dick. I don't need to know this stuff."

"I think you like it. In fact, I bet you are turned on right now."

203

Frank unbuttoned his girlfriend's pants and shoved his right hand into them. He entered her with his first two fingers. With his other hand, he fondled Klaire. He was looking at Klaire and fingering Camille.

"See, I told you that you would like this. You're just as sick and twisted as I am."

Frank took his hand off Klaire for a moment and pulled his member out of his own pants, already hard as a rock; he started stroking it.

"You want to suck it, bitch?" he asked, while looking at Klaire.

"You get that fucking little stick anywhere near my mouth, and I'll bite that mother-fucker right off!" she screamed back at him.

He hadn't actually thought of that possibility, and he certainly didn't want that to happen. He did want to finish, so he kept looking at the naked woman. Right before he was about to climax, he pulled his right hand out of Camille's shorts and finished with his dominant hand and blew his load right in his girlfriend's face.

"Goddammit, Frank, fppt," spit Camille.

"You liked it last night, why you complaining now?"

CHAPTER 61

Samantha had a good week. She was starting to realize the fact that her and Jackson were probably never going to be a thing, and just friends. A very nice man who she met at Hy-Vee in Rochester had asked her out. She was looking exceptionally cute that day for having worked all day and just stopped quick for a few groceries.

This guy was going to take her to the local comedy club in Rochester. He told her if the date doesn't go well, at least she should get a couple laughs in.

She was getting ready to go on her date when her phone rang. It was him. She knew he was cancelling on her. That was her luck.

She clicked the answer button on her cell. "Hello," trying to be as chipper as she could be, pretending she didn't know she was going to get cancelled on.

"Uh hi, Samantha, this is Tyler, your date for this evening."

"Hi, Tyler, did you forget to write down my address?"

"Well, I'm not sure if you know what I do for a living. I'm a TV reporter."

"Oh my god, I thought I recognized you!! You are on KTTC!"

"Yes. It is my day off, but there is a huge story that I'm on my way to right now, and I have to take it. This stuff doesn't happen around this area, so I can't miss it. I'm going to have to cancel our date. I will make it up to you. I promise!!"

"What is this huge story? Another murdered woman? I probably know her. I know the main suspect I bet too," Sam said sarcastically.

"Well, kidnapped actually. Two of them, one in Dover and the other from a home in Preston!!" Tyler said excitedly.

"*Get the fuck out*!! Two women? Preston and Dover?!!"

"Yup, why?"

"One named Klaire and the other Camille?!!"

"*How* in the hell did you know that!?" said a confused man. "I just got the names a couple minutes ago."

"I have to go. I know them both!"

Samantha hung up and had Jackson's number pulled up and calling.

"Okay, we still on for our date some other time? Hello? Samantha? She friggin hung up on me!" Tyler said to his cameraman sitting in the driver's seat of the news van.

CHAPTER 62

They had just reached Jackson's home when his cell began buzzing. It was Samantha?

"Hi Sam."

"Jackson, are you okay? What the fuck is going on?"

"Long story. Short version is that both Klaire and Camille have been kidnapped. Frank is also missing. And whoever the dick fuck is that did this, killed my dog. Both Haley and Mandi were in the houses and were left alone."

"I'm so so sorry. If there is anything I can do, you let me know. Camille is one of my good friends, and I think you know you are too. You let me know if I can help. I bet you are busy, I'll let you go."

"Thanks, Sam, means a lot to me, I appreciate your support."

"Oh, Jax, FYI, the news crews are on their way. I just talked to one of them."

"Crap, just what we need. Okay, thanks. I'll talk to you soon."

He hung up, and they walked back into Jackson's house. Most of the forensic people had left. He could still see Raider, lying in the garage. Flies starting to collect around him. He hoped that his dog's soul wasn't hanging around wondering where the F his owner was, as he was just lying there on the cold concrete floor, not being helped.

Haley noticed, and she ran into the garage to see him.

"Can I touch him?" she asked.

There was an officer standing just outside the garage door answered. "Go ahead, sweetie, we are done with him."

She picked the dead dog's head up and held it. She slid up as close as she could, without getting into the pool of blood. Sitting beside the dog, she talked softly and lovingly to him. Shooing the flies away as she sat there.

It broke Jackson's heart seeing this, and he went over and sat next to her and pet his dog also.

"He must have died trying to protect the house," Jackson said softly.

"He was the best dog ever. Ever."

"He sure was. We will take him out to Grandma and Grandpa's tonight and bury him."

"Okay, I'll go write something to say. I'll come up with something nice."

"I know you will. I will try to think of something to say also if I have time."

"Can you close the big door. I just want to sit here with him for a bit, Jackson. By myself."

"Sure, honey," Jackson walked over to the wall and hit the garage door button, and the door went down.

Jackson walked into the house to meet up with the Sherriff.

"The little girl's grandparents should be here within a half hour."

"Okay, good. I'll walk to the park and get them."

"No need. I'll do it," said the trooper. "Otherwise, I'm just a glorified security guard here. I need something to do."

"Is it okay if I go upstairs and have a look around? Maybe I will notice something that could help?" Jackson asked the Sherriff.

Before the Sherriff could answer, they heard a voice call from up the stairs. "Yes, please send Mr. Ackerman up, he could be useful."

"Who the hell is up there?" called the Sheriff. "All of my crime scene people left already."

"Special Agent Angela Caprilla. I've been here for hours. You can come up also if you wish, Sherriff."

The two men looked at each other, and the Sherriff motioned to Jackson with his arm, as if to say, after you. The two men climbed the stairs single file and walked around the bannister to the main bedroom in the house. They saw the FBI agent staring out the window.

"Mr. Ackerman, can you tell me if anything is missing from the room?" the female agent asked. She was midforties, straight black

"Haley!!! What on earth? How did you? I'm confused," Mary exclaimed, clearly not knowing what had happened in Dover that morning.

"Well, Mom, Emily must not have the connections in Dover, like she does Preston. We believe the same person who took Klaire from my house also took Camille and possibly Frank."

"My heavens, who is this person? Why are they doing these bad things to good people?" cried Mary.

"The police don't have any clues, Grandma, they are stupid. The FBI will have to figure it out I guess," Haley chimed in.

"Hey, Dad," Chad said impatiently. "We need a couple shovels. We need to bury Raider. The bastard hung him in the garage. I hope he took a big bite out of his ass before he was hung."

"I'll get them, meet you guys out behind the barn, in the grove. That will be a good spot for him," Dan said, trying to find something to do other than talk about all this stuff.

The whole family walked back behind the barn, Jackson carrying Raider in his arms, with everyone following. Dan was waiting there with two spades. He and Chad dug a hole in a matter of a couple minutes. Dick had wondered off into the barn, where they could hear a couple rips of a saw, and then four nails being hammered in. He got back right as Jackson was laying the dog into the hole. Still inside the blanket.

Haley was the first to speak. "Raider" she began, "was a wonderful dog. He was a part of our family. I remember him as a puppy, biting my hair and playing fetch all the time with a ball. He loved running in the woods when we would go for a walk and chasing little animals. We love you, Raider."

"Very nice, Haley," Mary said, as she patted her on the back.

Chad was next. "You weren't officially my dog, but we had a pretty tight bond, you and I. Everyone knows it. I'm going to miss you, my friend. Rest in peace, Raider."

Dan just said, "I'll miss ya bud, love ya." He had a single tear roll down his cheek. Nobody had ever saw Dan cry, and nobody dared say anything about it this time either. He was leaning on the shovel, and with the sleeve of his shirt, he reached up and slowly wiped the tear away, hoping that nobody would notice.

There was a silence for a few seconds, and finally Jackson spoke, "You were my little boy, Raider. You were my first dog I ever had after I moved out on my own. Haley and I picked you up down the street. You were in a pen with five other pups, and you stood out, we both knew you were the one from the start. We have been through a lot, but we always had each other. I'm sorry I wasn't there for you this time. I love you, my friend."

Jackson and Chad each grabbed a shovel, Jackson taking the one Dan was leaning on and slowly filled the hole with the loose dirt that had been dug out of the hole. Emily got down on her knees and gently tamped the soil down solid with her hands. Not too hard because she didn't want to feel like she was smashing the dog beneath her.

Jackson's father walked over, grabbed the shovel from him, and pounded the cross that he had just made a few minutes ago into the ground. The cross was made out of a couple of old barn boards; it was aged and rustic looking. "I'll chisel out his name tomorrow," he said.

The small group silently walked back to the house, leaving Jackson just standing by himself, staring at the freshly dug grave and the newly erected cross.

"I'm going to kill the bastard that did this to you. He will know pain before he leaves this world. I promise you. I'll bring you one of his bones to chew on."

CHAPTER 64

I t was starting to get dark, and Jackson was walking to the house to join the rest of the family. He needed to make a phone call. He pulled out his wallet and dug out a white business card with blue lettering on it. He dialed the number on the card and leaned against his pickup.

"Detective Holmes."

"Detective, this is Jackson Ackerman. I'm sure you have heard about my girlfriend and my ex-wife and her boyfriend."

"Yes, I have, and I am sorry."

"Thank you."

"What can I do for you, Jackson?"

"Well, I'm not sure about this, but this guy has been dropping all the bodies at your mailbox, right?"

"Yes, so far I've received them all I believe."

"Well, let's assume the worst, and that he will be paying you another visit tonight, or soon. Does the FBI have anyone stationed there?"

"No, sir, they do not."

"Don't you think that would be a logical place to station someone?"

"I would think so, but I'm not officially on the case you know."

"Do you officially live at your residence? You have the right to sit, or hide, anywhere on your own land, right?"

"You are correct, sir. I think that I will go out and check for some critters tonight. I have my ghillie suit that I use turkey hunting, I know right where I can hide. I'll look like another bunch of weeds."

"I'll call again, if I hear anything else, so you aren't out there for nothing. But if that bastard shows up. Do me a favor and call me first before you call it in. I need to have a little man-to-man with him."

"You do know that I'm a police officer, right?"

"Yes, I also believe that you are also pissed that you were taken off this case, and that he keeps shitting on your reputation by dumping bodies at your door and mocking you. You don't have to do anything other than just let me talk to him before anyone else."

"My official response to that is, I will call it in to my superiors, just as soon as I retain knowledge that the correct suspect has been apprehended."

"Thank you. I'll be in touch."

"Hopefully I hear from you, and you don't from me."

CHAPTER 65

T he cabin was getting cold. Klaire was still as naked as she was when she went to bed with Jackson the previous evening. Camille was nodding off and on, while Frank was outside doing something. They couldn't see much of anything. The plastic beneath them didn't do much to help with keeping Klaire's feet warm. She wished she could curl up in the blanket, until the cops kicked in the door. She didn't want anyone else to see her naked. Bad enough that Jackson's ex-wife had been tied up right next to her all day. She could feel her checking her out. It creeped her out but thought nothing of it other than curiosity. She wondered if she would check out Camille had the roles been reversed? Just to see what Jackson used to look at and compare herself. Camille was a pretty lady physically, but from the couple times they had met and from stories she heard, her inside wasn't as beautiful.

The door opened, and Frank came in. He announced, "This may take longer than I thought, he must not have found my clue. I left your pink phone under his pillow, and it had a text message from you to him that I didn't send, just left as a draft. It said, I'm at the cabin with your ex and her bf, come join us, no cops."

Klaire just looked at him dumbfounded, "Let me get this straight, you left a message at a crime scene as to where to find you? How are the police not here already?"

"Well, I left it for him, not the police."

"Wow, you are dumb."

"Maybe you could use my phone and just text him? If the cops find that phone, they will be all over you before he gets here," said Camille.

"*Why* are you helping him?" asked Klaire.

"I just want this over with, maybe he will let me go. I don't know."

"Good idea, where is your phone?"

"Over there on the table, I think," replied Camille.

Frank walked over and grabbed the phone. He picked it up and found Jackson's number in the text messages. He read through a few of the old texts between Camille and her ex. "Still have a thing for him, don't ya? I can tell by the way you talk to him."

"I do *not*! I only want you, Frank, now just let me go, and we can move on together."

"You mean, let *us* go, right?" Klaire said, trying to correct her.

"I'm all about me. If he lets me go, that's all I am worried about. I have a little girl I need to take care of."

"I have a little girl who I need to take care of!!"

"Girls, girls!!! If you are going to fight, we should strip Camille and let you do it on the bed over here, and I can film it!" the perverted captor said excitedly.

"No, thanks," stated Klaire.

"I'd kick her ass, and she knows it," Camille boasted.

"Speaking of filming, I should take some pictures since I have your phone out." And with that, Frank started taking pictures of Klaire, bound and naked. He used the zoom and got real close ups of her privates. Then he lifted up Camille's shirt to reveal her breasts and took pictures of the two of them together, then a couple of selfies between the two. He even took a selfie with his tongue licking Klaire's nipple. "I should send this one to your lover. That outta get him here quick!"

He decided against it, just in case the police didn't know who he was, so he wouldn't show his face in the picture. He finally sent a text from Camille's phone to Jackson's. It read, *Come alone. Frank's cabin, we are all here.*

Jackson received the message almost instantly.

CHAPTER 66

Jackson was in his dad's bedroom calling for his father. "Dad!!! What is the combination to the gun safe!"

"My Lord, why are you digging in there?"

"I have to go somewhere."

"Do you need help, brother?" Chad asked.

"I was going to say yes, but if this is a trap, I need you here to defend everyone here. Give Dad a gun, it will make him feel good."

"Dad! Come on!!" Chad yelled.

Dick came walking in. "The combo is your mother's birthday."

Both Chad and Jackson just looked at each other.

"Jeezus Christ, boys, you don't even know your own mother's birthday?!"

"Well, yeah, it's like November something," said Chad.

"He'd never get it figured out, Dad, there isn't a November on the dial," Jackson laughed.

"You two are dumb. 11-7-45," the elder male stated. "Learn it because I may forget in my old age, and I'll need to be reminded myself!"

Dick opened the safe, and Jackson dug out a Colt 45 and a box of shells and a 7-mm rifle, with shells. Chad got two 12-gauge shotguns out and a 20-gauge shotgun out, two boxes of ammo for each. He handed one to his father and took the 20-gauge to Dan, who was still sitting in the living room.

"Why is yours bigger than mine?" Dan asked.

"Genetics," replied Chad.

"Walked right into that one," mumbled Dan.

"You, boys, always measuring your dick size," Emily chimed in from the floor where she and Haley were playing Scrabble.

"Girls measure their brains, guys measure their"—Haley pointed to her area below the belt—"I'd rather have a brain."

"Me too, Haley, me too," added Mary from her recliner.

CHAPTER 67

Detective Holmes was hiding out in the ditch near his mailbox. He wasn't right on top of it, but he was within range to be able to do whatever he needed to do. He was nestled into a small bush that was just a hair taller than the fence that it was up against. He knew that he would never be spotted by a man driving down the road because he just had two deer walk by him at six steps, and they never spotted him. They didn't smell him either. He had enough cover scent on the suit left over from when he did a spot and stalk during bow season last deer season.

His rifle was camo colored, so it didn't stick out and wouldn't glisten if a headlight happens to shine on it.

He had sat there for a while now, and it was dark. He didn't know how long he would sit there, and he hoped that he wouldn't have to do anything other than just sit and be bored. He really didn't want another dead woman to show up. It didn't even matter if he was no longer on the case, people were still dying, and he was over it already.

His phone was on silent and vibrate. When it started vibrating, he damn near shot the pile of grass in front of him. He had been so concentrated on watching the road that his phone surprised him.

"Holmes."

"Change of plans. I'll be pulling up to your mailbox in a couple minutes, don't shoot me."

The detective just sat there. He assumed the person who just called was Jackson Ackerman. He hadn't plugged his name into his phone, so he wasn't positive. But who else could it be. He decided to stay put, just in case, until someone pulled up, and he could identify them.

The Ford pickup pulled up from the wrong direction, which put Detective Holmes on alert. It came in hot and slid to a stop right in front of his driveway. The door popped open, and Jackson jumped out.

"Holmes! Let's go!! Come on!" shouted Jackson.

"Coming."

Jackson heard the voice but didn't see anyone. It was dark, but the moon was bright enough to see fairly well. He didn't even see the man dressed head to toe in what looked like a pile of grass, when he stood up. He did finally see him when he got to the bottom of the ditch and was walking toward him. He was about thirty yards away.

"What's going on, Jackson? Did we find the girls?"

"No, but I got a text telling me where they are. Let's go, they aren't too far from here."

"Seriously? Okay, I'm in."

The two men jumped into Jackson's truck, the detective still holding his rifle. They went down the road two miles, and they turned left, farther off the highway than they already were.

The truck rolled another mile, and they were about a mile or two from Big Rock, where everyone always went to swim, camp, and party.

"Okay, Detective. Do you see that driveway up here on the right about one-half mile? It doesn't have a mailbox."

"Yes, I think I see it."

"There is a cabin, about halfway across the block, set back in the woods. I've only been there one time, so I'm not very familiar with it. It belongs to my ex-wife's bf, Frank. I think he may be behind all this, but I'm not 100 percent sure. But this is where I was told they all are."

"What's the plan, call the FBI and have them storm in?"

"No, I think he would kill both girls for sure. Honestly, if Frank isn't behind this, and he gets killed, no skin off my back. But I have to save Klaire, and I have to save Haley's mother."

"Well, I have to worry about all three of them."

"Well, I'm not going to try to get him killed, but he isn't my priority."

"I understand."

"So I'm going to drive up the driveway. I think you should get out here, hike across the field, and come in from behind."

"All right, and then what? I just hide out? If they are inside a building, how do I cover you?"

"Well, I'm not sure. We will probably just have to play it by ear. Who knows what is going to happen."

"Okay, well, good luck."

The detective hopped out of the truck, headed down through the ditch, and crossed the fence. He snuck along the fence line as stealthily as he could. The first couple of hundred yards were pretty open, but after that, it was impossible to see the man, once the cover got better.

He snuck around the side of the cabin, giving it an extra wide distance so that he would not be seen or heard. He found a place that had good elevation for better shooting angles, and it also allowed him plenty of cover. It was around one hundred yards from the cabin. He was in place well before Jackson started up the driveway.

CHAPTER 68

Having hunted with his brothers, father, and friends his entire life, Jackson knew enough to give the detective enough time to get into place. Just like when they used to do a deer drive, let the people going on stand, get there so when they chased the deer out, they were ready and not moving. Not that Jackson was going to drive the killer out of the woods, but he wanted his help to be there, in case he needed him.

Jackson waited a good twenty minutes, and then he finished his drive, pulled into the long driveway, and slowly drove toward the hidden cabin. While he was waiting, he loaded both the forty-five caliber handgun and the 7-mm rifle. The handgun he placed in his waistband. How many movies had he seen, and that is where everyone kept their gun. He wished he had a second smaller gun to hide somewhere else, in case he was frisked. The 7-mm rifle, he placed in the bed of the truck, if he somehow had to run without his handgun, he could grab it quick out of the truck bed.

This was not a good situation, and Jackson didn't really have a good plan. All he knew is that he needed to try and free Klaire, Camille, and Frank, if he wasn't the goon behind all this.

Jackson finally stopped the truck, a little short of the cabin, so he had a little room to maneuver if he needed to. The driveway was narrow but widened when it got near the cabin. The driveway spread out into an area where you could park. There was only one vehicle there, and it was Frank's truck.

The cabin had two windows on the front of it, one on each side of the old door. It had a wood-shingled roof and was quite rustic looking. Jackson had been there one other time, when he dropped

Haley off because Camille had been drinking, and she didn't want to drive.

Jackson looked around, surveying everything, making sure nobody was hiding to surprise him. He knew that there was a detective hiding nearby, so that made him feel a little more at ease, while he was outside anyway.

The door swung open and out stepped Frank, he was holding what appeared to be a machete. The light was on inside the cabin, and it illuminated his figure and made it hard to see his face.

"It's about time! I was beginning to think that you weren't going to show up, or you would be a puss and bring the cops with you."

"What are you doing, Frank? You got the girls inside there? Are they all right?" Jackson asked.

"They are both here, and they are fine. They would come out and greet you themselves…but they are a little tied up at the moment." The man laughed at his corny joke. He always was quite a funny person; other people just didn't appreciate his sense of humor though.

"So, what's the plan, hard to frame me for these murders too if you brought me out here to kill me too."

"Why don't you just come inside. We can discuss how this will end. It is purely up to you, Jackson. You have to make the decisions."

"I'm just supposed to trust you?"

"Well, if I were you, I wouldn't. But then again, what other option do you have? I guess you could hop back into your truck and leave. Call the cops, and they could come pick up a couple of dead women. That is an option I guess. Is that your choice?"

Jackson had no idea what this fool's plan was, but he decided that there was only one way to try and save the women, and he had to just go with the flow and try to save them somehow. He figured he was smarter than this dirtbag, so maybe he could outsmart him.

"Okay, I'm coming," Jackson stated as he started to the door. He was about five feet away, and he heard Frank again.

"Far enough." And he produced his own gun, which he had been hiding behind his back. Jackson hadn't noticed as he was focusing on the machete in his other hand. "Let's have a look to see where your weapon is. I'm assuming you are armed. You aren't that stupid to come here without something."

"I may have something," Jackson admitted.

"Real slow, with your left hand, reach and place it on the ground. Real slow now, don't make me nervous."

"Wow, do you watch too many movies or what? Real slow now… Jeezus Christ, man, you are such a cliché."

"Is it cliché to have your girlfriend tied up naked in my hunting cabin because if it is, then yes, I probably am cliché. Now shut the fuck up unless I ask your opinion."

Jackson reached into his waistband and pulled the gun out and slowly placed it onto the ground. This left him defenseless for the moment, but he needed to see this thing through.

"I'm a cliché? Mr., I have a handgun in my waistband. Do you have a little gun strapped to your ankle like a fag too?" Frank continued, "You can step inside now, don't do anything stupid and don't touch either of them."

Jackson did as he was told, and as Frank stepped aside to let him in, he stepped through the door. It smelled like bleach. This had to be where he did his killing. This had to be where he must have killed Brandy and the others. He hadn't thought about that fact until that moment. It gave him the chills instantly.

Klaire looked at him and started to cry. "Jackson! You shouldn't have come, now we are both going to die and neither of our girls will have you!"

"Well, if we do die, it will be together. I had to come for you."

"Hi, Jackson, don't forget about me over here," Camille pouted, clearly put out that he hadn't even bothered to look at her yet.

"I came for you also, Camille, don't worry."

"All of you shut up! Go sit on the bed over there, where I can see you," Frank commanded.

Jackson walked a couple steps and sat on the edge of the bed that was on the left side of the room, closest to Klaire. He noticed that the blanket was draped on the bed, like it belonged there.

"Nice bedspread, I used to have one just like it."

"Used to," replied Frank.

"So what now, Frank," Jackson asked. "We going to sing cum bi ya and make s'mores?"

Frank smiled, "No, I thought I'd give you the opportunity to save one of these lovely women. It is all up to you, like I said."

"What are you talking about? Why don't you just let them both go. I can take them both home, and you can just leave and go into hiding or whatever it is that you plan on doing."

"Oh, you would *love* that, wouldn't you, Jackson? Jackson Ackerman always gets the hot girl. This time he takes two of them home, probably have sex with them both."

"No, I would just take them home to their daughters."

"Well, I do have to admit, you must be swinging because you have had some fine-looking women in your life. I've never really had anyone good looking in my life until Camille here. Hell, one of your women was a friggin model. Then the lovely naked Klaire here. She may be the best of them all."

"Frank, you need to stop looking at her! You may have me tied-up, but I'm still your girlfriend," Camille spouted.

Jackson found it odd that even now, Camille was still a jealous bitch. When they were married, she would bitch at him whenever a good-looking woman was within sight. Half the time, he hadn't even spotted the woman, and he would be getting cussed out. She was always jealous. She even stopped inviting her own friends to go with her, especially Samantha, because she figured Jackson wanted her, even though he hadn't thought of it at the time. Now, yes he had thought about it.

"So what are the conditions of you letting one of them go free?" Jackson inquired.

"All you have to do is choose correctly, and one of them gets to go home, and you get to take her place."

"Let me get this straight, I choose one of them. But I can choose wrong? What if I choose wrong? And what is it that you consider wrong?"

Jackson had no idea what this madman was talking about. Choose wrong? What the hell does that mean?

"Well, you see. You get to choose one of the girls. If it is the correct one, she will get to go home to her little girl. You will get tied up in her place. Then, the party *really* begins!!" and Frank laughed and laughed. He almost dropped the machete he laughed so hard.

Nobody else was laughing.

"Best part is if you happen to choose incorrectly. Well then, I just kill all three of you. You two ladies have a minute each to plead your case to your savior over here. Camille, you go first. One minute on the clock, starting…now."

Frank looked at the second hand on his watch.

Camille was already talking. "Jackson, you have to pick me, we've shared so many memories. Haley adores you, but she needs her mother. I know you love me still. We could get back together. I'll even let you do that thing you like. I need you to pick me. I'm too young to die, remember our wedding vows, for better or worse. I love you, Jackson, you have to pick me. We could get remarried. I'll be the best wife you ever could hope for. Haley needs us both. Oh crap, if you choose me, you have to stay here. Haley will really need me without you! You can't leave her to go to her father's. You have to choose me!!"

"Holy shit! Shut up!!" Frank interrupted, "I never realized how long a minute was, you've said enough."

"You didn't give me my whole minute!" Camille bitched.

"You've said enough. You are supposed to be in love with me, so you clearly are lying to one of us. Klaire, you get fifteen second. Go."

Klaire craned her neck and looked directly into Jackson's eyes. "Thank you for these past few weeks and for showing Mandi and I what a good man is. I haven't told you this yet, but I love you."

That is all she said, and it was all that needed to be said. She wasn't going to beg for her life. She figured with his history with Camille and his love for Haley, his only choice would be to pick Camille, even if he couldn't stand her. He would do it for Haley.

CHAPTER 69

L ying in a prone position for this long was one of the most uncomfortable things Detective Holmes had ever done. He didn't dare move, but he really couldn't see much. There was only one window on the back side of the cabin. He had positioned himself at a pretty good angle though, considering this. He could see about two thirds of the cabin, and he could see the two women tied up in the middle of the room, facing the door. Jackson was sitting on the bed, nearest the window, which pretty much blocked any good shot he would have on Frank.

God, he wished he could hear just what the heck they were talking about. He could see a machete in one of Frank's hands and a small handgun in his other hand. He was frozen in his position and didn't know what to do. He wasn't doing anyone any good where he was.

He decided he had to take a chance and do something. It was bold and could backfire, but he had to do something.

He pulled out his phone, found the number he needed. He contemplated what he was about to do again and hit the call button and placed the phone to his ear.

Detective Holmes could actually hear the phone ringing.

*****

Inside the cabin, it was silent. Jackson was still looking into Klaire's eyes. She had just told him that she loved him. He didn't know what to do. He knew that he loved this woman also, and he would literally die for her. On the other hand, he wasn't going to be

229

leaving this place alive, in all likelihood, and Haley needed a parent. Sure, she could go live with her dad, but he was always traveling, and she would be on her own a lot.

Then, there was plan B. What if he could somehow get all of them out of there? But how?

"Okay, Jackson, I am going to need your decision," Frank demanded. "Which one do you want to go free, and you take their spot."

Jackson hadn't made up his mind yet, so he decided to try and stall for a bit. Didn't evil villains in the movies always want to tell the people why they were doing what they were doing? Frank obviously watched a lot of movies; maybe he would feel this need to divulge his motives also. This could give Detective Holmes more time to do something, or him more time to think.

"Before I make my decision, I'm going to need some more information. I can't rush a decision like this. I need all of the facts first."

"What are you talking about? You are just stalling."

"No, I just need to know why you were trying to pin these murders on me. Then you end up just killing me anyway? Why not just kill me? Why did the other women have to die?" Jackson asked, and he actually did want to know this before he died.

"Well, I guess you do need to know this. Your decision would be greatly helped by having this knowledge. I can't tell you everything, but I will tell you this much." Frank walked over to the table where there was one more chair. He set the machete down and grabbed the chair and dragged it back to where he was standing. He swung it around backward and sat down, straddling the back of the chair, leaning over the chair back, the handgun dangling, not pointed at anyone now.

"I guess that I was always a bit jealous of you, Jackson. Even though you and Camille were divorced, I see that she still lusts after you. I see how all of these gorgeous women just fall for you. I don't get it, you aren't that good-looking, you aren't rich, and you're not famous. But yet, they fall for you. Then Haley thinks you are like a god. I could never measure up to good-old Jackson. Jackson does this, Jackson does that. It pisses a guy off always hearing about how awesome you are. So I decided that I needed good-old Jackson to not look so good in the world's view. So I'd pin a murder on you. It was just going to be one, but they didn't arrest you. So I picked out another one, which ended up being two more. Still, no arrest. These cops were either really good at their jobs, or really bad. Why didn't they arrest you? The bad part is, I really started liking this killing, and it became more about that than framing you. I still tried, but I just couldn't stop killing."

Jackson was listening to Frank talk, but he was looking at Klaire and Camille. He looked at Klaire, who looked like she was completely broken, scared, naked, and ashamed. She was tied up, and her wrists were raw from trying to work the ropes loose. She stared at the floor and appeared to just be tired.

Jackson's focus changed to Camille. She was dressed in clothes like what she would wear out on the town. She was also tied up, but he noticed that her wrists were not raw. Maybe she just didn't try to break lose as much as Klaire. But that really wasn't her personality; she loved to fight, she should have been trying to get lose. He noticed that Camille didn't appear to be as broken as Klaire either, possibly because she wasn't being humiliated by being naked all day long in front of strangers. What bothered him the most, though, was her face. She was hanging onto every word Frank spoke, like she still loved him. That is when Jackson knew. He had to choose her.

Frank kept on talking and telling his tale, but Jackson had somewhat stopped listening, and Frank noticed. "I watched you, you know. I watched from outside your window. Watched you guys have sex. I watched you and Tami have sex. She thought she was being so sneaky, coming in through the back like that. She literally walked right under me, while I was sitting in the tree. It did surprise me. I hadn't noticed her coming until she was right under me."

"You are a sick bastard!" Klaire said softly. "That is private between us. You had no right to do that."

"You need a life, man, just sitting around watching my house?"

Frank laughed, "Camille loved it when I would come home. I'd be all horned up from watching you have sex, and she would take it even though I was thinking of Tami and Klaire the whole time. But you knew, didn't you, hun."

"I knew you were different. I knew something was going on," Camille admitted.

"I even kept some trophies," Frank admitted and walked over to the shelf where a small wooden box was sitting. He pulled it off the shelf and pulled out a couple pairs of women's underwear. He put Klaire's up to his nose and took in a deep breath.

"Fucking sicko," Jackson mumbled.

CHAPTER 70

Special Agent Dulfino was absolutely shocked to hear his phone ringing. He was both embarrassed and shocked that it was going off. Who the hell would be calling him; everyone on the task force was with him. It rang only one time before he hurriedly answered it as quiet as he could.

"Agent Dulfino, who is this?"

"*How* the fuck did you know to come here?"

"Who is this?"

"Oh sorry, this is Detective Holmes. I'm behind the cabin, camping out with my rifle."

"You are what? How did you get here?"

"Ackerman picked me up. He is in the cabin with the two women tied up. The ex's boy toy looks like he is the one running the show in there."

"How did you know we were here? Did you spot us?"

"No, actually I was calling for your help, but I heard your phone ring, and I knew you were here already."

"Well, stay clear, we are going in hot in a few minutes after we all get into position," the agent stated.

"I have a pretty clean shot right at the moment. If you want me to take it, just say the word."

"No, don't do that, we want everyone alive."

"Dude has a gun on hostages. Do you really think nobody is going to die here?"

"If we do it right. But don't move, you are plan B if our initial plan doesn't work. I'll be in touch."

"Agent?"

"Yes, Detective."

"Turn off your ringer, he may hear it next time."

"Roger, turning it off now."

The FBI had a squad of twelve men, not counting Agent Dulfino. All former Navy Seals, experts at sneaking in on unsuspecting people. They had snuck within feet of the cabin, just waiting for the word to storm in and make the rescue.

From Detective Holmes's vantage point, he saw five of them moving in. He admired their stealth and wondered how well that would work deer hunting. He hadn't even noticed them before, but now he knew they were there and was looking for them. None of them had his shot angle, or could see in any of the windows from where they were, so he stayed put like he was told.

He felt like he had been on stake out for days, but he knew this was all going to come down to the next few minutes and seconds would make or break this.

Inside the cabin, not one of the people knew that the FBI was closing in on them. Jackson knew Holmes was out there somewhere; Klaire knew nothing and was silently saying prayers for her little girl to grow up strong and to be brave. Camille was laser-focused on every work Frank was saying, so she had no clue anyone was outside coming to save her. Frank was in charge of everything and was in no hurry.

CHAPTER 71

Frank was busy digging in his box of trophy undies, and Jackson took the opportunity to slip a small hunting knife out of his boot. It was a camo-colored pocket knife, still folded closed. He palmed it. He was already leaning forward on the bed so that he could dig the blade out of his boot, so he just continued his left arm moving slowly toward Klaire.

The view of about half of Jackson's body was blocked from where Frank was standing, and he didn't notice Jackson's movement. He placed the trophy box down on the shelf and brought his attention back to the three captives.

Jackson was already back to his original sitting position by the time Frank was done admiring the different undergarments. He had carefully placed the closed pocket knife into Klaire's hand, which was tied securely behind her back and behind the chair.

"Now, Jackson, I'm going to need your decision. Which one of these two is going free and being replaced by you?"

"Okay, I've come to a decision. This is the hardest thing that I've ever had to do, but…I'm sorry, Klaire. I have to choose to let Camille go. I love you, Klaire, and if we have to die, I can't think of anyone who I'd rather die with."

Frank was a little surprised, "So you are picking Camille? Over this lady here? Are you still in love with Camille?"

"No, but I love her daughter, and she needs her mother. Klaire's daughter will have to get by I guess with just her dad."

Klaire had slowly opened the pocket knife and was working the knife blade back and forth across the ropes that bound her. She had

235

no idea if the portion of the rope that she was working on would free her or not, but she was trying.

Camille's focus had changed from Jackson to Frank and now back to Jackson. She was unaware of the naked lady next to her trying to free herself.

Camille inquired, "I was hoping you would pick me, you made the right decision."

"Okay, time to make the swap. I'm going to untie her, and she is going to tie you back up. Then she is free to go. She can drive your truck back home. Not like you will be needing it. Maybe Haley can keep it for when she can drive?"

Frank walked over and untied Camille. Klaire had quickly hid the knife so he wouldn't see if when he walked behind to untie Camille.

Camille was untied rather quickly, and she gently rubbed her wrists where she had been bound. Frank motioned for Jackson to take her place in the chair. Jackson slowly stood and walked behind Klaire, when he got closer to her, he leaned in around her and gave her a passionate kiss. They both closed their eyes while their lips joined, and they both felt as if it could be the last time they ever touched. There was nothing sexual about this kiss. Her lips were dried and cracked, and Jackson could taste the lingering sweet taste of the chloroform that was used to immobilize her.

Frank pulled them apart and yelled, "Just sit down, you two can kiss all you want when you are dead."

Camille took the ropes that had bound her and began tying her former husband up. "You never let me do this to you when we were married," she joked.

"I would prefer to not let you do it now either," Jackson replied.

There was one rope that tied his hands together behind the wooden chair. It was a farmhouse type of chair with a rounded top on it. After his hands were tied, another rope was fastened around the sides of the chair and ran between the small gap between his two hands. Another rope tied both legs to the legs of the chair and crisscrossed around his body a couple times and around the chair.

He wasn't going anywhere unless he managed to walk on his tiptoes somehow.

Jackson noticed that he was tied up much better than Camille was, and it almost felt like she was enjoying doing this to him.

CHAPTER 72

The FBI was in place now for a couple of minutes. They had men stationed at each corner of the small cabin and others behind trees that were within twenty yards and making for very comfortable shooting ranges if needed.

The men at the corners of the house were listening in on what was transpiring within the building. The four of them could all hear fairly clearly what was being said and gave hand signals back to the others and the commanding officer as to what was going on. The wait signal was given as they wanted to see what was going to happen. It didn't seem that the gunman was in any sort of hurry, and it didn't look like he had any idea that they were there.

Detective Holmes was growing extremely uncomfortable now. He thought that this would be over by now. He couldn't hear anything going on, other than the crickets and some frogs in the woods. He wasn't able to recognize what the hand signals that were being given between the agents meant. He was just too far away to see their black gloved hands to know what they were telling each other. He could see fairly well into the cabin and that was the only reason why he hadn't made a move. Jackson Ackerman was now completely clear from his view, and he had a very good shot angle to take Frank out if he needed to.

From what the Detective could see, it looked like one of the ladies had been let go. He had no clue what was going on in there.

His body ached, but he was going to see this through, and he would lay there until morning if he had to.

CHAPTER 73

Camille walked around to the side that Frank was on, and she walked up and gave Frank a peck on the cheek. "See, I told you that he would pick me."

"As usual, my dear, you were correct. I thought for sure that this cute little piece of ass would make him pick her, but you won. He picked you."

Klaire who was working on her ropes again with her knife, actually stopped for a second, "Wait, what in the hell is going on here? You knew about all this? You bet that Jackson would pick you over me? What the...what was your reasoning behind that? Why did you think he would choose you, who he detests over me?"

"Simple, my dear. He loves Haley more than anything, anyone in this world, and any pain he can save her, he will take that route."

Jackson interjected, "Actually, I picked you because I wanted to know for sure that you were in on this with him. So technically, I was also right. You are correct, I would literally do anything for Haley, and Klaire even knows this, so I knew that she would understand my choice. But if I had to choose between the two of you under other circumstances, it isn't even close. She is such a better person than you could ever be."

"*Shut up!*" screamed Camille. "You are an asshole!"

"Maybe, but I'm not the one killing people. So tell me, Camille, what is the real reason that you started killing these women?"

"I wanted you to go away!! You just don't go away!! Most men, when they get divorced, don't want anything to do with their step-kids. Not Jackson Ackerman. No, he sticks around. He is always there. Every time I turn around, I see you. At her games, at her concerts. You have visitation for Christ sake!! Who does that? I wanted you to just go away!! Every time I see you, it reminds me that my daughter thinks you are a goddamn saint! *You are not a saint, Jackson!* I had to show her that you were evil so she wouldn't want to see you anymore. I picked out the targets too since Frankie doesn't know your life like I do. I didn't kill anyone, but I told him who to kill."

Frank could see that Camille was about to lose it, so he wanted to get this over with. "Okay, let's get this over with. Do you want to kill them, or should I? I have a gun and a machete. Her, I get to do with the machete. You can use either one on him, or I can do it for you if you want. We just need to wrap this up and figure out what we do from here."

CHAPTER 74

Detective Holmes could see some more hand signals being waved around down below. He still didn't know what they meant, but they were a lot more excited now than the previous ones he had seen. Suddenly, his pocket was vibrating.

"Yes, Holmes here."

"Do you still have a clean shot?"

"Yes, sir, do you want me to take it?"

"We are going in now, if he makes any movement that looks like he is going to take out any one of the hostages, you take the shot. Otherwise, you let my boys do their thing. Understand?"

"Yes, sir, if at any time he looks like he is going to kill someone, I shoot, otherwise, your men will bust in and take him."

"Correct. Okay, we are going in ten seconds from now," and Dulfino hung up.

Holmes could see the hand signals flashing again below him and now that Agent Dulfino had given the sign to go in. He pulled up his rifle and looked through the scope. He had a shot at the head of Frank and a shot at his chest. His last proficiency test was close to a year ago, and he did just well enough to pass. As a detective who rarely draws his weapon, he wasn't a range junkie like some of the other officers. He could hit a deer at three hundred yards, but this wasn't a deer. He decided to shoot for the chest and go with the larger target.

CHAPTER 75

"You kill the bitch, and I'll just shoot him when you are done with her. He can watch her die," Camille demanded and took the gun from him.

"Okay, you are the boss," replied an obedient Frank.

Frank raised his machete to take a swing, at that same instant, the cabin door exploded off its hinges and fell to the ground. Klaire had just finished cutting her way free from her ropes and turned the knife in her hand and tried to lunge at Frank with it. The first FBI agent came in through the door as Frank's arm was coming down to sever Klaire's head from her torso. Detective Holmes seeing him swinging took the shot.

There was blood everywhere. Nobody seemed to know what was going on. Three ex-Navy Seals tackled Frank to the floor, bouncing him off the side of the bed before reaching the floor. The bloody machete that he had swung was knocked out of his hand.

Klaire was now on the floor covered in blood. She wasn't sure who was all bleeding, but she didn't think she was. But she was bleeding. The bullet meant for the killer had grazed her shoulder as she lunged for him. It was superficial, but it was bleeding pretty well.

Frank had three large men on top of him, and blood oozed from underneath the pile of men. The bullet had caught its target, even though Klaire had got in the way a little bit. Frank was not moving.

Camille just stood there screaming, not knowing what in the hell was going on. Another ex-Navy Seal grabbed her and took the gun away from her and took her outside, all in one fluid motion. She had some blood on her also but not as much, and none of it was hers.

She was quickly cuffed and patted down to see if she had any other weapons on her.

Jackson was still tied to his chair; he was bleeding profusely from the deep cut on his back, near his right shoulder blade. Frank had missed Klaire as he swung since he got shot, and she had lunged at him. Hit Jackson but not with all of his force, like he had intended for the woman's neck.

"Hey, Frank, nice of you to cover the floor in plastic so your blood doesn't ruin the woodwork," Jackson said mockingly, as he also was dripping onto the plastic.

Frank was in the process of being cuffed by the three men who tackled him. He wasn't resisting at all. Frank was dead.

Klaire reached for the pocket knife that was now on the floor in front of her. She was stopped by Agent Dulfino. He picked up the knife, which was still clean as a whistle. Klaire had not been successful in her attempt to stab the man who was trying to kill her. She had gotten her hands free, but the other ropes around her body prevented her from getting to the man. She managed to get up a little bit before her momentum and the ropes holding her still made her fall to the floor. The ropes most likely kept her from getting the bullet that grazed her, from hitting her in a spot that wouldn't be as superficial.

"Let me help you out of these ropes, ma'am, and we'll get you a blanket to cover up with," Agent Dulfino said to her. "Are you going to die, Jackson?"

"No, sir, but I might need a bandage...or two," Jackson replied.

"We'll get you looked at. The ambulance has been dispatched and will be here soon. We had them on standby, so they won't be long."

It was just starting to calm down, and a man who was dressed like a small shrub burst in, still holding his rifle. "Is she okay? I didn't hurt her, did I?" and excited detective yelled, out of breath from running down the hill.

"I'm fine, just a scratch," Klaire reassured him.

"I'm sorry, I didn't know you were going to jump at him like that."

"I'm just glad it wasn't a very good jump," Klaire chuckled a little bit as she was handed the bedspread off the bed. The one that she had been curled up in before she was brought to this place in the first place.

"Oh yeah, hun, I forgot to tell you. I picked up this walking-talking shooting tree on my way here. *That* is the only reason I didn't chose you. I knew he was here looking out for us both, and I had to know if Camille was a part of this," Jackson explained.

"I was wondering, but I wasn't going to say anything!" laughed the woman, and she hit Jackson in the shoulder in fun. Jackson winced. "Sorry, sorry!"

"Need I remind you that I have recently been struck with a large sharp object?" Jackson tried to pull away from his attacker. "By the way, can someone untie me before the ambulance gets here?"

"Right away," replied one of the ex-Navy Seals who was just standing there doing nothing.

CHAPTER 76

Jackson woke up around noon, after not getting home until early in the morning. He actually only slept about five hours. He crashed on his couch since Haley was in her bed upstairs, and Chad chose to sleep on his bed, rather than the old air mattress that didn't like to hold air all night.

Klaire had decided to go home and clean up and hold Mandi for a little bit. She said that she would come back later that afternoon, and she was calling in to work for both of them, so he didn't have to worry about doing that. They were not going to work on Monday.

As Jackson opened his weary eyes, there was a face staring at him.

"So, Mom's going to jail, huh?" asked Haley.

"I'm afraid so. I don't know for how long, but I'm sure she will for a while."

"How could she do that to those women? I know she didn't kill them, but she told stupid Frank who to kill. Almost as bad!" Haley said, clearly disappointed in her mother.

"I don't know what to tell you, it is hard to believe."

"I'm glad they didn't kill you and Klaire. I'm going to need someone that I can look up to."

"I am always going to be here for you. You know that."

"How about Klaire? I think I may need her too. You should probably just marry her."

"Whoa, hang on, let's slow down on that one. We need to date a little longer before we start talking about that stuff."

"Well, don't wait too long. You can't let her get away," Haley smiled.

A voice from the kitchen called out, "Don't you ever cook? Where is all of your nonprocessed food?"

"I cook sometimes!" exclaimed Jackson.

"No, he doesn't, Uncle Chad. Frozen pizza isn't cooking!"

"I'm going to the store. Is your grocery store open on Sundays in this little hick town?" asked Chad, still in the kitchen.

"Yes, it is open. Get me some pop while you are there please!"

"Can I go with you?" asked Haley.

"Yup, and yup. Let's go."

The two of them left for the store, leaving Jackson with only his thoughts and a sore shoulder. His ex-wife was probably going to jail for a long time. He needed to figure out how to get custody of Haley, but he didn't have any legal rights to her. He would have to go talk to her father and see what he thought. Then he knew a lawyer who worked pretty cheap. He hoped.

His life had changed so much in the last couple of days; he didn't even know where to start. He decided to go out for a smoke since Haley was gone. He went to the kitchen to look for his pack of smokes. He usually hid them in his leather riding jacket's inside pocket, which hung year round on a hook near the door.

There wasn't anything in the pocket, and he remembered that he was out. He went and sat back down on the couch and turned on the TV. The Vikings game had just started, and he decided to watch it since Chad would be back soon, and that was his team. The Raiders didn't play until later in the day.

It was probably twenty minutes later when the two food runners returned. They came through the front door, each with two bags of groceries, and Chad carrying a twelve pack of Diet Dr. Pepper for his little brother, and Haley had a two-liter bottle of Orange Crush for herself. They went to the kitchen to put away the purchased items, and Chad started cooking homemade boneless spicy chicken wings.

"Your Vikings are already up 20–7! Your crappy kicker missed an extra point and then followed that up with a short kickoff that the Lions returned for a TD."

"That guy, why don't they just cut him? He sucks."

Haley walked into the living room and tossed something on her stepfather's lap. It was a pack of Marlboro Lights.

"What the?" exclaimed Jackson.

"I figured with all the stress of the last couple days, you would need one, considering you are out. By the way, you don't need to hide that you smoke from me anymore. I've known for years. You and Mom aren't as sneaky as you thought you were. I know you both smoke."

"You've known all along?" a shocked Jackson asked.

"Yes. And here," she tossed a lighter to him. "Get rid of the lighter with a half-naked woman on it. Klaire is way hotter than that lady anyway."

"Maybe I should get a half-naked picture of Klaire to put on it?"

"I might start smoking if you want to start making those lighters!" yelled Chad from the peanut gallery.

They all laughed, and Haley sat and watched the Vikings with her stepfather.

It was halftime and the food wasn't quite ready, so Jackson decided to step outside and have a smoke. He went out back and stood on the deck. He looked around and realized something was missing. Raider... His dog was always there with him, when he went out back to smoke, waiting to get some attention and maybe a treat. Jackson became sad and thought about his dog. Of all the people killed in the last couple months, his dog would be the hardest for him to get over.

Jackson pondered whether or not to get a new dog right away. He decided against it and was going to wait and see if he got Haley full time, or what was going to happen there. Then if he did get her, they would find one together.

He finished and walked back inside and was told that the food was ready. He washed his hands in the sink and grabbed some boneless wings. He didn't know how or where his brother learned to cook, but he was glad he did. They were delicious.

Haley volunteered to do the dishes, and the boys just sat and watched football.

There was a knock at the front door, and Haley ran to answer it. Nobody had even noticed anyone pull into the driveway.

"Klaire and Mandi!!" Haley exclaimed. She hugged Mandi and then hugged Klaire extra tight. "I'm sorry for everything my lame Mom and her skuzzy boyfriend put you through."

"Oh, sweetie, you don't need to be sorry, you didn't do anything wrong…did you?" Klaire teased.

"No, ha, guess I didn't. I just want you to know that it upsets me that they did that stuff."

"Well, we are okay, I will be just fine. Besides, I get to tell everyone that the cops shot me." And she pointed to the small gauze bandage on her shoulder. She had on a spaghetti strap blouse, which showed the bandage in its entirety. She had tried to put a regular blouse on but the slight pressure that it put on the wound from just touching it drove her nuts, so she changed.

They walked in and closed the door. Mandi had a grocery bag, and she plopped it down on the coffee table.

"We brought chips and dip. I can't watch football without chips and dip," Mandi explained. She started digging the bags of chips and two containers of dip out of the bag. "We got Doritos and Top the Tator because Momma said Jackson liked that, and we also got plain chips and sour cream and onion dip because it is nummy."

"You guys are awesome!" Jackson said. "Pass those Doritos and Top the Tator over this way, Mandi!"

Everyone dug into the chips, and there was lots of chomping and snapping sounds being made. Klaire was still standing watching the people devour the food.

"Chad, we just want to thank you for taking care of Mandi yesterday until my parents got here. She told me that you were fun."

"Oh, anytime. Just get me one of those new lighters, and we will call it even."

Jackson spit Doritos out his mouth, and Haley, who was drinking her glass of Orange Crush, had pop come out of her nose as they both started laughing.

"I take it I missed something?" Klaire said not understanding what was so funny.

"I'll tell you later," said Jackson as he started for the kitchen to grab a wet rag to clean up the pop and chips that were now all over the coffee table.

CHAPTER 77

Samantha was at home watching the Vikings as well. All decked out in her Vikings gear, complete with a knit hat with yellow braids coming out of it. She was sporting an old school #28 Ahmad Rashad jersey. The players now days weren't as loyal to their teams as they used to be, and she couldn't wear a jersey of someone who might leave as a free agent next year.

She was still full from her spaghetti lunch that the man from TV had made for her. He had showed up and made her lunch and was sitting with her watching the game with her. He was dressed up because he was getting picked up after the game by his cameraman. They were heading down to Preston to take some footage in front of Jackson Ackerman's house for the six o' clock news that evening.

"Well, I hate running out on you, but I need to get down to the Ackerman house for some footage. That story is messed up. You said you know those people? Did you know both Jackson and his ex-wife…"

"Camille."

"Yes, that's her name. You knew both of them?"

"Ya, I was in their wedding."

"No shit! Wow."

"Do you want an exclusive interview with Jackson? Pretty sure he owes me. I could set it up for you if you promise to cook for me again."

"Really! Wow, heck yeah!! That would really help my career! That would be pretty awesome of you. You must really like me if you want to suffer through my cooking again."

"Let me give him a call, and you are a pretty man. I can put up with your cooking at least one more time I think."

"Pretty man? You mean rugged and handsome, right?"

"No, I think pretty is more fitting," Sam smirked as she teased.

Sam pulled out her cell during the next commercial and dialed Jackson's number. It rang twice before he picked up.

"Well hi, Sam, how the hell are ya?"

"How's the shoulder?"

"It is sore, but with all the stitches, at least it isn't bleeding anymore."

"Say, I have a favor to ask of you."

"Anything for you, my dear friend. Name your favor, as long as it doesn't include me using my right arm."

"Well I kinda just started dating this guy named Tyler, and he happens to be a field reporter for KTTC. Would you be willing to do an exclusive interview with him today?"

"Normally, I would say absolutely not, but since you are asking, I'll do it. I'm sure Klaire would be okay with it to since you are asking."

"You are awesome! He will be so stoked. It will probably get me some brownie points with him too."

"It better!! Ha. I only have one condition."

"And what would that be, Jackson?"

"He has to wait for the Raiders game to be done because it is about to start, and I am watching that. They are playing the Chargers, so we need to win this game."

"Okay, so he probably won't make the six o'clock news then."

"So, he will make the ten o'clock news. He can just mention that he will have an exclusive with both of us coming up at ten, and that will give him a chance to promote himself."

"Not only are you a handsome man, Jackson, you are pretty smart."

"Well, I try. Will you be coming down with him?"

"Oh, hell no, I'm not going anywhere close to a TV camera."

"Okay. Well, Klaire and I will have you two down next weekend for a grill out or something. Just to say thanks for everything."

"We will be there. Catch you later."

"Bye."

Samantha turned to Tyler with a big old smile. He had heard most of the conversation as her cell was pretty loud. He was so excited he could barely contain himself.

"You got me the interview, didn't you?" he asked very excitedly.

"Well, of course, I did."

He grabbed her and kissed her very hard. He held both of her arms by their biceps and held her to him as he kissed her with as much excitement as he could have mustered.

He released her and looked away shyly. "I'm sorry, that was our first kiss, and I just grabbed you and made you kiss me. Probably not what you were expecting."

Sam's face was flush, and its redness stood out against all the purple that she was wearing. She was not expecting that at all. Her arms hurt a little from where he had grabbed her so forcefully.

"It certainly wasn't what I was expecting our first kiss to be like." As she fanned her face with her hands. "Is it hot in here? Can you do that again?"

Tyler grabbed her again, this time with more passion than brute force, he pulled her to him slower this time, with her looking at him, wanting him to manhandle her again. As their lips touched this time, she had time to wrap her arms up around his broad back and pull him into her. They kissed passionately for what seemed like eternity, but it was actually only about forty seconds.

As they released their lip lock on each other, they continued to hold each other and look into the other's eyes. Tyler asked, "Was that better?"

"It will do for now I guess," Samantha teased.

"Hey, I'm just curious. How come he is a handsome man, and I'm 'pretty?'" Tyler air quoted the "pretty" part with his fingers.

"Seriously, that is what you are thinking about right now? Well, I guess he just volunteered to switch spots with his ex-wife, who he hates, so she wouldn't be killed. What have you done lately?"

"I cooked spaghetti for the sexiest woman in Southeast Minnesota."

"Oh, you are smooth, did they teach you that in reporter school?"

"No, but I'm pretty good at thinking things up on the fly."

They snuggled in together to watch the last few minutes of the game. Sam didn't even really watch the game, she had her eyes closed and was enjoying having a good man with her for the first time in how long. She hadn't even slept with this guy yet, but she was hoping that it would be soon.

"So, again. I'm curious, what did you do that he thinks that he owes you something back?"

"Oh, nothing much. I may or may not have figured out that Frank was the one behind everything, and I figured that I knew where Frank was holding the girls. So I drove to Preston and told the FBI agent in charge where the cabin was. They took a tactical team out and rushed the cabin and saved everyone. Well, except Frank I guess, but who cared about that D-bag, right?"

"Did you know that Camille was in on it too?"

"No, that was a surprise to me too. I can't know everything you know."

CHAPTER 78

The Raiders game was just starting when the first news van pulled up. Some small-time station out of Lacrosse, Wisconsin. It wasn't long after that and a station from Austin, Minnesota, pulled up, followed by a news team out of Mason City. Jackson figured that since a lot of this had gone down in Iowa, they were going to report on it.

Jackson walked over and closed the shade on the picture window. Haley hurried up and closed the rest of the shades in the other rooms.

Klaire had snuck up the stairs into the master bedroom. She hadn't thought twice about it, but as soon as she stepped inside the bedroom, she stopped cold. She stood and looked at the bed. The last time she was in this room, she was abducted, completely naked. And that slime ball probably touched her. She was grossed out and she wanted to cry, but she didn't. She touched her shoulder where her bandage was and thought, *He won't be touching anyone ever again.*

She shook herself from her thoughts, and she slid open the closet door as quietly as she could. She didn't know if they would be able to hear downstairs, but she didn't want to take the chance. She found his jerseys that he had hanging together. Four of them, three black home jerseys and one white away jersey. She decided on the white one, Tim Brown's No. 81. She pulled it off the hanger and slowly closed the sliding closet door. She laid it on the bed, and she reached down and grabbed the bottom of her blouse. She stopped as she had started to pull it up over her head. She let go and walked over to the window and looked out to the trees lining the property. She picked out the tree that she thought he would have been sitting in, and she pulled down the shades of both windows that were there. Nobody needed to be watching her ever again.

She changed and walked down the stairs, and she stood in the entrance of the living room where everyone was engulfed fully in the Raiders game. Jackson sensed her presence, and he looked first. Chad and the two girls followed and soon all four of them were looking at Klaire, standing there in Tim Brown's white jersey, with black numbers on it, and a Nike swoosh on the sleeves.

Chad was the first to say anything. "Fuck me, I think I just became a Raiders fan."

Jackson smacked him with the back of his left hand, which was open, so it was more of a backhanded slap than anything. "I've been trying to get you to convert all these years, and all it took was a pretty woman in a jersey?"

"Yeah, I'm actually surprised you hadn't thought of that before. It is a powerful argument."

"It sure is, brother, it sure is. Klaire, I kinda want to take you upstairs right now and forget about watching the game."

"Eww gross!" exclaimed Haley and Mandi at exactly the same time.

"I read something about guys liking their women in their jerseys, I guess it is true," she giggled.

Just then one of the Raiders linemen broke through and sacked Phillip Rivers, and Jackson erupted with excitement. "*Yeah!!! whoo hoo!! Take that,* Rivers!!"

"So much for going upstairs, I guess," snickered Klaire.

"What, hun? Did you just see Rivers get destroyed?!"

"Yes, yes I did," and she snuggled up with him on the couch, making certain to not touch his shoulder where the stitches were. She leaned in and gave him a kiss on the cheek. She was happy that she had her child and her man both with her, and they were all safe. She would get Jackson upstairs after the game, and he could take his jersey back.

ABOUT THE AUTHOR

Kelly Masters is an employee at Mayo Clinic in Minnesota, where he works in the Accounts Payable area. He also co-owns a flower/gift shop with his wife. In his free time you can find Kelly attending rock concerts, local high school sporting events, or out in the woods hunting. He is an avid motorcyclist and is nearing his lifetime goal of riding to each of the lower 48 U.S. States. Kelly and his wife reside in a small community in rural Minnesota, along with the two youngest of her five children, their cats and pair of ducks.

CPSIA information can be obtained
at www.ICGtesting.com
Printed in the USA
LVHW011338130519
617615LV00006B/526/P